SOUL PURPOSE

Book 1

The city of lost beings

Anthony Bunko

Copyright © 2024 Anthony Bunko

The right of Anthony Bunko to be identified as the Author of the work has been asserted by him in accordance with the Copyright, Designs and Patent Act, 1988

All the characters in this book are fictitious, and any resemblance to hideous creatures and evil demons is purely coincidental. This book is also available to read on the back of weird Goth people's tee-shirts sitting in coffee shops in any shopping centre in the world on a full moon.

All rights reserved. No part of this publication may be reproduced, stored in a retrieval system, or transmitted, in any form or by any means without the prior written permission of the publisher, nor be otherwise circulated in any form of binding or cover other than that in which it is published and without similar conditions being imposed on the subsequent purchaser.

First published 2024 by STRUMMMER PUBLISHING

anthonybunko@gmail.com

SOUL PURPOSE

Book 1

The city of lost beings

Other titles by Anthony Bunko: -

1. The Tale of the Sh*gging Monkeys – Trippin'
2. Two Sh*gging Monkeys – The Siege of El Rancho
3. The Belt of Kings
4. Boy, Girl, Fruitcake, Flower (renamed – TV, Tarot Cards and George bloody Clooney)
5. Working up to the Slaughterhouse
6. Demons and Cocktails - Stuart Cable's autobiography
7. Hugh Laurie Biography
8. Hugh Jackman Biography
9. 2 Hard to Handle – the autobiography of Mike Spikey Watkins
10. Dic Penderyn and the Merthyr Rising
11. Lord Forgive me but I was a Bullsh*t Consultant
12. Ma'am Anna – Anna Rodriguez's autobiography
13. Nerves of Steele – the Story of Phil Steele
14. The Boy who Cried Sheep
15. The Wizard of GurnOZ
16. Frayed Around The Edges
17. I Could Have Been an Astronaut if it Wasn't For Malachy McAleer
18. The Man Whose Hair Grew Black
19. Lucky – the Luckiest, unlucky Dog in the World ever – Book 1 – Lucky Goes to Ireland
20. Lucky – the Luckiest, unlucky Dog in the World ever – Book 1 – Lucky Goes to Egypt
21. Fighting To Speak – Mark Jones autobiography

Dedicated to: -

*Mam and Dad
for bringing me up on the
'right' side of Love Street
xxxxx*

Trigger Warning
This book deals with issues
Such as mental trauma,
eating disorder and suicide

List of Chapters: -

1. roll up, roll up to see the...
2. the Creep and a Coward
3. bloody teenagers
4. the art and soul of ...
5. I don't do small talk ...
6. I want souls...understand?
7. his face the size of a balloon
8. you call that music?
9. the black eye dude
10. who's the loser now?
11. just another shipment of souls
12. that's for Johnny
13. reservoir demons
14. they can't run from me
15. this is personal now
16. living on a prayer
17. the queen of the prom
18. I've almost been run over by a train
19. anymore bright ideas?
20. reservoir demons
21. I hope I've got this right
22. can the parents of the following come with me please?
23. Its soul time

Who is that?

1

Roll up, roll up to see the...

'Breathe Leo. Breathe.' The voice bounced around my head like a silver metal ball dancing frantically inside a pinball machine. Fingers gently smoothed my thick wavy brown hair.

'Oh, not again,' I cringed.

'Leo.... Leo.'

'Get off me mam, it's embarrassing,' I wanted to say. But I couldn't. I couldn't because I lay there motionless on the supermarket floor. Next to aisle seven and this week's special offer of bog roll (or 'bath tissue' as they call it here in America) stacked neatly up towards the ceiling. I must have looked like a dead fish on a dinner plate. My eyes wide open. One side of my face covered with spaghetti sauce from the broken jar I must have accidently knocked over when I fell.

'Is that boy going to die, daddy?' a young girl innocently asked. She hung onto the side of the shopping trolley. A strip of red lights flashed in the heels of her shoes.

'No, I'm not going to die, you cheeky little tike. I'm…I'm…I'm not well that's all, so there,' the voice inside me screamed out. 'And, if you must know, those trainers look stupid,' I wanted to add.

'Shhhhhhh, Emily' came back her dad's reply.

The silence around me felt deafening. I could sense everyone standing. Staring. Ogling. They always did when this happened. Nosy so and so's. In Wales, where I used to live before my father got a 'better' job in the U. S, OF A, no one would dare just stand there gawking like I was a bloody monster in one of those scary films. Rubbernecking as if I had grown two heads or turned into a human beetle. No, they used to look away. Look away and make the sign of the cross and pray for my poor soul. But in this hick town where we now lived, the small-town population seem to love things like this. Love a bit of drama. Probably because they are all addicted to television. It's a wonder they haven't all got square bloody eyes,

'Haven't you got something better to do,' my mother snarled at them.

Still, no one moved. Even the wheels of their shopping trolleys swiveled to face me. Mocking me. Mocking the skinny teenager flat out on the floor.

'Leo, I'm here for you darling,' I could just about hear her soothing voice and feel her gripping my hand tightly.

'Go away everyone...just, just ... go away,' my words filled up any spare space left in my mind. At my age it was bad enough to be seen out shopping with your mother, never mind having a major fit in the process.

'I hope no one recognizes me.' My left leg started to twitch. Followed by my right. I knew what was coming next. My eye lids began to get heavy. As if someone was lowering the blinds over a window. I fought with all my might to keep them open. But it was no good. They slammed shut like the door of a prison cell. I try to force them back open. They wouldn't budge.

'Oh my god,' a girl shrieked, 'isn't that, that Australia nerd from third period.'

'I'm Welsh ... I'm bloody Welsh.' These hicks were so thick at times. Since moving here, I found out that most Americans could only name a handful of places that existed in the rest of the world. Australia, Ireland, Scotland and Paris Disney, which by the way, most thought was an island created by the Disney Corporation.

'It is...it is...Leo...Leo Young,' another girl piped in. 'What's the loser doing?' They nudged and giggled to themselves.

My entire body ceased up. My embarrassment complete. I wish I could have crawled under the nearest shelf and never come out like an old shriveled up grape that had dropped from someone's cart and rolled off to safety. 'Why am I such a loser? Why can't I just be normal like everyone else?' It was a question I had asked himself a million times and a million times the answer came back the same. 'Because you are Leo Young, and Leo Young isn't normal. Leo Young is a big loser. A massive nerd. Quotation marks, a freak.' I pictured all of the shoppers standing in a circus tent eating popcorn and clapping politely at the main attraction. 'Roll up…roll up to see the epileptic boy doing his shaky breaky dance…it can't be missed.'

The image slowly faded. The blackness slowly crept over me. It engulfed me in its arms. I tried to fight it off. It was no use. It was way too strong.

I drifted in and out of consciousness. The last thing I felt was my body stiffening up like a board. Then the dark silence took over.

******

Several miles away, a scrawny eighteen-year-old girl in a long flowery dress strolled through the foyer of one of New York City's most prestigious hotels. The man behind the reception was busy checking in an overweight businessman to notice the sadness etched on the girl's features.

By the stairwell, she slipped off her flip-flops before climbing the thirty-odd floors to the top without once stopping for breath. With a struggle, she eventually opened the old rusty metal door leading onto the rooftop. The sudden dash of sunlight lit up her face. The gentle breeze blew through her long, silky, black hair. A faint smile turned up her lips. Stretching out her painfully thin arms, she twirled around and around and around until the surrounding buildings merged into one big blur. Slightly dizzy, she wandered towards the edge of the rooftop.

Sitting on the edge, she dangled her long legs over the side. Down below the hustle and bustle of the city streets rose up to greet her. She pulled the front page of a magazine out of her pocket. The stunning model in the skimpy red swim suit smiled back at her with a mouth full of perfectly white teeth.

'I hate you … I really do hate you.' She ripped the page into tiny pieces. Letting them all go. 'I never wanted to be like you anyway.'

The fragments of paper rained down between the buildings. Fell like confetti being thrown over the happy couple at a wedding. Bits floated towards the hot dog stand. The hot dog stand where the girl often walked past holding her nose so she didn't have to breathe in the delicious smell. The smells that make her stomach rumble and ache for a bite of the junk food.

Wiping the tears from her eyes, she got back up to her feet. She nearly toppled forward. But quickly gained her balance.

'That was close,' she breathed out a sigh of relief.

Smoothing out the creases in her dress, she looked over the edge at the sidewalk below for the second time. Then looking up to the heavens, she smiled before stepping off into the fresh air.

******

SCCCREEEEEEEEEEEEEEEEEECCCCCCCCCHHHHHHHHHH!!!!

A loud screeching jolted me out of the blackness. I was back on my feet. A yellow taxi cab, several feet away from shattering the kneecaps of two elderly people. Its blaring horn pierced my eardrums.

BBBBBEEEEEEEEEEEPPPPPPPPPPPP!

The driver wound down his window to hurl a barrage of abuse at the couple. 'Get out of the way you two idiots!'

The elderly pair stood frozen in the middle of the road.

'Oh,' I shouted at the driver, 'you shouldn't be allowed to drive into a supermarket ... that's dangerous. You nearly hit those two old people.'

The driver shook his head and gave them the finger. The aging couple hastily stepped back onto the pavement. The taxi moved on.

'You were lucky there,' I said to the man and woman.

They both ignored me. They stood waiting for the traffic to stop.

How rude I thought. I looked around. 'What the he....lllllll?' The light from the afternoon sun burnt holes in my eyelids. Something red dripped off my cheek on to the concrete. Oh my god I'm bleeding. I touched the side of my face. The red substance covered my fingertips. For some reason, I licked it. The old couple must have thought I was insane.

'It's not blood.' I held out my finger. 'It's not... It tastes like...like ... tomato sauce'. A flashback of me laying in the supermarket floor next to a jar of spaghetti sauce popped into my head. The inconsiderate sound of the traffic shook the image away.

My eyes quickly scanned my new surroundings. Tall buildings, with their flashing animated neon signs, stretched up into the sky for what seemed like a mile. My heart raced on catching a glimpse of the M & M store and the Hard Rock Café where my parents took me on my fifteenth birthday.

'New… York…. City?' the words crawled sluggishly out of my mouth. 'What the hell am I doing here?' The shock of it all smacked me across the face causing my body to tense up. I had never been alone in the city before. My parents wouldn't allow it. Not in my 'condition'. Not even with my best friend, Josh.

'Excuse me,' I turned to a woman carrying several shopping bags. She completely ignored me. She walked straight past, trying to hail a cab. I asked someone else, but got the same blank response. I felt disorientated. Confused. Scared. I staggered aimlessly around. Dodging the steady stream of human traffic flowing in the opposite direction. No one talked to each other. People trudged about like zombies with their heads down. Most stared into cell phones. On the road, cars crawled bumper to bumper. The racket of the constant blare of their horns filled every inch of space. I stopped at the red light on the sidewalk. I stood in the middle of the waiting crowd.

Afraid to speak. Afraid to make eye contact with anyone. My head spun as I wondered where my mother had gone.

Suddenly, I felt someone, or something, watching me. I looked up. A loud gasp escaped from deep inside my guts. A large figure stood perfectly still across the other side of the road. It looked like a man. A very large man. He stood about eight foot tall with a dark hood masking his features. Only the intense white glow of two eyes gave any clue there was a face there at all. A few strands of wild scraggly black hair hung out of the hood. Tattered clothes hung loosely on his massive frame.

'I bet he plays basketball,' bizarrely that was the first thought which crossed my mind.

He remained perfectly still. Just standing there, glaring. Glaring at me. No one else seemed to notice him. Only me. A massive shiver raced down my spine and settled somewhere down near my Converse trainers.

The impatient crowd around me blurred past as the light on the lamppost changed to green. I couldn't move. I was stuck to the concrete. My legs wouldn't work. I stood transfixed by the creature's piercing gaze. The noise from the busy street diminished to a murmur as the world carried on around me. Rushing past me.

The hood covering the thing's face dropped to its shoulders. It was ugly. Really ugly. Uglier than my Uncle John's pet pig. Now that took some doing, let me tell you. I rocked back on my heels. The man-thing sneered while exposing a mouthful of outrageously grotesque teeth with two long fangs protruding from each side. My heart thumped madly in my chest. My legs turned to jelly. The man-thing turned its deformed head to the sky before letting go of a bone chilling cry.

'UUUUUGGGHHHHHHHHHHH.'

Pigeons flew away. Dogs howled. I stood stationary. Then, then it headed towards me. Bounding across the road. Six black hairy legs sprouted out of the side of its body as it moved. It scurried onwards like some kind of human spider, clambering over the tops of the cars.

I staggered backwards. I bumped into the large glass window of a hotel.

The creature crossed the road in seconds. I closed my eyes. I put my hands up to my face. I waited for the attack. Waited for the creature to devour me. But then…..

BOOOOOOOSH

A loud thud like a heavy sand bag hit the concrete in front of me. I was too afraid to look. My body stiff with fear.

'Arrrggghhhhh,' a woman's scream forced my eyes open. The female in an expensive fur coat stood shaking. Her hands over her wide-open mouth. I followed her stare down to pavement. The splattered body of a teenage girl lay on the sidewalk in front of me.

'She ju…ju…jum…jumped from up…up… up there,' some guy stuttered while pointing up to the roof of the hotel.

I looked at the bloodstained body and then back towards the man-thing with the spider legs. It stood about 5 feet away. Its eyes fixed on me. I gulped. It shook its huge head and then transformed back into human…ish form again. It pointed at me. Then at the body. It growled before disappearing down the steps of a nearby subway.

I still couldn't move. Petrified amongst the crowd of shocked people that had gathered around the poor lifeless girl. It was the first time I had ever seen a dead body before, let alone someone whose head looked like a freshly cracked egg. Dark red blood sipped into the cracks of the pavement. A bellhop from the hotel rushed over to place a blanket over the girl's crushed skull. The blare of the police sirens broke the silence. A minute later, a cop car snaked its way slowly through the traffic.

Some members of the crowd jostled around for a better position. A few looked like they were getting some kind of morbid kick out of it all. One guy in a baseball cap, manically chewing gum, relayed the tragic event into his cell phone. 'Yeah...splattered...blood everywhere...I'll get a pic and send it to you.' He aimed his phone ready to snap the lifeless girl lying on the ground.

'What the hell are you doing?' I yelled at him.

He ignored me. I walked towards him to slap the mobile out of his hand, but then I stopped dead in my tracks. Terror gripped me. My mouth dropped open. The dreamlike sight of the gray, chalky spirit of the dead girl rose up from her human remains. I tried to scream. Nothing came out.

The spirit brushed herself off. She smiled weakly at me. 'Hello, I'm Helen.' She stepped over her own lifeless body. Her hand extended.

'Mam,' I whispered to myself, 'mam, where are you?' I wobbled backwards into the hot dog cart. Two bottles of ketchup toppled onto the ground splattering more red sticky substance onto my shoes and all over the street.

'That's much better,' the dead girl confessed. She appeared oblivious to her own transparency. 'I feel so light … so weightless.' She danced around the pavement. Her hair flowing behind her like the tail of a stallion.

'Why…why...why did you do that?' I stuttered.

'Do what?' she smiled at me.

'You know...jump.'

The girl turned her back on me. She looked up at the building. Her features changing. 'Because…I was…I was so…so fat…so ugly.'

'What?'

'Fat…flabby, chunky, you know.'

I could almost see the bones sticking out of her painfully thin legs. 'Fat! Are you crazy? There's more meat on a toothpick.'

The girl sighed. 'I thought you would understand.'

'Understand what?'

'What I was going through, not like those stupid talent agents.'

'I don't know what you are talking about,' I muttered.

'They said I was too overweight to be a model. They said I needed to get in better shape. Try next year, they said.' The frustration evident in her voice. 'I tried everything. Eating less. Not eating at all. Sticking my finger down my throat. Pills…more pills. And still no one wanted me.'

I struggled to get my words out. 'You killed yourself because…because…someone said you were….fa…' She turned sharply to face me. 'a….a….little overweight?'

'Yeah. You got a problem with that?' Licking her lips, she spun back around. 'But now, I could go for a burger…with fries and…cheesecake…mmmmmmm cheesecake with a big dollop of fresh cream'

In the background, two paramedics tried to get the dead girl up onto the stretcher. A piece of her skull flopped onto the sidewalk.

I felt queasy. 'Arrrggghhh.' I needed to be sick. 'Arrrggghhhhh.' I heaved, spewing into the stainless-steel container full of hot dogs. Chunks of what was once deep inside of me covered the contents in the metal pan. I apologized to the vendor. He just disregarded me.

'Hey…I wanted one of those,' the spirit of the dead girl shrugged her shoulders.

I wiped my mouth. I felt like throwing up again, but my stomach was empty. I looked around. Confused. Scared. Then I ran. Ran as fast as my legs could carry me. I sidestepped in and out of the shoppers and business people. I could hear the spirit girl shouting after me. I kept going. I needed to get away from this nightmare.

'This is just a bad dream…. Bad dream, that's all. I'll wake up soon… I will.' I tried to. No change. I was still in New York. Still getting chased by a dead girl. I sprinted around the corner. Down a gloomy, narrow alleyway lined with graffiti, I slipped on some garbage. I clambered to my feet. In front of me, a brick wall.

'Oh no, a dead end.' My heart raced. Crouching, I hid down behind several bulging trash cans. The place stunk of garbage and urine. I shut my eyes tight. Praying it all away.

'AAAAAAAAAHHHHHHHHHHH!' I screamed out as something tapped me on my shoulder.

Helen sat next to me. Cross legged. Large grin on her face. 'Well?'

'What do you want?' I poked the girl's arm. My finger retreated on touching her cold, clammy flesh. I shuffled away from her on my backside. The butt of my jeans soaking from the stagnant putrid water lying on the ground. 'Go away…please….go away.'

'What's that?' The spirit pointed to a piece of paper sticking out of my pocket.

'I don't know. I haven't seen it before.' I unrolled it. It appeared to be a map of some kind. I studied it before my head suddenly shot back violently. 'What's that smell?' It was the most disgusting, pungent odor I've ever smelt. It reminded me of a mixture of rotten potatoes, eggs and my best friend Josh's taco farts.

Holding her nose, the dead girl looked at me accusingly.

'It wasn't me,' I protested.

'Yeah right. I don't see anyone else here and I didn't do it.'

A strange gurgling sound emanated from the entrance of the alley. I jumped to my feet. A look of terror raced across the dead girl's eyes. Two small gruesome looking creatures emerged through a steam cloud rising up through a drain cover.

'Holy crap!' I muttered.

The blue hazy light given off by an overhead neon sign revealed how hideous the creature's features really were. Their naked hairless bodies were dark purple in color and blistered like a pig's skin roasting over a spit.

The bigger of the two ugly pigmy faces hissed, 'She's mine…not yours, boy.' Globules of spit sprayed out of its deformed mouth.

'Tell him Zotto … tell him.' The smaller one jumped up and down.

'Shut up.' the leader hushed his companion. They both strolled closer.

The girl's spirit hid behind me. Her sharp nails dug into my skin. I tried to pry her fingers from my flesh. The mysterious paper map fell to the ground.

'Give her to me boy or I will hurt you.' The demon creature's words were coated in menace.

'I don't want to go with them,' she squawked on the verge of hysteria. 'Please…please don't let them take me.' Her bottom lip quivered uncontrollably.

The demon creatures edged forward. Repulsive grins on their faces. The small one swung around a lamppost. It landed on top of the trash can with a bang.

'What do you want?' I asked.

My question was met with silence. Zotto stood only three feet from me. I stared in dismay at a face as repulsive as the odor it emitted. One blank empty socket and a strange yellow eye stared back at me. Saliva dripped from the few black, rotten teeth left in the beast's mouth. It pointed with its stubby, charred fingertips. 'I want…her…the jumper…she's mine.' Both creatures made terrible noises like wild banshees screaming at the first sight of the full moon.

The girl's head jerked from left to right. Looking for somewhere to run. She bolted but the demons were on her tail. The anguish evident on her face on realizing her escape route was blocked by the ten-foot wall. In panic, she tried to scramble up over it. The demons were too quick. The smaller one jumped on her back. It tore viciously into her neck. The girl's piercing cries filled the alley. Her effort to fight it off fruitless. The creature was too strong. It dragged her to the ground. Zotto joined in. Both monsters ripped her to shreds with their bare hands. Tearing at her skin. Breaking her spirit bones with ease. The girl's shrieks sailed up into the evening sky. Then it stopped.

Quiet.

I thought of running. Again, my legs wouldn't work. I stood gazing at the lifeless mangled body lying motionless on the ground for the second time. Zotto rammed his hand into her chest. 'I HAVE IT,' he loudly announced. With a grin on his ugly face, he held up a pulsating, glowing glob-like thing high above his head in some kind of victory pose.

'You've got it…another one for you.' The other demon bounced up and down like an excited little child.

The pair strolled back towards the entrance. I shook uncontrollably. I stood, staring at the object pulsing in the demon's tight grip. The blob changed color from dark red to bright yellow before Zotto rammed it into a small bag draped around his shoulder.

'Shall we keep this one?' the smaller one quipped. It lightly stroked my cheek with the palm of his stubby hand.

Zotto's good eye ate into my brain. 'Nah…he's a pussy cat…he's no threat to me, to us.' He pushed me hard. 'See you again, boy.'

I stumbled backwards. Clattering into the trash cans. I lay there afraid to move. My eyes shut; I could hear the creatures swaggering away. I felt a warm sensation run down my legs. Seconds later, the sound of a police car siren wailed off in the distance.

'Leo…Leo.'

'Get away…get away,' I slapped out at the hands touching my face.

'Leo…it's me.'

I opened my eyes. My mother's tearful and concerned face stared down at me 'Leo…thank God.' She hugged me. 'You frightened me to death. That was a long one. At least five minutes.'

I could feel the wet patch on my jeans. Mortified, I glanced over to see the faces of the onlookers in the supermarket still staring. My mother helped me to my feet. We left the shopping cart full of groceries. We walked out of the store. I looked back. The little girl with the flashing shoes raced to where I had been lying. She reached down to pick up a piece of paper off the floor. She handed it to her father. He opened it. 'It's a map honey,' he told her, 'A map of New York City.'

2

The Creep and a Coward

The rest of the class snickered behind my back as another object bounced off the top of my head. It was the fourth time since I'd sat down. I didn't need to be a rocket scientist to guess who was responsible.

'Just ignore him,' Josh, my best friend, tried to blow it off. 'By the way Leo, we've totally got to go to McDonald's after school. My mom's got me on some kind of cabbage patch diet that just makes me fart.' I raised my eyebrow. 'Ok…fart more than normal. I just need real food before I waste away.' He sucked in his chubby cheeks. This only made the rest of his head look fatter.

I glanced at the half-eaten Snickers bar he held in a death grip. 'I'm not sure, I'll have to ask my mother first,' I replied. Another missile hit me above my left ear.

'Got the creep…five outta five.' Ethan Jackson stood up at the back of the room. Raising his large grubby hands high above his head while twirling around like a prize fighter who had just won his first title fight. Several of his cronies clapped and hollered.

'Real funny Ethan…you could have put someone's eye out with that,' Josh bravely spoke up for me.

'Let it go Josh,' I pulled on his sleeve.

'Real funny Ethan…you could have put someone's eye out with that,' the bullying boy mocked. 'You sound like my grandmother, Fatty.'

The laughter in the class rose up again. I knew Josh would be searching for a witty comeback. A witty comeback that would probably get both of our faces smashed in.

'Don't Josh…don't,' I knew from bitter experience that neither of us were in the same league when it came to face smashing as the stocky bully boy with the shaven head. To be truthful there wasn't anyone in the school in the same league as Ethan when it came to smashing faces. Even the teachers. He would definitely get an A plus and a big gold star if violence and intimidation were legitimate subjects in school.

'Josh, it's not worth it. He's a dick' I thought I had whispered the words under my breath. Unfortunately, it was louder than I'd planned. Much louder.

My classmates all breathed in at exactly the same moment. There seemed to be a loud, 'Oooooooing' sound filling the classroom. Ethan's face morphed from grinning intimidator to irritated psychopath. Pushing desks out of his way, he stormed from the back of the room. I jumped up. Automatically covering my face with my trembling hands.

'So, I'm a dick...huh?' The bully pushed me hard in the chest. 'Not worth the bother, am I?'

I toppled back. Crashing into the blackboard. Knocking the board eraser and pens onto the floor. Ethan flexed his muscles. His knuckles clenched. Screwing his face up tightly like a cabbage patch doll.

The room fell silent. Not for the first time. Definitely not the last. All eyes stared at me. The bully boy's number one crony, Johnny James, egged Ethan on. Always dying to see a fight. Well, not so much a fight, more of a one-sided massacre. To get a better view, a few of the other kids stood on their desks. One held up a cell phone to film the event. I shot a glance over to where Beth Patterson sat. The punky-looking girl had her head down. Reading her magazine.

Ethan came at me again. Slapping the side of my head hard.

'No, I didn't...I didn't say, mean...that,' I replied. The fear in my voice evident to all.

'You did punk...least I'm not a creep and a coward.' The bully puffed out his chest. 'Am I?' He poked me again. His finger bruising my skin.

I eyeballed the floor. Wishing it would open up and swallow me up whole. My face bright red. The embarrassment two thousand times worse than the humiliation I felt on wetting myself on the supermarket floor a few days before.

'Well punk?' Ethan grunted. Twisting my left ear. 'Am I?'

'No…No…No,' the words dribbled from my mouth. I fell down onto one knee in agony.

Grinning with sadistic pride, Ethan twisted my ear lobe like he was trying to unscrew a cap on a water bottle. I wanted to boot him. But I was too scared. I wanted to yell at him. But I suspected it would have just made him angrier. He took great pride in his torturing. The thick-set boy didn't have much else to be proud of in his life. So bullying was his perverse way to show everyone he was someone. Someone like his father who was now serving a stretch in prison for armed robbery. His mother took in 'renters' on a regular basis to help support her five kids and her spiraling drug habit. He used the excuse of a broken home to wage war on the world. Unfortunately, that world seemed to revolve around making me and Josh's own existence a living hell.

'Ok…punk, tell the class how much of a creep and a coward you really are.'

'What? Owww!'

'You heard me,' the bully pulled me up from the floor by my ear. 'Come on dork…say it!'

The room fell deadly silent. This time, the smiles slowly slipped from the kids' faces.

'Stop it Ethan…you…you…' Josh spoke up.

The bully let go of my lobe. He turned his attention to my mate. 'Want some of it as well do you fatty?' He marched towards him. Kicking the rubbish bin out of his way.

Josh held the remains of his snicker bar up like a sword. It didn't do him any good as it got walloped out of his grip. It flew across the room. Smacking into the window.

I stood behind Ethan. My heart beating. I tried to motion to Josh to stop. Too late. The bully boy grabbed him in a headlock. Rubbing his knuckles aggressively on his scalp. 'Let's see what you got then, lard ass.'

Classmates giggled.

Josh struggled to get free. Ethan pinned his face against the wooden desk top. The noise level in the class grew louder and louder.

'Smash his head in, Ethan,' at the back, Johnny chanted.

I leant back against the wall. Watching. Silent. Wishing I was brave enough to stand up to the bully. Brave enough to fight my own battles for a change. I bit my lip. My breathing heavy. I stepped forward. Again, my legs refused to function. My friend was getting a beating because of me and I couldn't do anything about it.

'Ok…ok…Ethan,' I quietly mouthed the words. My legs shaking. Tears welling up in my eyes. 'Ok…I'm a creep…I am a coward,' my voice grew louder with each word.

Just at that moment, Mr. Hubbard, the geography teacher, strolled through the door. In his arms a pile of books and a brief case. The sound of chair legs scraping the wooden floor was the only sound as kids scurried to get back into their desks as quick as possible.

'Jackson, put poor Josh's head back on his shoulders and take a seat or it's detention for you … again!!'

The bully boy muttered something inaudible under his breath. Ambling to the back of the room like a gorilla in a white vest. Not taking his eyes off me or Josh, he squeezed into his chair,

'Thanks, Josh,' I murmured to my friend.

'No problem … you would have done the same for me,' Josh winked.

I looked away. I knew deep down; I probably wouldn't have.

'Right, everyone,' Mister Hubbard wasted no time with pleasantries. 'I still haven't received all the consent forms from your parents for the class team building trip to Teatown Lake Reservation on the twenty first of next month. If you don't hand them in, you will not be going. I repeat, you will not be going. No exceptions.' He slid up in front of my desk. Trying his best to whisper in the quietest voice he could. 'Leo … do you think you will be able to come? You know, with your condition and all…' He stood there waiting for a reply in his old well-worn tweed jacket with tan leather elbow patches.

The colour drained from my cheeks. Mr. Hubbard had a habit of making me feel like a two-year-old. Painfully reminding me, and everyone else, I wasn't like the others. I was the kid from that other country who had the shiver and shaking disease. I sighed. This was turning out to be just another typical crappy day at school. And it was still only bloody nine fifteen.

'He can't go sir.' Ethan grinned. 'He may have one of his...his fitttttssssss.' The bully started to shake. Spit dribbled from the corner of his mouth. He banged the desk with both hands. Pretending to convulse.

Except for a few snickers from his hardened cronies, everyone else stayed silent.

'Jackson ... I wish you would have a f...f...f...Just sit and down and shut up,' Mr. Hubbard snorted. He turned back to me.

'Of course, I can sir,' I lied. Sinking down deeper in my seat, I stared at the top of my desk. I hadn't even asked my parents yet. Afraid of what they would say. I know the answer would be no. I didn't know how but I was determined not to miss another school trip. I was definitely going, if it was the last thing I did.

'Good, good Leo,' the teacher tapped the desk. 'Ok everyone, books away,' he said. Retrieving a stack of papers from his desk in the front. 'You have twenty minutes. No looking in your books. No talking. No cheating. That means you, Mr. Jackson,' he quipped while passing out another one of his infamous un-announced geography quizzes.

Moans and groans escaped from the students' mouths. They got louder on reading the title on top of the paper; 'Places Around the World.'

'But sir,' injected Josh.

'No buts … just do it,' the teacher cut off Josh's sentence.

Twenty minutes later, I sat there staring around the room at the others struggling to finish the test. I had sailed through it. In fact, I had completed it in about eight minutes. I didn't want the others to know so I pretended I was still doing it by doodling on a blank piece of paper. Things like that came easy to me. I didn't really know why I was so good at general knowledge, the world, and people and stuff like that. The answers would pop into my mind. It was as if I had been to the places before. I knew that was stupid because the furthest I had ever travelled was from the United Kingdom to living a few miles outside of New York City. Oh yeah, and once me and my family went to Boston to the funeral of someone who had worked with my dad.

I looked over at Josh. His head down, sweating profusely. He looked up. 'Are you done already?' he hissed. I nodded my head.

'You, big suck up,' Josh grunted. Scratching his head while trying to figure out how many countries made up the United Kingdom.

I held up 4 fingers.

'What?'

'There's four countries,' I whispered.

He winked.

I liked Josh. I had become his one and only friend in the world. Two years ago, Josh had been the only kid in the school to talk to me on my first day. I soon realized his friendliness may have had more to do with him finding out what I had in my lunch box as much as him liking me.

Our friendship had grown in gym class. Well, more like in the bleachers during gym class. I had to sit in the stands and watch the other kids play basketball. I longed to join in. But wasn't allowed. It was so unfair. I didn't have glowing aspirations to be the captain of the baseball team or the star quarter back. Or anything as ambitious. To be honest, I just wanted to be part of the team. Any team. Even if it was the part that rode the bench or helped out with the water bottles. But due to my condition I had as much chance of being the first epileptic teenager to walk (or knowing me, shake) on the moon. The nearest I got to competition was playing Madden NFL on my X-Box. Or an occasional game of chess with my dad. I hated chess with a passion.

On the other hand, Josh did everything in his power not to join in. In fact, he was proud of his laziness. Each week he forged his mam's name on notes excusing him from any form of physical activities at all. His idea of exercise was carrying a full plate of ribs to the table in one hand and a large plate of fries in the other at the all-you-can-eat restaurant. He wasn't really obese. Yet, overweight enough for his parents to try everything, unsuccessfully, to get him to shed a pound or thirty!!!

Weighty or not, what I really liked about my friend was he was the only one who treated me like a normal human being. Even when he saw me having my 'blackouts' he would laugh them off. Usually making some wise-crack when I came around.

'Let's go for something to eat,' he would normally pipe up, 'you need to get your energy levels back up.' Always looking for any excuse to go for something to fill his face with. To Josh, I was just Leo, his best friend and nothing else.

Back in the classroom, Mister Hubbard walked by. Without stopping, he tapped my head gently when he saw I had finished. 'Good boy,' he uttered.

Again, I could feel everyone looking. Scorning me. Loathing me. I couldn't win.

I began to scribble onto another blank piece of paper. 'Good boy. Good boy…. Special boy. Freak. Loser. Loser. Loser….' I repeated the words over and over. Digging my pencil into the paper so hard the nib broke.

I was sick of being the 'good boy'. Sick of always being the only one to do his homework on time. The swot of the class. Tired of being the nerdy one. I wondered how it would feel to be bad. Bad like Ethan. Well maybe not quite that ghastly. I didn't like the idea of spending most of my afternoons in detention for sticking other kid's heads down the toilet. Maybe a little left of center would have been enough for me.

I rolled the paper up into a ball. Turning my attention towards the window. Outside, I spotted the janitor, Mister Allen, picking up trash in the yard. I wondered if the old guy was happy. Happy with his life. Or unhappy like me. My eyes got heavy. I yawned. Resting my head in my hands. Just then I saw something moving in the bushes. A blur. I straightened up in my seat. My eyes scanned the perimeter of the yard. I saw it again. There. Running from tree to tree. Whatever it was, it was fast and small.

It stopped behind a trash can. The thing appeared to be sneaking up on the janitor. 'Demons!' I yelled out. I glanced around at my class mates. No one looked up at me. Not even Mister Hubbard took any notice. He continued to stroll around the class like a prison guard.

'Demons!' I shouted again. I turned back to see the hideous creature deliberately edging towards the poor janitor who leant over drinking water from the fountain. I sprung out of my seat. Pressing my face up tightly against the glass, Banging on the window. 'Mister Allen…behind you…look out!'

The hideous small creature vanished. The old man carried on with his cleaning up tasks.

'I'm going nuts.' Wiping the sweat off my brow. I breathed out with relief.

BANG

All of a sudden, the demon's head smashed up against the window. Its mouth wide open. Blood running down its chin. 'Hello boy,' Zotto the demon hissed at me.

'Aarrrrrrrgggggggggghhhhhhhhhhhhh! I stumbled backwards onto the floor. I lay there. Too afraid to open my eyes. I could hear giggling. Turning into full-on hilarity. When I finally looked up, Josh stood staring down at me. A huge grin on his face.

'You fell asleep you, idiot,' Josh snorted. Laughter tears rolling down his cheeks. The rest of the class joining in.

'No, but…there was something…a demon…out there.' I pointed at the uninhabited window.

'Quiet everyone,' Mister Hubbard took control. 'Mister Young, please pick up your pencils and get back in your seat.'

Embarrassed, I gathered my stuff back up. Then slid, red-cheeked, back into my desk. I peered out of the window. The janitor sauntered back to his truck. A full garbage bag over his shoulder. No signs of demons anywhere.

I slumped down in my seat. Someone poked me in the back.

'Hey,' Beth's whisper brought me back to some kind of reality. 'Nerd-face, what's the capital of Peru?' She glanced at Mister Hubbard to make sure he hadn't heard.

'What?'

'Capital Peru?'

'Lima.'

'Lime?' she replied.

'No, Lima,' I wrote it down on a piece of paper. Inconspicuously as I could, I shoved the paper towards the edge of her desk.

She read the note. I stared at her jet-black hair with streaks of pink pulled up in a pony tail high. She wrote something on the paper and slipped it back. I blushed from head to toe before I even read it.

'You are my hero,' it stated. I guessed she was being ironic. Underneath it said, 'but next time kick Ethan the dog face in the nuts.'

She winked at me before going back to the quiz. My heart missed a beat. It always did whenever Beth Patterson acknowledged my existence. It usually meant her teasing me. But in a nice way. She was the love of my life. Unfortunately, she didn't know it yet. Worse still, she probably never would because I was too shy to talk to her.

Beth was so super cool. Not one of the false pageant parade girls like Sharon Bell. The girl from first period all the guys liked. No. Beth was miles better than that. She was smart. Funny. Lovely. She didn't need gobs of makeup or gaudy jewelry to look pretty. She looked great in old camouflage pants and black tee shirts which she always wore. I had never seen her in a dress or doing any girly stuff.

'One day Beth Patterson,' I stared at her, 'One day I will be your hero for real.' A ball of rolled up paper hit the side of my head. Muffled laughter from the back of the class rose up again.

'Six outta six,' Ethan boasted.

3
bloody teenagers

A long black limousine with blacked-out windows majestically pulled onto the avenue. The clock on the dashboard flashed 22:08. In the back of the vehicle, Alex White took a long drag on his cigarette before flicking the still lit stub at the man seated opposite him.

'That gig was shit, man. The sound was awful. I couldn't hear myself talk let alone sing.'

The older man picked up the discarded cigarette. He placed it in the ashtray. 'Sorry Alex, I'll sort it out for tomorrow night…I promise.'

Alex lowered his sunglasses. 'You better had man…or I will be looking for another tour manager…understand?' The man nodded. 'Now pour me a drink,' the star demanded. Placing his sunglasses back over his eyes. 'A double.'

Through clenched teeth, the tour manager did exactly what he was told … yet again!

For the second time in as many days, I found myself standing on the sidewalk in New York City. A black limo glided past. Normally I would be wondering who was inside? Were they famous? An actor or a basketball star? Or just rich? But tonight, I had more important things on my mind. Like the last time I was here. Seeing an ugly monster running towards me with spider legs. A dead girl appearing in front of me before she got 'killed'…. again, by two demon creatures with bad breath and a worse attitude. So, to be honest, wondering who was sitting in the back of the shiny, black limo was the last thing on my mind.

My heart thumped in my chest. A lot like a bass drum bashing it out at a rock concert. I cupped my hands over my eyes in disbelief. I looked down. 'Oh no.' I was still wearing my pyjamas. Thankfully at least, like the first time I had been in this situation, no one could see me. Which could be a good or a very bad thing. Only time would tell.

Minutes earlier I had been at home eating a late dinner with my parents. My dad rambling on about how his boss had stolen one of his brilliant ideas. Mam telling us about the family next doors trip to Florida. The last thing I recalled was reaching across to get a second helping of mashed potatoes when the darkness crept up on me. Crept up like a murderer emerging out of the shadows in a big, black cloak. It's murkiness way too strong. Too cunning for me to shake off.

For whatever reason I was back on the mean streets of the city. Nervously looking up and down. And left and right for clues. The warm night air clung to my skin. The hairs on the back of my neck standing on end. I inched slowly onward. Checking for anything out of the ordinary. Out of the ordinary such as suicidal jumpers, eight-legged spider men, or hideous demons.

Thankfully, except for a few cars driving past, the sidewalk remained almost deserted.

Then from around a corner, a gang of drunken sports fans headed in my direction. 'We shoulda wasted them,' a rowdy middle age man slurred to his buddies. His big beer gut hanging over the waist of his pants. 'We were robbed…that was never a penalty.'

I stepped back into a doorway. Holding my breath. Waiting for something to happen. But nothing did. The men disappeared, without incident, into a bar for probably another round of aftergame drinks.

I breathed out a big sigh of relief. Across the street I spied a large, modern-looking hotel. A red carpet lined with photographers, teenage girls and several large bouncers surrounded the plush entrance. The long black limo pulled up to the curb.

'Aaaaaaaaahhhhhhhhhh!' the sudden loud screams from the girls frightened me half to death.

Although I wanted to keep walking, I was curious as to why there was such a frenzy. I headed across the road towards the commotion. Nearby stood a homeless man rifling through a trash can. The tramp wore a dirty, old purple beret on top of his dirtier matted hair. A long, soiled army coat and well-worn holey boots made up the rest of his attire.

'Gross,' I muttered in disgust. I watched the man lifting out a half-eaten hot dog from the trash can. He wiped off some of the dirt. Swallowing it in one gulp.

The vagrant looked over. 'Who're you looking at?' he snarled, before continuing to rummage for some more free dinner.

I stopped dead in my tracks. 'You can see me?' I asked. The tramp already munching on some more half-eaten nosh, ignored me. 'Maybe he can't.'

At that moment, a heavy-set bloke, in a raincoat, walked past me. It broke my concentration. The man headed towards the hotel. Muttering anxiously to himself.

One of the bouncers opened the back door of the limo. A good-looking. young guy with long, blonde hair, dark sunglasses, a tight-fitting black leather jacket and ripped jeans stepped out.

'Aaaaaaahhhhhhhhhh!' The second round of screams from the girls reached fever pitch.

I didn't recognize him. I wasn't into good-looking, young guys with long, blonde hair, dark sunglasses, a tight-fitting black leather jacket and ripped jeans. I guessed whoever it was he must have been super famous.

'Only famous people can get away with wearing sunglasses in the dark,' Josh had once informed me after seeing some super cool rock star perform with his shades on during the Super Bowl half time show.

The good-looking star snaked his way along the red carpet. Only stopping to sign autographs or posing for pictures. The posse of young ladies shrieked enthusiastically.

'Alex, I love you!' one of the girls yelled out.

A quick-thinking bouncer caught another teenager near the front who fainted.

I wandered closer. Standing in amazement, and more than a little jealous at the reaction this person had over the line of wide-eyed young women. 'Why him God? What makes him so special?' I thought. 'Bet no one ever watched him flop around on the supermarket floor and pee his pants.'

Feeling a little resentful, I turned to walk away. My attention got pulled back by the sight of the muttering man in the raincoat standing at the entrance of the hotel. I'm not sure why but I could sense something wasn't quite right about him. He didn't look like a fan. He looked out of place. His eyes too intense. Shifty. Continually wiping sweat from his forehead. The star walked towards the hotel doors. His perfectly white teeth glistened from the flash bulbs. The muttering man stepped out to block Alex's path. He reached into his pocket. Producing a shiny, black pistol.

'Watch out!' my warning fell on deaf ears. 'I think he's got a gu...,' I didn't even have a chance to finish the sentence. The man raised the handgun and started firing.

BANG!

The first shot got lost on the stunned crowd. But not on the rockstar who fell backwards onto the ground. Blood gushed from a deep stomach wound. The screams of excitement turned to squeals of terror as more shots continued to ring out.

BAM! BAM! BAM!

At first the bodyguards stood frozen like statues. The killer fired shot after shot into the stars dying body. Only stopping when the chamber ran out of bullets. Two security guard dived on top of the gunman. Struggling to restrain him.

It was as if a large panic button had been activated. People raced around aimlessly. Girls cried. Many screamed. Some just watched in silence. I stood there in shock. Stood there, just staring at the star lying on the red carpet. His bullet ridden body seeping blood.

I turned my head away from the bloodshed.

From out of all the confusion, the spirit body of the rock star sat up. He removed his shades. Staring disoriented at me. 'What's happening man?'

'Not again…please, no,' I ignored the star's question. My eyes darted around the panic-filled streets.

Behind him, the bodyguards forcefully disarmed the killer. One minder, the size of a police horse, rammed the assailant's head into the concrete. Alex's tour manager kneeled over the celebrity's lifeless body. His face white with shock.

The spirit of Alex clambered up to his feet. With confusion written all over his face, he stared down at his own crumpled dead body. 'I don't understand man.'

'You better run,' I pushed the star. 'Run…and hide…hurry.'

'What?'

'I…I…think you've been shot to…shot…to…death,' I looked into his eyes. 'And it's not over…quick, hurry they will be coming for you…quick…I've got to go.' I didn't want another run-in with the demon tag team.

The spirit of the star tutted. 'Don't be so stupid, dude, I can't be dead' he argued 'I have a second sell out show at Madison Square Garden tomorrow night and a new album to promote.'

He looked at his manager. 'Bert…Bert.' The star pulled at his manager's arm. Hs hand went straight through it.

'It's no use, he can't see you,' I noticed the tramp at the end of the street gesturing for us to come his way. I continued, 'look, none of them can see you…you're…you're…. dead.' A police siren wailed off in the distance. 'Now go…go.' I pushed Alex away. 'Run…run as fast as you can.'

As if he was strutting onto stage at Wembley, Alex put his dark shades back on before wandering in the direction of the tramp. I tried stopping him. 'No, not that way.' I think he could see the danger in my eyes. I pointed in the opposite direction. The star turned and half ran, half walked towards Central Park.

'No...No!' the tramp waved his arms about. 'This way...idiot. This way.' He threw his beret to the ground. Kicking out at a trash can in the same movement.

I eyeballed the irate hobo. Then glanced back at the rock star who had disappeared around the corner. I decided it would be safer for me to go in the opposite way to both of them. I strolled towards a metal bridge. Quickening my pace with each stride. I noticed the rolled-up piece of paper clutched in my left hand. I dropped it as if it was a red-hot potato and marched on.

From out of the shadows, five small, hideous demons appeared. They purposely blocked my path. Zotto, the leader, stood at the front. Smirking. Puffing on a cigar. 'Lost your prize have you boy?' He motioned his stubby fingers in the air.

Instantly the rest of the creatures darted forward. I turned and sprinted back in the direction I came. Racing in and out between the parked cars. The demons closing in. I dashed around a corner near Central Park. Losing my footing, I fell to the ground. With my hands over my head, I waited for the attack. For the creatures to rip me apart. Nothing. Instead, they rushed straight passed me. Straight in through the big metal park gates.

I scrambled to my feet. Quickly heading in the opposite direction for the second time that night. At the end of the street, for some bizarre reason, I slowed down. Then against all the logic screaming out in my mind. The logic demanded that I forget about the popstar or whoever he was, I turned around and headed back. I couldn't stop myself. Amongst the trees in the park, without any street lights, it was almost pitch black. It was unnerving. Why didn't I just run away? Run away from the monsters. Yet, something drove me on. I didn't know which way to go or what I was going to do. I quietly tiptoed on. The vile smell of demon much stronger.

'Hello…hello,' I whispered. 'Alex…are you here?'

A bone chilling scream sailed into the air. Goose-pimples broke out all over my body. Without thinking, I ran through the trees towards the cries. My legs just about holding my weight. By the time, I reached the children's play area, the star lay dead for the second time that night. Several demons sat astride Alex's body. Pulling and biting at him. Lumps of spirit flesh hung from their mouths. I stepped backwards. Back into the shadows. Too late. Zotto had already spotted me. The creature slid the rock star's expensive sunglasses onto his own deformed face. He yelled out some kind of instructions in a strange language. Three of the demons immediately stopped what they were doing. Bounded towards me on all fours like a pack of hyenas. This time I knew they were coming for me. I turned but was still too slow to react. One hopped on my back. Knocking me to the ground. Within seconds they were all over me. Punching and kicking. I rolled myself up into a self-protective ball.

'Wake up, wake up wake up,' I tried to convince myself it was just a nightmare. It didn't feel like much of a dream when one of the demons sank his teeth into my arm.

'ARRGGGHHHHH,' I yelped out in pain.

'CRACK!'

The sudden sharp sound near my head. Followed by a whimper. A demon cried out in agony. The walking stick hit it again. I peeked through my fingers. The old tramp stood hunched over. Whacking the demon, like a baseball player hitting a homerun. The other demons backed away. Hissing violently. Eyes red. Fangs dripping spittle.

Near the star's body, Zotto snarled with aggression. A dozen or so bats flew overhead. The demon's fangs exposed. He clicked his stumpy fingers. All of his gang of vile beasts scurried back to him. Within a blink of an eye. they all disappeared off into the darkness of the park.

I lay on the ground shaking. A sharp pain in my side. Blood ran down my arm. 'Thank you.' I looked up at my rescuer. I held out my hand for a help up. The tramp brushed it away.

'Thanks,' the tramp's voice was as course as his clothes. 'If my leg wasn't so messed up, I would have kicked you myself.' He huffed and puffed while hobbling away. 'You must be the worst one I have ever had the displeasure…to…to.' He went out of ear shot before I could hear what he said.

Gingerly, I got up. My side hurt but I wasn't hanging about. I limped after the tramp. 'Wait…wait…I'm the worst one at what?'

'Go away kid. I've got others to collect.' He changed direction sharply.

'Please?' I pleaded. I stopped myself from tugging at the old man's stained and torn sleeve. 'I don't understand.'

The tramp picked up a cigarette butt from the ground. He placed it deep in his jacket pocket. 'Ask your mentor.'

'Mentor?' I innocently asked, 'who?'

The tramp spun around to face me. His wild dirty hair covering most of his unshaven face. 'Don't diss me kid.' I noticed bits of food and probably insects lodged in the man's beard. 'Horace William James…or Jezzie to his friends.'

I racked my brain. I didn't know anyone by that name. 'I've never heard of him?' I said quietly. Stepping backwards from the smell from the man.

The hobo took off his beret. He ran his hands through his greasy locks to reveal his weather-beaten features. It shocked me how someone could have so many deep lines engrained on their forehead. 'You're looking at him kid?' The tramp puffed his chest out. I shook my head. 'Now go back home.' He rambled away.

I hesitated. Confused. Continued walking stride for stride with him. 'Sir…sir.'

The tramp marched on. Completely ignoring me. A few choice words muttered under his breathe 'Bloody teenagers…hate them all…can't be trusted…any of you.'

I stopped. I called out his name. 'Jezzie.'

The tramp turned around on a dime. Surprisingly agile for an old battered hobo. He poked the tip of his cane into my face. It made me go cockeyed as I focused on the wooden stick inches from my nose. 'The name is Mister James to you, kid. You ain't my friend. Never will be' He stared long and hard into my eyes The contempt evident through his gaze. Jezzie plonked himself down on a step near a water fountain. He fiddled with his holey right boot.

I plonked myself down as well. But not too close. 'I'm the worst at doing what?' I enquired again.

'What?' the tramp snapped back. Lighting the butt of one of the half-smoked cigarettes he'd found on the floor.

'You said I was the worst you have even seen…worst what?' I picked up a stone and threw it across the grass. It skidded several times before hitting the stump of a tree.

Jezzie puffed out a ring of smoke. 'Soul walker.' He rested his head back on a step. Looking up at the stars.

'Dog walker?'

Jezzie snorted. Shaking his head violently. 'No chance kid…I wouldn't allow you to go anywhere near my dog.' He tried to get back up to his feet. I jumped up to help. The tramp pushed my hands away. 'No! Watch my lips, kid…a soul walker.' He spelled out the words. Letter by Letter. 'S.O.U.L.W.A.L.K.E.R. Well, you're supposed to be anyway.'

I felt my forehead squeeze up into a frown. His words spun around my brain refusing to settle. 'Soul walker...what do you mean a soul walker?'

'What do you think it means? You walk the dead's souls to the station.' He rolled his eyes to the night sky. 'Don't you know anything?'

A loud voice whistled through the trees. A familiar voice which baffled me even more.

'Leo...Leo.'

I looked up towards the sky. 'Who said that?' I stuck my finger into my ear and wiggled it around.

'I think he's coming round!' the woman's voice rang out.

'Mam, is that you?' I carried on with my conversation with Jezzie. 'What do you mean? I don't understand.'

'Wake up Hon,' the voice echoed in my head.

'Mam...please I'll be there in a minute,' I blurted out. 'This is much more important.'

The tramp exhaled. He flicked the cigarette butt at me. 'You ain't even listening to me now kid.'

'I am, I am...honest...it's just I'm hearing other...other things! Can't you hear her?'

Jezzie spat on the ground. 'Look, people's souls are depending on you,' the tramp spoke. 'You can't afford slip-ups in this job. You've got to get yourself ready for the next time. Be prepared'

'Next time! I don't want there to be a next time.' I kicked my foot into the dusty ground.

'There will be kid, so you better read up on your role…I presume you can read?'

'Of course, I can,' I snapped back.

'Well, if you want to stop being such a loser…study it. Understand the craft. The pitfalls.'

I scratched my head. 'What?' I began to feel quite dizzy. I steadied myself against the step. My head spinning.

'Leo…Leo.' The words got louder.

'Mam.'

'Huh…why am I bothering?' Jezzie grunted. He began to hobble off as fast as his gamy leg could carry him. 'Ignorant…the lots of them.' He muttered then turned back. 'Learn how to handle yourself kid…get some lessons.' He looked at my pyjamas. 'And start looking the part.' He disappeared off into a bunch of trees.

I looked up at the bright glare from the moon overhead. It burnt into my brain. Struggling to keep my eyes open. I lay back on the grass. Licking my lips. 'That's nice.' I could taste gravy.

I opened my eyes. My mother stood over me holding a towel. I lay stretched out on the carpet in the dining room. Smashed dinner plates and bits of food surrounded me. My father positioned by the door not saying a word. Anguish on his face. Tears in his eyes.

4

The art and soul of …

'Open up,' my mam shoved a spoonful of medicine in my mouth. It tasted disgusting. Smirking like a Cheshire cat she handed me a glass of water. 'There you are, wash it down.'

I felt weak. My head was banging. Not only from where I bumped it on the floor when I blacked out, but also from the experience of travelling through whatever world I had just arrived back from.

'I'm a soul walker, mam' I muttered into the glass. 'I walk the dead's souls for a living.'

'What did you say honey?' my mother replied, picking the food-stained table cloth up off the shag-piled carpet.

I continued babbling. 'Well, when I say "for a living" I don't actually make money from doing it. I don't think.' I saw the weird look my mother gave me. She walked towards the kitchen door. 'Sorry Mam…just talking to myself.' I lay down on the couch. Switching on the TV set.

In the kitchen, my mam slumped herself on one of the stools. Silent tears flowed down her cheeks. My father stopped filling up the dishwasher. He came over to her. A dirty plate in his hand. I turned the sound down to hear their conversation.

'Don't worry honey…he'll grow out of it.' He avoided looking into her eyes.

'When?' she snapped aggressively back. 'It's been ten years now of him "growing out of it."' She emphasized the point with finger quotations. 'How much longer do we have to wait?'

'But…the doctor said,' his words of encouragement were stopped by her cold stare before he had time to complete his meaningful sentence.

'I don't care what the doctor's said. They don't know what they are talking about. He's getting worse. You saw him in there…it was like he was…he was dead.'

My father mooched up to her. 'Maybe it's his new medication.' He knew he was clutching at straws. 'They said it could have some side-effects.' He placed his arm across her shoulders.

She pushed it away. 'It's not his medication.' My father trudged off towards the back door. 'Go on walk away…ignore it,' she added, 'like you always do. You've never accepted his condition…always walking away. Leaving me to cope with it.'

'That's unfair,' his father replied. 'I do my share…'

An image on the TV screen dragged me away from their argument. 'Aaaaaaarrrrrrgggggghhhhhh!' a loud cry left my lips.

They both rushed in to the living room. 'What's wrong?' my mother was the first to speak.

I stood there bolt upright. The glass smashed at my feet.

'What is it darling?' she asked again.

I pointed at the screen. A woman reporter stood outside a hotel in the city centre. Surrounded by other reporters and a handful of policemen. The lights from their cars flashed in the background.

'In breaking news today,' the pretty lady reporter looked directly at the camera lens. 'Alex White, lead singer with The Cowboy Disciplines, was gunned down in front of The Plaza Hotel about ten minutes ago. A 57-year-old man has been arrested.'

'I knew he couldn't sing, but that's taking it too far.' My old man's attempt at humor was wildly misplaced. The stretcher with a body on it covered by a blanket was wheeled past.

'Not funny, Roger.' My mother sat down. Her hand to her mouth. 'Who would do such a thing?'

'Police are still trying to determine the motive in the case....' The reporter added.

The room spun. My entire body wobbled. 'I was there,' my admission fell randomly out of my mouth.

Both of my parents stared at me. They looked at each other. My mam shrugged her shoulders at my dad.

'What son?' my father chipped in.

'There,' I nodded towards the TV. 'I saw it all. I saw the killer. I tried to stop him.'

Mam gripped my hand. 'Leo, what are you talking about? You haven't gone out all night.' Tears welled up inside of her yet again. 'That's in the city honey…miles away.'

They must have thought I was possessed or gone off my trolley.

'No, you don't understand…when I blacked out. It happened then. It's happened before. In the supermarket. On the weekend. The girl. That girl who jumped off the building…I saw her too. She did it because she thought she was too fat,' I mumbled.

'Stop talking crap, Leo,' my father barked.

'Roger!' mam yelled

'Well, it is crap…total baloney.'

I didn't even look at them. Instead, I stormed up to my bedroom. Ignoring mam's concerned pleas. I slammed the door shut. By the time I had reached the confines of my room my heart pounded hard in my chest. Irrational thoughts bounced around my head like jumping beans in someone's warm hand. 'I should go to the police. The police? What would they say? What could they do? I could tell Josh? Yeah, I can tell Josh. No, he'll think I'm just trying to be cool. Maybe I go and try to tell my parents again? Are you kidding? They think I'm crazy as it is. And I'll never be allowed to leave the house again.'

I stretched out on the bed. I stared up at the ceiling. The earlier conversation with the tramp played out in his head. *'Read up on your role…I presume you can read boy?*

'Of course, I can.'

'Well, if you want to stop being such a loser...study it. Understand the craft. The pitfalls.'

What was the old guy talking about? What did I have to do with all these dead people? And why me?

I sat down at my computer. After a full two minutes, I typed in the words 'soul walker.' I held my breath. Nothing came up except a link to some old Korean computer game which was set in the 18th century. It wasn't what I was looking for. I tried again. This time putting the words together. Still nothing.

'How am I supposed to read up on it, when there's nothing to read up on.' I banged my hand on the desk in frustration. Mister Carter, our English teacher's face popped into my head. 'What did he always say in class. "If you want to know the real facts about something, read a book from the library, never mind all this made-up rubbish on your computersssssss. Books are the source of the truth" He always emphasized the word 'computers' as if they were public enemy number 1. In his mind, they were. Technology wasn't his thing. But Mister Carter did look about hundred and six years old!!!

That's it. I decided to go to the local library first thing in the morning. I climbed into bed.

I was too much on edge to sleep. I paced the floorboards until daybreak. As nine o'clock rolled around, I bolted out of the door. I didn't tell my parents. I raced without stopping the three blocks over to the library.

The old building stood deadly quiet. More quiet than normal when I entered. Two librarians shuffled around near the counter. An old woman in mittens muttered and grumbled continually to herself near the fire exit. I watched her moseying out of sight towards the section on animals at the back of the ground floor.

Right. Time to get started. I placed my bag on a chair. I began my quest to try and find out what the hell was going on in my life. I searched and searched the lines of books on the various shelves in the non-fiction section. I couldn't find anything. The closest I came was a book about the undead in Manhattan. That turned out to be about vampires working in the office blocks in the late 1950s. Sounded quite interesting. Maybe another time.

'This is stupid,' I told myself but I carried on looking. After an hour of rummaging around, I made a decision to approach one of the men behind the desk. The man wore a bright red sweater. Head down. He sat diligently stamping the inside of the books. Then stacking them into two neat piles.

'Excuse me sir.'

The man rolled his eyes to the ceiling at being interrupted from doing the most important job in the world. 'Don't roll your eyes at me,' I wanted to tell him, 'I'm a customer.' I purposely lowered my voice. 'Do you have any books on…on…on soul walking?'

'Have you checked the pet sections…loads in there.' He carried on branding the inside covers of the books.

'No…not dog walking ... soul walking,' I repeated a little louder.

The librarian heaved a heavy sigh on placing a book in the wrong stack. 'Well try horror…fiction…Stephen King's got something called dead something-or-other. Don't know what the fascination is personally.' He pointed to the racks on his left-hand side. He carried on.

'No…it's….'

From out of nowhere, the other librarian emerged behind the desk. A wicked twist in his left eye made him look quite comical. A lot older than his work colleague, the man was dressed all in grey. Pants. Shoes. Shirt. Sweater. The drab colour matched his complexion. The only real colour to him was a dab of red blood on his chin which I assumed must have been a cut from shaving.

'What was the book called you were looking for?' he spoke slowly. Very deliberately. His eyes drilled into mine.

I didn't want to go through the whole rigmarole again. 'Forget it. It was a stupid idea anyway.'

As I turned away, the man caught my hand. His skin felt cold. Clammy. 'No…tell me. I'm sure I can help you.' His expression didn't alter. His left eye floating aimlessly around in its socket.

'Okay…it's a book about soul walking or soul walkers. Or soul something or other. Apparently, it's about people whose job it is,' I paused, '….is to walk the…'

He squeezed my hand. 'I know what they do,' He turned to his colleague. 'Rob, I'll see to this.'

The other librarian was still too engrossed in putting ink in the ink stamping device to listen. Or even care about what we were talking about. The grey one motioned his head for me to follow him. I grabbed my bag. Shadowing the strange man up to the second floor.

'Who told you about the book?' he asked while continuing walking to the far corner of the room.

I dithered. 'Oh…just some… Hummm… homeless person.'

'Old Jezzie was it?'

I dropped my gym bag onto the floor. The thud it made echoed around the building.

'Do you mind?' the mumbling woman cried out from somewhere down below the mezzanine floor.

I snatched at the man's arm. 'Do you know him? Do you know Jezzie?'

'All the soul walkers in this area know Jezzie. He's quite famous,' he added, 'has he whacked you with his cane yet?' I shook my head. The librarian looked me up and down. 'It won't be long I bet. A couple of short, sharp blows to the cranium.' Chuckling, he trudged onwards.

I stood puzzled. 'Hang on, so, are you one too? You know…a soul walker?'

'Shhhhhh,' the librarian glanced left and right before nodding excitedly. 'Seventeen years now,' he boasted. 'I was about your age when I started. One hundred and twenty-three souls successfully taken to the station. I've only lost four in all that time. What about you?'

I felt too embarrassed to tell the odd-looking man the truth. The truth that I wasn't really sure what the heck he was talking about. 'What souls? What station?'

Instead, I played along. 'Oh…I'm new to it all. Just learning the ropes.' I quickly changed the subject. 'Do you have epileptic fits too?'

'Narcolepsy,' the man said so matter-of-factly. 'Can't control it. I just fall asleep; doesn't matter where I am…'

'Lucky you work in a library then,' I joked. The man stared at me obviously not amused. For once, both his eyes pointed in the same direction. Pointed straight at me. Sending a shiver down my spine.

He sauntered on. I followed. He unclipped a red velvet rope from across the entrance to a set of winding iron stairs. A sign attached stated that 'staff only' were allowed beyond that point. We both leisurely climbed the stairs to the third floor. Our footsteps reverberating around the old historic building. At the top, a small, spooky looking attic style room greeted us. It smelled of mothballs and loneliness. The only light made its way in through two dusty skylight windows.

The librarian grinned. 'I think what you are looking for may be in here.' He pointed to an extremely old book shelf. 'Good luck.' He winked at me with his gamy eye before disappearing back down the way we had come.

I glanced about. The place was eerie and spooky. I wanted to follow him. To race after him. But I knew I had to find out what this was all about. I scanned the small space. The shelves appeared stacked full of old hardback books. Books of all shapes and sizes. Many covered in dust or spider webs or both. I squinted in the poor light to read the titles. There was some really weird stuff. Books on the occult. Demons. Torture. Death. The war of angels. I explored the shelves for a while. Handling each book with care. I still couldn't find anything on soul walkers. The man reappeared again about fifteen minutes later. He gently tapped me on the shoulder. I almost jumped out of my converse.

'Everything ok?' The man's one eyeball now completely at a right angle to the other one.

'You frightened the life out of me.' I clutched my heart. I added, 'There's nothing here. Nothing at all. I've checked the shelves twice.'

'Maybe you are looking too hard.' He smirked.

'Maybe I'm just wasting my time,' I wanted to reply. I resisted. Instead, I simply shrugged my shoulders in a 'I don't know what you are talking about' sort of way.

The librarian pulled a comb out of his pocket. He stood there running it through the several strands of hair left on top of his head. His comb looked disgusting. Full of loose hair and other weird things.

'Perhaps you need to close your eyes to find it. Feel for it. Believe in it,' he squawked. Then as if by magic, he was gone again.

'Great,' I grunted, 'I've got to feel for it. Feel the force. Let the force be with you. I'm in some kind of Star Wars movie, like Luke Skywalker. I'm Luke Soul Walker or Leo Soul Walker. That's it I'm Leo Soul Walker.' I chuckled to myself.

I wasn't falling for the weird bloke's advice. His black magic tricks. Stubbornly, I searched one more time with my eyes wide open. Still nothing. I glanced about to make sure I wasn't being Punk'd. Or filmed for one of those other TV shows. The ones that show stupid people doing stupid things. 'Only in America,' my dad would always say when watching them. 'Only in America.'

After convincing myself there were no cameras, I reluctantly tried the way the weird dude had suggested. I closed my eyes. I opened them again. Just in case someone was waiting to pounce on me. I was alone. I tried again. This time I closed them tight. Carefully I moved my hand along the shelf of books. Lightly touching them one by one. Halfway along, my fingers stopped. I touched the spine of a book. Without thinking, I gently pulled it out. I opened my eyes and stared at it. The book was entitled, 'The Art of Soul walking'. Butterflies flapped around in my stomach. My knees wobbled 'Now that's weird!' I studied it curiously. 'Where were you hiding?'

Instantly it felt a lot colder in the room. I shivered. I decided to take the book back downstairs to the less creepy second floor. Once there, I sat at a table on a small balcony overlooking the main doors. It was light. I felt safe. Well, safer than where I had just come from.

The book wasn't very big. Only about ten pages thick. It fitted into the palm of my hand. The cover, a dark brown colour. The title written in old italic style with faded yellow wording. Nothing else appeared on the front or the back. Downstairs, a large clock ticked and tocked away. My hands soaked with sweat. I took a deep breath. I pulled back the front cover. At exactly the same time, a door creaked slowly open somewhere down below. It made me break out in a cold sweat. It reminded me of a badly made horror movie. I breathed out and started reading.

Soul walking. Chapter one: Your Role.

A soul walker's role and responsibility, in the process, is to assist the spirit of your carefully selected client from the Earth world to the Station of Discovery. You are to provide security and balance during the death transition process.

I stopped reading for a second. I considered what it was telling me. Assuming it meant I, or whoever, had to take these dead people's souls to some kind of station where they get discovered. I gulped hard. 'Those pieces of paper I kept finding, and throwing away, must have been some kind of map,' I muttered. I really was an idiot.

I read on.

You will simply act as a guide and aid the person, or persons, through the maze of non-physical realms, to the cross over point, where the client's soul will be stripped bare by the purest of angels. Only then will their future be decided.

I didn't have a clue what this bit was going on about. Although it sounded like these 'people' were being transported like cattle to the slaughterhouse.

'Person or persons,' I re-read the line again. I slumped back in the chair. Puffing out my cheeks. To be honest I didn't want to deliver one of them, never mind a pack of them, or whatever a group of dead people's souls were called. A shoal. Maybe, a soul of dead people, I thought. My mind alive with energy. My knees knocking nervously under the table.

I moved quickly through the next chapter. It explained in detail *how the clients would basically shred their outer 'jacket' they wore (commonly referred to as their skin). The dead spirits would no longer breathe and would sometimes appear full of life and energy.* I chuckled at the irony in what I had just read.

I suddenly felt hungry. I opened up a bag of chips I had brought with me. I ate quietly so I wouldn't get in trouble. Down in the entrance, the main revolving door deliberately moved around. That's strange. I stopped munching. I watched the doors come to a stop. No one came in or went out. I dismissed it and carried on reading. Engrossed.

The large creature with the hood covering its deformed features emerged from the door. Invisible to the human eye. Once inside the library, the man-thing sniffed the air. Still inhaling, it headed to the back section of the ground floor. It didn't bother to look right or left. It's pace quickening with each stride.

Near the back wall amongst the shelves of books on animals, the shopping bag dropped from the mumbling woman's hands. Tins of cat food rolled along the wooden tiled floor. She quickly bent down to retrieve them. Not paying any real attention to the pins and needles spreading up her left arm to her shoulder. It was only when the pain hit her full force in her chest, did she realize something was wrong. She rocked backwards on her heels. Grabbing at the shelf to stop her fall.

Seconds later, she lay spread-eagled on the floor. Her eyes open. Her last breath about to leave her body. The hooded creature loomed over her. It waited patiently for the spirit of the dead woman to rise up.

Upstairs I sat absorbed in the book. My lips moved as I read the bit called 'Taboos and Dangers.' I muttered the title of the last chapter over and over before daring to turn over the pages.

The journey to the stations is full of danger and distractions. There are many things you must learn and there are many rules you must obey.

Your role is to take the dead's souls to the stations and nowhere else – no distractions, no straying off the route.

'Where else would you take a bunch of dead people's souls?' I asked himself. 'Disney Land?' I imagined me and a load of dead individuals all sitting on a bus with Mickey Mouse ears on our heads. I shook the stupid thoughts from my mind. I read on.

You are not to judge, just deliver.

Only take the clients you have been assigned. No one else.

Never tell your client where you are taking them.

Never ever get personal with your clients.

I placed the book on the table. Biting my lower lip until I felt a slight pain. I wondered how I would remember all the things I had to do. Should I write them down? Or better still could I ask the grey-looking librarian if I could copy the pages. I carried on. Carefully placing my finger on each word.

Souls are a rare commodity in the non-physical realms and there are many interested parties ready to block your path. The main ones to be aware of, and avoided, are: -

I *t*urned the page quickly to find a sketch of a demon facing me. It looked exactly like Zotto, but with two evil eyes not one.

The soul stealers – Lucifer's little foot demons on Earth. They will stop at nothing to steal souls because with each soul they steal they will get rewarded with gifts of beauty or entry to sit with Satan in the fires of hell.

'Gifts of beauty,' I pictured Zotto with his one yellowy eye and purple skin. 'No chance, not even a full make-over on one of those TV shows would help him.' Now at least I knew why the leader of the demons wanted the souls so badly. It started to make sense in a rather outlandish kind of way.

I turned the last page. Downstairs, the revolving door opening for a second time broke my concentration again. It must be windy outside I assumed. Although the branches of the near-by trees looked quite still. I carried on.

Once again, invisible to all humans, a gang of evil demons came darting through the revolving doors. They spilled into the large foray. Tripping over each other as they ran. Four of them in total. 'This way… this way,' one of them pointed towards the back wall under the mezzanine flooring.

They sprinted off through the various racks housing the selection of assorted books. They howled and cheered as they ran. They scurried into B rack. Stopping dead in their tracks. Bumping into each other. A bit like a gang of dumb policemen in some old black and white silent movie. Sitting on the recently deceased old woman's chest, the large man-spider creature hissed at them. The last remains of her spirit body hanging out of its mouth. The demons backed away. Growling. Spitting. Hissing. The spider creature returned the snarl. Followed by an almighty roar. The demon's turned and fled empty handed back out into the street.

Back upstairs, unaware of what was going on below, a strange feeling crawled all over my skin. I looked around nervously before finishing off the last page. The words 'Efil Shadows' was printed on the page.

Efil Shadow – this creature is the deadliest. They can swallow up an entire spirit in one bite. They are more cunning than the soul stealers. Beware of them. They can appear at any time and from anywhere and take many forms.

An image of the large man-spider creature that rushed at me on my first experience with the girl who had jumped from the building popped into my mind. I definitely didn't like the sound of them. I finished the book. Placing it on the table top. I felt quite exhausted trying to take it all in. I still wasn't sure why I was involved in it. Why now? Why me? And importantly, where would it end?

A hand touched my shoulder.

'WHAAA…' I screamed. Everyone in the building stared up at me. The book stamping librarian shook his head. Placing his finger up to his mouth.

'I don't look that bad do I?' Beth whispered in my ear.

I gripped my chest for the second time that day. My cheeks turning the colour of a ripe tomato. She pulled up a chair next to me.

'What are you doing here brain box?' she asked. 'And what is it that you are so engrossed in?'

I tried my best to hide the book. She was too fast. 'The Art of Soul Walking.' She looked bemused. 'Wow!! I didn't realize you were into all that Goth stuff, Leo.' She seemed quite impressed.

'I…I…I…,' I stuttered, 'someone told me it was a good read.' It was the first stupid thing that popped into my head.

'Who was that?' she joked, 'Marilyn Manson.'

I placed the book out of harm's way. 'Well, what are you doing here?' Changing the subject.

'Looking to buy some shoes,' she sarcastically replied. I glanced down at her feet. 'No, idiot, I'm reading up on Teatown for the school trip in a couple of weeks. I wanna see if it's worth being stuck with Sharon Bell and the rest of the airheads all day or not.' She glared at me.

'I'm going,' I spluttered my words out.

She rocked back in her chair. 'Another reason to stay home then,' she joked. Keeping a straight face.

I sighed. I looked down to see a spider crawling up the table leg onto the wooden surface. It scurried across the top. Zigzagging as it traveled.

Beth stiffened. I could tell she was trying not to show me she was scared. She scooted her chair closer to mine. I breathed in. She smelled so fresh. Her hand felt so soft on my bare arm. I gently picked the small insect up. Placing it back down gently on the floor. Trying my best not to show her I was fearful as well. I hated spiders.

'My hero,' she said. 'Do you want to go to Starbucks?'

'M…m…me?' I stuttered again.

'Yes, of course you…unless there's another spider catching hero here.'

'Hang on, a minute.' I bounded up the stairs to place the book back on the old dusty shelf. I didn't even like coffee. But I would have had a cup of lighter fluid to be with the girl of my dreams. The grey librarian nodded knowingly to me as we left.

We walked out of the library. Strolled out into the bright sun light.

'What's the gym bag for?' she asked curiously.

'Karate lessons,' I hesitated before adding, 'Me and Josh.'

I could tell she was dying to laugh. I was right. She couldn't hold it in any longer. The laughter escaped from her pretty mouth. 'No way! Not only are you a secret Goth but also a kung fu fighting warrior.' She playfully karate chopped my neck. 'Anymore skeletons in your closet, Leo Young?' She grabbed my arm. Leading me in the direction of the coffee shop.

In the background the Efil creature sauntered out of the library door. Licking his lips. It pulled up its hood and disappeared down into the subway.

5
I don't do small talk ...

45 minutes later, I stood alone in the street. Checking my watch every couple of seconds. As usual I was waiting for Josh. Waiting outside the old convenience store which had been converted into a new martial arts academy. I paced up and down. Muttering to myself. Twenty minutes late. I knew he would be.

'Hey Leo,' Josh called out. Strolling across the road. Munching on a double cheese burger. By the time he reached me, the burger had gone.

'Come on Josh…we're gonna be late.' I noticed he didn't have his duffel bag with him.

'Well…it's like this…I…I can't go tonight,' he hesitated. Licking the sauce off his fingers.

I glared at him. Waiting to hear what new and laughable excuse my friend had devised this time. He had already missed half of the lessons since we had agreed that if we were going to stop getting beaten up by bullies like Ethan, we better do something about it.

'I've got a meeting...very important. Big family thing,' Josh looked down at the pavement.

I couldn't be arsed to listen to anymore of his pretexts. I picked up my bag. Storming off, I muttered back. 'Yeah? With who? Mr. Nacho Belgrande?'

Josh piped up. 'Don't be like that Leo. You know I've never been into all this karate chop stuff. It's just not for me. I'm more laid back.'

'Yeah...laid back. Laid back on your recliner eating Doritos and watching Family Guy,' I berated. 'I'm going. Some of us have bullies to fight,' I added quietly, 'and demons to overcome.'

'Leo.'

'Forget it Josh.' I opened the door to the building.

'Oh, thank you,' he shouted back. 'Thank you very much. Don't forget if it wasn't for me faking your parents' signature on the consent form, you wouldn't be doing it at all.' Josh ambled off in the opposite direction.

Inside the building, I quickly changed into my white karate suit. I rushed into the studio as fast as I could. Taking my place with the other kids sitting crossed legged in a circle on the floor. Master Kang the instructor ignored me. I knew he wouldn't be happy. Being on time was one of the unwritten rules in Master Kang's lessons. 'Bloody Josh,' I whispered under my breath.

A tough looking Puerto Rican kid wearing his white suit tied up by a brown belt stood in the middle of the circle. Doing stretching exercises.

Master Kang pointed to me.

'What?' I looked at the others.

'You late, you fight,' the instructor turned away.

'No…Mister Kang…I've only been here four times…I don't…'

'Fight,' Master Kang glared at me. So did the rest of the kids. Most I suspected were quite pleased I had got picked instead of them.

Wearily, I stood up. For a split second, I considered racing out of the building as fast as my legs could motor. Although it was hard not to, I fought the urge. I did come here to toughen up. Nervously I stood opposite the brown belt. The larger boy's expression hadn't changed. He looked hard. Much too hard for me. Much too hard for many grown men I imagined.

'Ready?' the instructor questioned.

'No…' I stood there in shock. 'I can't fight him.' I pointed at the boy. 'I'll get my butt kicked.'

'Fight,' Ignoring my plea, Mister Kang clapped his hands.

'But…but,' my protests were in vain.

The brown belt bounced on the balls of his bare feet towards me. I backed away trying not to look like a sissy. I didn't like this one bit. It was all too real. I'd enjoyed whacking the punch bags while pretending to be Bruce Lee, but this was way too scary. Way too real.

The bigger teenager kept coming. He never took his eyes off me. The aggression evident in his features. His long gangly tattooed arm whizzed past the side of my head. I glanced around for an escape route.

'Move,' someone shouted from the back. 'Move, Leo.'

My legs felt like lead. I stepped back. Fortunately for me, I blocked another jab which would have knocked my teeth out if it had made contact. The image flashed into my mind of Josh sitting in a restaurant. A plate of ribs stacked in front of him. His mouth covered in BBQ sauce.

'Why didn't I go with him?'

Another punch jarred my shoulder back. The brown belt lunged forward. Ready to finish me off. I reacted with a wild aimless counter punch. A punch which somehow caught the on-rushing boy squarely in the chest. It rocked him backwards on his heels.

Everyone in the hall looked stunned at what they had just seen. No one more so than me. The Japanese instructor winked at me. That only made the brown belt madder. Madder and a lot meaner. He stepped in again with a series of jabs.

'Sorry…sorry,' I mouthed the words while ducking down to miss the violent blows. 'I didn't mean to hit yo…uuuu.'

That was the last thing I remember. A beast of a roundhouse kick from the older kid walloped me on the jaw. The thudding sensation pierced my ear drum. The pain travelled quickly to my brain. I could feel myself falling but couldn't do anything about it. My arms and legs shut down. My head hit the floor first. Followed by the rest of my body.

I lay there for a while. Listening to the shouts echo around my semiconscious brain. I felt as if I was floating. The voices in the sports hall were quickly replaced by the distinctive sound of a moving train. My eyes shot open. I found myself lying out on the ground under a railway bridge in a rundown part of the city.

'Stop lying around and follow me.' Jezzie poked me with his cane.

'What?' I staggered to my feet. My jaw aching. My head in a daze.

'You heard. This is going to be your one and only lesson from the master.' The tramp hobbled away towards a line of boarded up houses.

Although the sky was overcast, it was still warm. Warm and humid. I was still in my karate uniform. Barefooted, I rushed to the old man's side. 'How did you know I was going to be here?' I stepped on a stone. I let out a cry.

The tramp ignored the question. 'Listen kid I don't do small talk…especially with your kind.'

'Kind…what kind?' He made me sound like an alien being from outer space.

'The hooligan kind…teenager punks with no thought for other people's lives.' He limped on.

'Huh?' The tramp's outburst confused me.

'Never mind, just step on it,' his tone aggressive. 'Keep up.'

We walked in silence past two blocks of desolate and rundown houses. Finally, Jezzie plopped himself down on a bench. I joined him. My bare feet hurting. The side of my head throbbing. We sat overlooking a basketball court. Graffiti from the local gangs covered the walls and the empty buildings that surrounded the play area. The concrete court stood almost deserted except for a couple of older kids playing a game of two on two. I looked on a little jealous as they raced up and down the court. Passing and dribbling. One player sank a lay-up from the edge of the court.

'Am I having another fit?' I asked him. He ignored me…again! His dark eyes scanning our surroundings.

'Well, why are we here?' I added. 'Is someone going to die?'

Jezzie twirled the cane in his fingers. 'You should have been a bloody detective. Now shut up. Watch. Listen. And learn.'

The ball game got quite competitive. I began to quite enjoy the game out on the court. So much so that I didn't notice, the group of punk kids appearing from out of nowhere. Hoods pulled over their heads. Tattoos crawling up their arms.

Jezzie stiffened. His knuckles white as he clutched his cane.

The gang stopped kicking around a tin can. Wandering deliberately forward like a disorganized army towards the court. The basketball players stopped. The ball hit the back board. It bounced towards the leader of the thugs. A lean muscular boy with olive skin. Menacing eyes. He wore a bright, yellow wife-beater vest. Baggy jeans. He stopped the ball with his foot. A wicked grin spread across his face.

'He's a nasty piece of work,' Jezzie muttered.

Although they appeared older, the basketball players nervously looked at each other. The switchblade in the gang leader's hand glistened in the sunlight. Without breaking his stride, he marched towards the boys. Picking up the ball, he stabbed it several times. He threw the deflated object back at them.

'Here you go,' he said arrogantly. 'Game over.'

His cronies snickered. Following on behind him.

Something else caught my attention. A large Efil stood behind the chain link fence. This one was truly enormous. It's head almost touching the top of the fence. Its white eyes glowed brightly in the surrounding darkness of the shadows.

'Jezzie,' I whispered. I completely forgot he had warned me about calling him by his nickname.

'Shut the hell up, kid.' Jezzie concentrated hard on the scene unfolding on the basketball court.

'But I think there's a…' By the time I pointed, the creature had vanished.

The leader of the thugs shouted out to the basketball boys. 'Your turn next unless you give us your money...' The players backed away. Scared. Ready to run.

'And their shoes,' another gang member demanded.

The gang moved in tighter. Like a pack of lions surrounding their prey. The basketball players suddenly ran. The chain linked fence blocked their escape. One of the basketball boys slumped forward. Hit over the back of the head with a club. Another one cried out. Collapsing against a fence. Several kicks rained down on him. The gang showed no mercy. Continued beating the poor boys savagely.

'Do something,' I pulled at the tramp's arm.

'It's out of our hands...just wait.' Jezzie showed little form of emotion.

I leapt up and ran at the boys. I froze on seeing one of the kids getting pummeled by two gang members with their fists and a heavy metal chain. I wanted to help, but I was too scared to take the next step.

'Sit down kid,' Jezzie pulled me back into my seat. 'No one can see you.'

Down on the court, the leader wielding the switchblade approached the poor boy forced up against the fence. The boy's face grimaced. The knife ripped through his stomach. He rolled about. Screaming out in agony. Blood gushed from his wound. The leader sneered. Plunging the six-inch blade in several more times. A look of hatred etched on his young evil face.

The play area emptied in seconds. On hearing the sirens of a police car, the gang scattering in all directions. Running through the maze of roads and alleyways

I needed to help. I rushed down to see if I could do anything for the dying boy. I got near him but the larger-than-life Efil bounded across the concrete court knocking me to the ground. The creature stood above the dying boy. It's teeth showing. It's eyes bright.

I got up. Sprinting back up to the tramp. Only now was Jezzie getting to his feet.

'Quick help him,' I blurted out. 'Help him…before it gets him.'

On the court, the spirit of the boy appeared. It was short lived. The Efil creature gnawed into his flesh. Chewing him up. Once the boy had fully disappeared, the monster roared out into the evening sky.

The tramp showed no emotion. He walked away. Unaffected.

'It said in the book, you were supposed to protect him. Take his soul to the station,' I yelled, 'What type of soul walker are you?'

The tramp turned abruptly. In one movement, he picked me up by the throat. He was much stronger than he looked. My feet dangled in the air. The veins in the hobo's neck pulsed.

'He is not the one we are here for.'

'What?'

'It's that one.' Jezzie pointed at the leader of the gang strolling nonchalantly away from the scene. Jezzie released his grip on me. I dropped to the ground on one knee. 'And don't ever talk to me like that boy…or else!' He limped off.

Catching my breath, I sulked behind.

On the main boulevard, the thug wiped his switchblade clean. He tossed the knife down the sewer. He ambled down the street. Bumping shoulder to shoulder with a businessman walking in the opposite direction. 'Watch it,' the thug barked like a rabid dog into the man's face.

Although it wasn't his fault, the businessman apologized.

'Better be.' The thug pushed him in the chest. Without looking, the boy stepped out into the busy road. The on-rushing truck flattened the thug. The vehicle dragging him several hundred yards before coming to a stop not far from where I stood.

'BWAAAAAAAA,' I puked again at the horrendous sight of the dead punk's bloodied body.

The tramp pulled me up by my hair. 'Look kid, you are in the wrong job if you are going to barf every time you see a bit of blood. Now come on…before they arrive.' His eyes darted about the street.

'What was that?' The spirit of the dead thug popped up from his lifeless body.

The tramp grabbed him in one movement. 'You are coming with us.'

'Hey Granddad…get your hands off. Who do you think you are?' The youth jerked his arm away. 'The police?'

The tramp twirled him around. He yanked the boy's arm up behind his back. 'I said come on. We have no time to waste.' Jezzie pushed him forward.

The boy resisted with each step. We walked a few blocks through the mass of human traffic flowing the other way.

'Haven't I seen you before Granddad?' the youth glared at the old man.

Jezzie ignored him. Looking left and right before spitting on the ground.

'I know,' the youth continued. 'I know where I've seen you.' His lips curled up into a smirk.

Turning around, the tramp pinned him up against the side of a shop window. 'If you want your soul to get out of here alive …you better shut that mouth of yours.' Jezzie pushed him hard again. 'Now move.'

'You're crazy…I'm out of here.'

'It's no use,' I chipped in. 'You're dead,' I changed my step to avoid a pile of dog poop on the pavement.

'Yeah…bite me.' the thug began to march away.

Jezzie's cane moved swiftly. He whacked the punk on the back of the head. The boy fell to the ground. Dazed.

'What is rule number five?' Jezzie spat the words at me. The tip of his stick waved inches from my face. 'Well…I'm waiting.'

My mind went blank. I stood staring at the dog mess on the sidewalk.

'Never ever tell them where they are or where they are going…understand Einstein?' The tramp's eyes wild with rage. The wooden cane tapped my head. 'I said… understand?'

'Yes…yes,' I muttered quietly. Feeling like a naughty kid caught pinching sweets.

'Yes what?'

'Yes Sir.'

Jezzie panged me on the head again.

'Sorry…yes Mister James.'

The tramp turned his attention back to the thug. He had pinned him underneath his foot to the ground. From somewhere deep inside his heavily stained overcoat, he threw me a length of thin nylon cord. 'Now tie this around his hands. Good and tight.' I did what I was told. Jezzie roughly pulled the killer to his feet. 'Now you… punk…start walking.'

I held the rope attached to the thug. Jezzie followed close behind. Every time the thug stopped or complained, the tramp poked him sharply in the back with his cane.

'There's a station close by. About four blocks over.' Jezzie checked the map. We continued to move amongst the New Yorkers and tourists that crowded the streets.

'What are you talking about Granddad?' the youth asked. 'What train station?'

I turned around to face him. 'Not a train station. It's a station where dead people's souls go to be…' I stopped when I saw the anger on Jezzie's face. His fingers clenched around his cane. Ready to strike. 'Beats me.' I turned. Faced front. Walking on.

'Move,' Jezzie whacked the thug with his stick again.

'Stop hitting me, grandpa.' The boy pulled hard on the rope. Dragging me backwards.

'Walk, I said.' Jezzie shoved the thug harder. 'Or I will drop you where you stand…for good.'

The thug and the tramp stared at each other for a full minute. I glanced at each of them as if I was watching a rally in a tennis match. Thankfully, the thug stared down.

We moved off. Staying close to the main road. Jezzie purposely avoided alleyways and dark deserted places. The traffic was heavy. The car horns bellowing out.

'Stop,' Jezzie grunted. His nose high in the air. Sniffing like a wolf on the whiff of a scent.

I unknowingly mimicked my new mentor's action. I couldn't smell anything except the exhaust fumes which tickled my throat. 'What is it?'

'Stealers.' The tramp's eyes searched the crowd. 'They are close…up there…go.' He pointed to a narrow side street between two large buildings. I didn't like the look of it. I didn't really want to be in the front. To be honest I didn't want to be in the line at all. I took small baby steps. My eyes darting from side to side.

'Stealers…is that a gang?' the tied-up thug asked.

I couldn't help himself. I was just too darn nervous. 'No, stealers are the creatures trying to steal your…' This time the blow from the cane connected with the crown of my head with a real force.

'Ouch!' I rubbed my skull.

'Don't you understand English, kid?' the tramp bellowed out. 'Now shut up.'

Out of the blue, two demons leaped from the fire escape above my head. One landed on Jezzie's back.

'Aaaaaaarrrrrrgggggghhhhhh!' I shrieked. Dropping the rope tied to the thug. I cowered in a doorway.

Jezzie pulled the beast over his shoulder. He booted it hard in the ribs. The thing rolled over and over before springing back on to its stubby feet. The second one bit into the hobo's neck. The thug stood in astonishment. Mouth open wide before fleeing into a laundromat. A look of terror on his face.

'Make sure he doesn't get away.' Wincing in pain, Jezzie pulled the demon biter over his head. He punched it as hard as he could.

I hesitated. I looked around for a possible escape route. I didn't want to fight. The road seemed like my best option to get out of here. I stepped forward. A muscular demon wearing a weight lifting vest blocked my path. It growled. Rocking back and forth on its powerful legs. Clicking its knuckles. Every hair on my body stood on end. Behind me, Jezzie wrestled with the other two demons on the ground.

'Look…I don't belong here,' I groveled. Moving back against a wall.

The soul stealer grinned. It charged towards me. Teeth glimmering. Instinctively I closed my eyes. I brought my fist up. More in self-defense than attack. My knuckles caught the monster firmly between the eyes. The accidental blow sent it spinning to the floor.

The creature lay motionless on the ground. I stood looking at my clutched fists. A huge adrenaline rush raced through my body. The best feeling I'd ever experienced. For some reason I raised my arm in the air like a captain of a team lifting up a trophy.

'Go on…get out of here,' Jezzie barked at the other two retreating creatures. They both scrambled away. Bloodied and battered.

'Did you see that? I knocked it out…knocked it out cold.' I stood in a glory trance.

The tramp looked around frantically 'Where's the thug?'

'Did you see that punch?' Hoping for some kind of recognition from my mentor.

'Never mind that…where did he go?' Jezzie screamed at me. He grabbed hold of my collar. 'You've lost him. The one thing I asked you to do and you screw it up.' He pushed me away.

I was speechless. 'But…but.' I pointed towards the shop. 'He went in there.'

'Leave a boy to do a man's job.' The tramp limped towards the shop entrance. Passing the unaware shopkeeper busy preparing to close up. 'Now,' Jezzie snarled at me, 'you stand here and if he comes out…you holler. Do you think you are able to do that?' he added sarcastically. I nodded. He entered the shop.

Once out of sight, I paced around. Moaning and kicking out at the metal shutters of a shop window. 'It isn't my fault…I didn't ask to be here,' I muttered. 'Who does he think he is anyway? Him and that stupid walking stick.' I pretended to play the role of the tramp. Limping around. Barking orders. 'Oh kid…do as I say or else…cause…I'm…the terminator…the homeless terminator.'

I stopped my improv performance instantly on seeing Jezzie standing there glaring at me. The thug by his side. The boy's nose bleeding. His left eye slightly swollen.

'What are you doing now?' Jezzie shook his head.

I could feel my face glowing bright red. I shrugged.

We walked the remaining blocks in silence. Heading towards the steeple of a church. Poking out high above the houses. Once inside, the church stood cold and intimidating. Dotted around in the pews, a few individuals sat praying. Near the large alter, an elderly woman cleaned wax from the candle holder with a blunt knife.

'Wait here,' Jezzie handed me the rope. 'On second thought.' He took it back and proceeded to tie the prisoner to a wooden pew.

'I'll do it myself.' He limped away towards the back of the building. 'Stay here and watch him.'

As soon as the tramp disappeared, the thug struggled to get himself loose. 'Let me out of here dude,' he half pleaded.

I ignored him. I was afraid to speak. Afraid to look up at him. Instead, I glanced up at the rafters. Several ugly stone gargoyles glared down. 'That's weird,' I thought. 'Things like that inside a church.'

Suddenly the thug toppled onto the wooden seat. 'Help…help.'

'What's wrong?' I turned to face him.

'I'm choking,' he gasped for air. Clutching his throat. 'I can't breathe…help me.'

I wasn't sure what to do. I stepped in closer to make sure he was alright. Grabbing me around the neck with his one loose hand, he threw me like a rag doll into the pew. 'Now tell me.' He tightened his grip. 'what's going on?'

'Let me go,' I was the one choking now. Choking for real.

The thug squeezed harder.

'Ok…I'll tell you…let me go.'

The punk released his grip. He placed his knee on my chest. Reaching inside his coat, he pulled out a pack of cigarettes and a lighter. Up above us, I noticed two stone gargoyles eyelids popping opened. Sharp nails appeared out of their paws. A low growl escaped from their mouths.

'Those dawgs look real.' The punk carried on lighting up the cigarette.

'You shouldn't be doing that,' I looked anxiously up at the creatures.

It didn't bother him. He sucked on the nicotine stick. 'What's the deal?' Pushing his knee in harder.

I stared at the orange glow of the cigarette. 'Ok.' I caught my breath. 'This is called a station of discovery. It's a cross-over point. It's where your sou…' I didn't finish my sentence.

The cane whacked the thug on his hand. In the same movement, it flicked the cigarette out of his mouth and also whacked me on the shoulder. 'Leo…if you don't shut up…I swear…' Jezzie yelled. Next to him, a priest stood. Quite small in size with a balding head. His eyes appeared too close together. On his face a friendly smile.

Up in the rafters, the gargoyle beasts barked loudly. Their teeth dripping spittle.

'Shhhhh my boys.' The man of the cloth motioned to the creatures. The gargoyles did what they were told. Yet they remained hunched up in their "ready to attack" stance.

The tramp and the priest looked the thug up and down. 'This is the scum-bag. Number 6154378868,' Jezzie announced. Reading the number on top of the map.

'Looks like he put up a bit of a fight Jezz,' the priest blinked.

'Not really,' Jezzie was short with his reply. 'He's just a punk. A no-good murdering punk.' He went to hit the boy with his cane but stopped himself. Untying the hooligan instead. Forcefully pushing him into the confessional box at the far end of the church. The door automatically locked behind the punk. A red light activated on the outside of the box.

'You going to watch this one Jezzie?' the priest opened the door of the box next door. 'Care to bet, say ten bucks?'

'No way, Father…that wouldn't be fair on you. I've got the inside track on this one. I already know where he's going.' They both looked at the floor and nodded.

I pulled at the tramp's sleeve. 'Sorry Mister James…how can he see us?' I motioned my head towards the priest.

'He's a fresh one, isn't he?' the priest stuttered.

'Straight out of the womb,' the tramp barked back. 'Probably still breast feeding.'

The priest laughed loudly. Stopping only to examine the bite wounds on Jezzie's neck. 'Let's get those cleaned up for you before they get infected. And maybe a quick shot of whiskey to celebrate.' The priest clicked his fingers. Two of the gargoyles leaped down from their position in the rafters. They sat guarding the outside of the confessional box.

Jezzie wandered towards the side door. Passing the statue of Mary. 'Wait for me outside kid,' he yelled. 'And no beating them demons up all by yourself.' His laughter filled up the church.

I sat down for a minute. Confused. Scared. I really wanted to go home. I headed towards the door. The loud banging noise turned me back around. 'Let me out of here. You'll pay for this!' the thug boy yelled from inside the box.

The gargoyles sat stationary. Protecting the door. I looked around. Curious to see what was going on inside. The beasts didn't bother me as I popped into the box next to the hoodlum spirit. Once inside I pulled back a small curtain. The punk sat glaring at a screen above his head. A film was playing. Clips showing gang fights. Shootings. Muggings. All kind of nasty stuff. It took me a while to realize the main character in the violent movie was the thug himself. This wasn't a film. It was real life. Real things him and his gang had done. Above the screen, un-illuminated, were the words, good soul, bad soul.

What I was watching made me sick to my stomach. I didn't want to see anymore. I got up to leave. Something on the screen caught my attention. The thug and his gang meandered into a small park. They walked towards the hunched over figure of someone rummaging around in a trash can. The person looked up. 'Jezzie.' My mouth dropped to the floor. The gang circled around him. On the screen the thug slapped Jezzie hard in the face. The rest of his gang laughed. The tramp fell on the cold snowy ground. Then the attack started. Brutal. Endless. They kicked and punched the defenseless hobo. Even after the rest of the gang got bored and moved on, the thug leader continued with his attack. He stamped on Jezzie. Leaving his victim for dead. The movie on the screen changed to the present. It showed the incident on the basketball court earlier in the evening. Then the screen went blank.

The thug turned and grinned at me. 'Did you like that?'

'No wonder you recognized Jezzie…you coward,' I shouted at him. 'Hope you rot in hell.' I wanted to say something worse. But it wouldn't have been suitable in a church.

BAD SOUL, BAD SOUL, BAD SOUL.

The words flashed in big red letters above the screen. Followed by a low buzzing noise coming from the box itself. The buzzing grew louder and louder. The thug began to shake uncontrollably. The skin on his cheeks began to quiver violently as if he was being blasted in the face by a strong air gun. His eyes bulged. His jaw opened up wide. Exposing his teeth. He grabbed hold of his head with both hands. I stood there afraid to move a muscle, Suddenly, his entire body exploded. Gunk covered the glass window. I scrambled out of the box. The gargoyles were already back up amongst the rafters. Back to stone.

I felt sick. I rushed towards the exit of the church. The last seconds of the thug's life imprinted on my brain. I struggled to open the heavy doors. My hands shaking. Once outside, the sunlight lit up my face. I retched hard. Nothing came out. On the street the rush hour traffic was already crawling home. My face white with fear. I sat down on the step. Placing my head in my hands. Tears filled my eyes. I sat there, wondering what I was going to do next.

6
I want souls...understand?

The demon that had been beaten up by Jezzie in the alleyway limped into the large room in the hotel. Its mouth bleeding. Its leg damaged. Over its shoulder, a soul bag dangled down by its side.

'Where is he?' it gestured to the two other creatures lounging around on the leather couch playing Commander 2 on the giant TV screen.

The one with the controls nodded towards the white doors leading to the bedroom. It went back to blowing up angel soldiers on the simulated computer game.

'Is he in a good mood?' the bloodied demon placed its bag onto the table.

'What do you think?' the demon grunted without looking up. 'Oh no man...I've been killed.' He punched the cushion. Handing the remote to its partner.

The doors to the bedroom shot open. Zotto strolled out. A towel around his mid-drift. On his face the outline of a new dragon tattoo snaked down his cheek all the way down to the ankle of his right leg. The image hadn't been colored in yet. However, even at this early stage it looked quite alarming. Engulfing his deformed body.

'I like it Zotto. Suits you,' the demon muttered. Its words cut off by the stare from its leader.

'Never mind groveling. How many have you got for me?' Zotto demanded to know. His one evil eye burned into the creature's face. He picked up a long glass of white liquid. Sipping it up through a straw.

The bloodied demon hesitated. Finally emptying out the contents from the bag onto the teak table. Zotto's disappointed features stared at the three souls pulsing on the shiny surface. 'Is that it?' his words short and concise.

The demon looked down at the carpet. It shrugged. The other two creatures stopped playing their game. They sat perfectly still. On the screen bullets and flames flew in all directions.

'Well,' Zotto's voice rose higher with every word. 'Where's the punk kid and the one he murdered?'

'It's that tramp, Jezzie. He was already there. And now he's got a helper with him. Some kid in a karate suit…looks mean.'

Zotto chucked the glass across the room. It smashed into a million pieces against the wall. In one swift movement, he picked the demon up by its throat. Its feet dangled an inch off the carpet. 'I don't want excuses, I want souls. Understand?'

The creature struggled to breathe. 'I…I…'

'Understand?' Zotto stuck his face up even closer. The half-finished tattooed dragon inches from the other demon's face. 'Now go and get me some more.' Zotto pushed the creature hard in the chest. It toppled backwards, crashing into the TV set. Sparks fizzed out of the back. The dazed demon got to its feet. It staggered to the door. The other two demons glanced at each other, before slumping quietly deep down into the curves of the couch.

Zotto marched back into the room. Slamming the door shut. The tattooist sat on the edge of the bed waiting to complete his masterpiece. His hands trembling in fear.

7
his face the size of a balloon

The minute hand of the clock moved so slowly I felt as though it was actually going backwards. Impatiently I sat waiting for my checkup at the hospital. My mother next to me. Her head buried in some glossy magazine.

I stared blankly at the poster on the wall. Informing the reader of the dangers of underage sex. I had too much on my mind to take it all in. Being tested and probed for what must have been the millionth time in my short life proved more of a distraction.

In the waiting room, a few other people sat around. A small boy perched on his mother's lap. His head buried in a Nintendo game. On the other side of the room, a smart blond woman in a business suit sat with her legs crossed. A stylish leather briefcase tucked neatly next to her expensive shoes. She smiled at me. Before going back to scribbling notes in a planner.

'I think I'll make us one of these for dinner tomorrow.' My mother rammed the magazine in to my face. The page showed a colorful photograph of a blackberry tart. 'Yes…I think I will.'

'Mam, you can't cook,' was what I wanted and should have said. Everyone knew that. Well except for her. She was the worst cook in the world…bar none. Instead, I politely shrugged and muttered, 'Yeah…that will be nice.'

The glass slid back on the receptionist's window. A plain looking nurse with short hair and a pointy nose called out a name. 'Sam Taylor.'

The mother picked the little boy up off her lap. She spat onto a handkerchief and began to wipe the little boy's face. I cringed at the woman's actions. It reminded me of how my own mother used to do exactly the same thing to me years before. She still would if given half the chance. I quivered in disgust at the thought of it.

Poor little Sam huffed and puffed all the way into the doctor's office. I knew exactly how he must have felt. It brought back bitter memories of when I first started to come to places like this. I must have been around 4 or 5. I remembered sitting on the floor in my bedroom unable to move. I just sat there staring up at the ceiling. All alone in my own little world. At the time no one else noticed. Being so young, I didn't know any better. I thought it was normal. Everyone did.

'It's just a phase,' my father often said.

That all changed after my first 'real' seizure. It scared my parents half to death. My mother and I were in a basement of one of my classmate's houses. It had been transformed into a dance area for her ninth birthday. The place was full of excited kids. Some of the mothers were teaching them how to do some stupid 'birdy' dance routine. I found myself attracted to the flickering radiance of the strobe light. The bright white light twirling around in the centre of the room. I stared at it long. Hard. Transfixed. Unable to look away. My face twitched first. Then my arm. Followed by the rest of my body. I woke up thirty seconds later. Flat out on the ground. My mother screaming hysterically. Then came the worst part of all. I never forgot the faces of the kids. Their mothers. My mother. Gawking at me as though I was a wounded animal.

My entire life altered forever that day. The blackouts got more frequent. More intense. In a bad week I could have two to three attacks. The kids stopped calling for me to go out to play. I rarely, if at all, got invited to anymore parties. There were lots of doctors to see. Each had their own opinion. Each of those opinions hadn't helped. Eventually a specialist pinpointed a bout of meningitis when I was three and a half. He reckoned that was the most likely cause of my epileptic fits. The doctor didn't see an instant cure. Telling my parents that as I grew older, the attacks could start to subside and even stop altogether.

That was ten plus long years ago and in a different part of the world. In all that time, I was as close to being normal as the elephant man. And now just to add to my dilemma, I had somehow become a soul walker. Or to put the record straight, a soul walker who couldn't actually walk a dead spirit's soul across an empty road without losing it.

Back in the waiting room, the nurse behind the glass bellowed out my name. It pulled me out of my memories of self-pity. I wandered along my own personal green mile into the doctor's office. My mother behind me fussing over my hair. I was sure she was just about to spit on her handkerchief and clean my face!!! I fastened up my pace.

'So, you say the seizures are lasting longer.' Dr. Price made no eye contact with me at all. As if I wasn't even in the room. Directing all his questions to my mam.

'But I'm not having as many now,' I jumped to my own defense.

The doctor ignored me completely. He sat waiting for my mother to reply.

'Yes…much longer,' she mouthed, 'and more aggressive.'

A concerned look took over the man's face. 'Aggressive…explain.' For the first time the doctor acknowledged me over his round spectacles.

My mother embarrassed to carry on. She lowered her voice. 'Well Doctor, there's more kicking. Rolling around. Screaming. Bruising.'

With the tip of his pencil, the doctor tapped his chin thoughtfully. 'Anything else unusual?'

'Unusual…how's this?' I imagined myself pulling a snarling demon out of my coat and slapping it onto the desk. 'When I do black out, I end up fighting these things. Well, not fight as much as getting beaten up by them…but you get the picture.'

My mother shook her head. 'No…other than that he seems fine.'

The doctor nodded his large silver-haired head. He wrote something in my file. Placing his hand strategically over it so I couldn't read what he recorded. 'When it happens again, give him some Diazepam as soon as he comes out of it. Right away. It will help.' He wrote out a prescription. Handing it to my mother. 'I would like to carry out one or two tests.' He picked up the telephone without waiting for any agreement.

'What kind of tests Doctor?' she asked uneasily.

'An MRI scan, I want to make sure that there aren't any new brain abnormalities. It's nothing to really worry about.'

'Nothing to worry about.' That was easy for him to say, 'I bet no one adds the word abnormalities when they talk about him.'

My mother squeezed my hand. A worried look etched on her face.

Forty-five minutes later, I lay on a cold narrow bed in a bright white room. Silver spotlights illuminating my body. A man with bright ginger hair, a bandana wrapped around his head, fiddled with dials on the wall next to the table.

'What's that?' I nodded towards the big white circular machine behind his head.

'A scanner…It's a big camera full of magnets. We are going to take some pictures of your brain…if you have one,' he joked. Gently, he slid me into the brightly lit tunnel. Once inside I felt like a broken train stuck in a tunnel. Broken down and waiting for the engineers to come and fix me.

For something which appeared to be so new and hi-tech, the machine was surprisingly noisy. A loud pulsating sound whizzed around my claustrophobic brain. The procedure only lasted thirty minutes. The longest thirty minutes of my life.

'Can we go now?' my mother asked the nurse.

Behind the screen I pulled on my tee-shirt.

'Sorry,' a nurse stated. 'The doctor says he wants to see these before you go. It will only take about an hour.' she added.

We both sighed.

We sat outside the doctor's office. 'I'm going to get a drink,' I told my mother.

I wandered around the halls. Searching for a vending machine. Two men in dressing gowns walked past heading to the TV room. One wheeling a drip. Behind them an orderly tried to maneuver a gurney through the crammed corridor. I moved to one side to let him pass. I glanced down at the patient lying on the bed.

'Jezzie?' I dropped the bottle of Coke on the floor. My heart raced around in my chest like a hamster running around on a wheel.

The orderly, IPod in his ears, hummed along to some tune while heading towards the elevators. I followed close behind. Glaring at Jezzie's face. He looked so pitiful. Helpless. And surprisingly cleaner than the Jezzie I knew from our soul walking experiences.

'Jezzie, sorry Mister James…it's me…Leo,' I rather stupidly announced to the man lying unconscious on the portable bed.

'Hospital staff only.' The orderly placed his hand on my shoulder. Stopping me from following them inside the elevator.

'What?' I jumped.

'Hospital staff only…public elevators over there.' The man pointed across the corridor.

Before I could argue, the elevator door closed in front of me. I stood there helpless. I rushed towards the stairwell. Clambering up the stairs. Two at a time.

'Oh no…what floor?' I slapped my face at my stupidity. I raced back down to the ground to check. Two…three…four. The elevator continued to climb. Five…Six. It stopped.

I sprinted back up the stairs. 'Excuse me…excuse me,' I pleaded with a couple blocking the path on the stairs. I burst onto the ward. Struggling to catch my breath. Sweat dripped from my forehead.

The corridor led off in both directions. The only noise came from the faint sound of a TV set in the visitor's room. At one end, two nurses were busy preparing a gurney. I headed the opposite way. Looking in the window of every door. Near the emergency exit I found Jezzie. Laying in a small room at the end of the hall.

I entered. Closing the door behind me. I quietly approached the bed. In the corner, several square shaped pieces of equipment blinked and bleeped at regular intervals. Two tubes protruded out of his arms. Snaking their way up to an intravenous drip. The only thing on the table, by the side of his bed, was a water jug and a bed pan. Both looked like they hadn't been touched. There were no flowers. Magazines. Get-well cards.

'So, this is where you have been hiding.' I touched the hobo's hand. It felt warm. For once he didn't smell like rotten cabbage. I leaned back. Half expecting the tramp to jump up and come back with some sarcastic comment. Or whack me on my head with his cane.

Nothing.

I studied my mentor's face. Jezzie's gray hair was a lot shorter. Neater than the matted locks of the Jezzie spirit I had befriended. His eyebrows were as bushy and wild as normal. I tried to guess his age. Maybe around fifty- five? Sixty? Or even older? It was hard to tell.

I picked up the folder dangling on the headboard of the metal bed. Reading the notes in front of me. They didn't make any sense.

'Mister James,' I whispered his name. Putting the folder back. 'Can you hear me?'

The life support machine beeping steadily in the corner was the only noise.

'It's me…Leo,' I tried again. 'I'm the moron you keep hitting with your cane.' I gently tapped the old man on the head with my finger. Mimicked the old man's voice, 'Hey Leo, you're an idiot, and it's Mister James to you, kid.'

My mischievous smile fell from my face at the sound of footsteps outside the door. I jumped to my feet. Panic overtook me. I managed to duck inside a small connected bathroom. I left the door slightly ajar. Two nurses walked in.

'Hello Horace…time for your sponge bath,' the older nurse commented. Joyfully whishing back the bed cloths.

'So, this is the famous Jezzie,' the younger one stated, 'what happened to him?' There was a hint of sadness in her voice.

'Terrible really,' the more experienced nurse spoke again. 'He was beaten up bad. Really bad. A terrible mess. His face the size of a balloon when they brought him in. You wouldn't have recognized him.'

Inside the bathroom, I closed my eyes. The image of the merciless gang savagely attacking Jezzie in the park lit up my mind.

'How long has he been here?' the younger nurse asked.

'About six months.' The older one replied. A sponge in her hand. 'And in that time, it's been my job to wash him each and every day. Hasn't it Horace? Now roll over my lovely man.' She pulled his unresponsive body onto its side.

The two nurses talked away while cleaning him up. I perched myself down on the toilet to listen.

'Does he have any family?' the younger nurse pulled the tramps gown back down. 'Or visitors?'

'That's the saddest thing. He hasn't had one visitor. Not one. And strangely all his medical bills are being looked after.'

'By who?'

'The church.'

'The church?' the older one nodded.

I wondered if there was a link with him getting his medical bills paid and his job of delivering souls in the spiritual world.

The younger nurse seemed curious. 'That's so sad…imagine having no one who cares for you,' she mentioned. 'I read it helps if someone tries to talk to them if they are in a coma.' She left a pause. 'And also playing their favorite music can sometimes bring them out of it.'

'I hope and pray he pulls through,' the older nurse spoke again. 'I really do.' They both stared at him for a few minutes. 'But it's only a matter of time until they decide to…to…' I could hear the dejection in her voice. She didn't finish her sentence.

I peeked through the gap in the door. The nurses finished up what they were doing and left. I waited for a minute until the footsteps had fully died away before sticking my head out. The tramp looked so peaceful laying there. Like an angel. An angel with a grouchy face. I said my goodbyes. Closing the door quietly, I left.

******

'What music would a homeless person like?' I asked my mother.

'What?' She appeared to be in a daze. She was. Pre-occupied with what the doctor had told her.

I repeated the question. 'You know…someone about sixty…ish?'

She heaved a sigh. 'I don't know. Why don't you ask a homeless person what music they would like?'

I paced about. I wasn't really listening. 'Don't worry…I'll think of something. What did the doctor say?'

I could tell my mother was fighting back the tears. 'He said everything was just fine.' I could tell she was lying. Although the scan had come back negative, he had warned her that the longer the seizures, the more risk of permanent brain damage or even worse.

8

you call that music?

I visited Jezzie at the hospital nearly every day after school for the next week. Plus, as much as I could get away with on the weekend without arousing suspicion. I told my parents I was at Josh's house. I told Josh I was taking extra karate lessons. I knew he wouldn't ask to come along.

Once there, I actually found it quite easy to talk to Jezzie. Well, mainly due to the fact he was comatose. I talked and talked. Not sure why, but I used the situation to offload some of my personal issues. I blabbered on about everything locked up in my mind. My overprotective parents. Being bullied at school. Even the problem I've got with zits. And of course, my love for Beth.

The nurses didn't seem to mind me coming. In fact, they seemed thankful. I did tell them a little white lie about being Jezzie's nephew. It did the trick though. They brought me food. Drink. Looked after me. On occasions they even let me help give Jezzie his daily leg massage.

One rainy Friday, I brought in my MP3 player. Hooking Jezzie up with it. I gave him a blast of Metallica at full volume. 'It's payback time,' I joked.

The tramp lay there immobile. With the aid of the machines, his chest moved up and down in time to the beat. I knew he would hate my choice of music. There was method in my madness. I hoped the heavy bass riffs and thumping drums would drive the lifeless Jezzie so insane he would wake up. Open his eyes. Throw the device across the room. Swear at me.

Nothing.

I sat next to the bed. The dim of the music in the background. I wondered what Jezzie was up to in the other world at that moment in time. Most likely beating up a pack of evil demons. Or wrestling with an Efil. Knowing him, hitting some poor rookie soul walker with his cane for not listening to his instructions.

'Whatever you're doing, please look after yourself.' I found myself getting quite emotional as the words tumbled out of my mouth. I snapped out of it. Picking up the local newspaper that someone had left 'I know,' I said, 'let's see who died this week.' I flicked through the pages. 'Here it is, Obituaries.' I scanned the list. 'This is a good one. Lester Brown, age 47. Died Eastern State Penitentiary. Lethal injection. What do you think Mister James? Good soul or bad?' I laughed out loud. Stopping only on seeing Jezzie laying there dead to the world.

'Ok…ok…you win…I'll let you sleep. I'll be back tomorrow.' I got up out of the chair. 'And I'm bringing someone with me so you better be nice to her or I'll unplug your life support machine.' I placed my hand next to the plug. 'Deal?'

Without warning, a black bird flew into the window. The loud bang almost made me jump out of my skin. I nearly landed on top of Jezzie. 'I was only joking…honest, I wouldn't do that.' I continued groveling to my mentor until I was half way down the corridor.

The next day, I led Beth up the street.

'You better be taking me somewhere nice,' Beth apologised on seeing the sign to the hospital. 'Oh sorry…is someone sick?' She turned to face me. A genuine look of concern in her eyes.

'You'll see.' I replied as we walked through the entrance.

Minutes later, we tip-toed into Jezzie's room. 'Who is he?' she whispered. I pulled two chairs up near the bed.

'Oh…he's just a friend.' I noticed her looking across at me. Then back at Jezzie. A puzzled look on her face. 'A family friend,' I quickly added.

She touched the tramp's hand. 'What happened?'

'He got beaten up.' I liked the way she wasn't afraid to touch him.

'That's terrible…I hope they caught whoever did this and threw away the key.'

An image of the thug's head exploding in the confessional box shot into my mind. 'You can say that.' I poured some water into a glass. I dabbed it on the old man's dry lips.

Beth screwed up her face. 'I'm sure I've seen him before? What does he do?'

My mind raced. 'He...umm...he...he works in the city...sanitation,' I gulped. 'He empties dumpsters and in his spare time he walks...walks... dogs.' It was the best explanation I could think of in the circumstances.

'He looks like he's had a hard life.'

I scratched my head. Staring nervously at the floor. 'Yeah, he has.'

We sat next to the tramp's bed for the next few hours. It was a neat way for me to get to know her more. We laughed. We smiled. We talked for ages. To be honest, Beth did most of the talking. I listened. Happy to be in her company. Now and again, she involved Jezzie in our conversation. She even pretended to answer for him in a strange voice. I felt relaxed. The most relaxed I had ever been while talking to a girl. Or talking to anyone really, well except for Josh. She made it all so effortless for me. I didn't want the afternoon to end.

Combing Jezzie's hair, Beth began to sing a song. I smiled at her. 'My mother used to sing this song to me when I was small. Always put me to sleep,' she added.

Trying to be clever, I piped up. 'Maybe you should sing it in reverse then.'

'Why?'

'You know… maybe it will wake him up.' I shrugged.

'Tree top, the baby bye a rock…' she sang.

I laid back in my chair and listened to her. I was impressed by her humanity. Her quick-witted humour. 'I'll be right back,' I headed to the bathroom. Once inside I splashed water onto my face. 'I need to tell her. Tell her what's going on.' I stared at myself in the mirror. 'Beth,' I practised what I was going to say. 'I'm a soul walker.' I shook my head. I tried again. 'Beth, don't be alarmed, but in my spare time I walk the souls of the dead to…to….to…. Oh that's no good, I sound like a lunatic.' I wiped my face dry and opened the door.

Back in the room, Beth stood up. Her face frozen. She pointed towards the bed. 'His eyes…' her voice quivered. 'Look.'

I rushed over. Jezzie's eyes were wide open. He stared blankly ahead.

'Quick go and get the nurse,' I motioned to her. I turned back to the tramp. 'Jezzie…Jezzie…can you hear me? Can you hear me?'

The tramp's eyes flickered slightly. Then shut tight again.

'No…no.' I tried to open them up with my fingers 'Jezzie…open them…Jezzie…It's me!' I was still trying when the older nurse raced in.

'Out of the way,' she cried. Immediately checking the tramp over. She shone a light from a small flashlight into his eyes. No reaction. Still motionless. She glanced at the two of us.

'They were open honest…' I insisted.

'I think it's time you both went home for the night,' She held Jezzie's hand. Checking his pulse against the watch attached to her blouse. 'And have a good rest…come back tomorrow…or…'

'You don't believe us,' I stated.

Beth grabbed my hand. She led me out of the room. 'But his eyes were open…you saw it too,' I repeated.

'I did…well I think I did,' she hesitated. 'Leo!' she cried, 'look out.'

I turned around. But I was not quick enough to avoid the open door in front of me. BANG

I smacked headfirst into the edge. A dull thud echoed in my head. Quickly followed by the sweet sound of nothing.

Silence

'What the hell do you think you are doing boy?' Jezzie pinned me to a wall. Hs strong hands fixed firmly around my throat. Fury burned in his eyes. 'Well…I'm waiting.' Spit from his lips sprayed over my face.

In the background, a large crowd cheered when the announcer's voice bellowed out over the loud sound system.

I couldn't speak. I could hardly breathe. I struggled to release Jezzie's grip. Eventually the tramp let go. I collapsed to the floor. Coughing and sputtering. 'What now?' I tried to get to my feet.

Jezzie stomped about. 'Don't what me. What are you doing snooping about into my life, kid? My life is my life...I don't need you in it.'

Catching my breath, I noticed we were stood high up in the stands of a football stadium. All around us, fans were decked out in blue and white shirts. Out on the field, the players were getting ready for the next drive. A few rows of seats over, paramedics were trying unsuccessfully to resuscitate an elderly overweight man wearing a baseball cap and a New York Giant's tee-shirt. They lifted the man's shirt up. Stuck electrical devices onto his chest. His body jerked at the jolt. But remained lifeless.

Jezzie grabbed my face. He turned it violently towards the steep concrete steps. There hanging over the railings was the mutilated body of the man's spirit. His chest already ripped apart.

'Take a good look. You made me lose his soul...you and that stupid girl.' Jezzie couldn't have pushed his face any closer to mine.

'You did see me?' I backed away, 'at the hospital...your eyes were open.'

Jezzie raised his cane. 'Yes...you...you and...what's her name. woke me up. I was leading the spirit away, and next thing...BAM...I'm staring at your ugly face. By the time I got back, it was too late. They had him.' He pointed towards two demons racing across the field holding the man's soul in their grubby paws. Jezzie hobbled up the concrete stairs to the exit. He disappeared out of sight.

The roar from the crowd reverberated around the old stadium. I watched the two paramedics carrying the sheet-covered body of the dead man on a stretcher towards the exit. I made the sign of the cross. Then raced after the tramp.

'Hang on...that's unfair.' I said quite meekly to start with. 'I was only trying to help you. I felt sorry for you.'

As soon as the words fell from my mouth, I knew I shouldn't have said them. Jezzie turned sharply. His knuckles white on his cane. 'Don't feel sorry for me kid...or I'll whoop your ass.' He smacked his cane on a seat. 'You don't know me...don't know the world I live in,' he paused, 'or used to live in.'

'But...'

'I don't need your help. I don't need anyone's help. Now go back. I don't want to see you again.' He stormed off as fast as his gimpy leg could carry him.

Disappointed, I followed him out into the concession area. I watched him bend down to pick up a half-eaten pretzel off the ground. I turned to walk away. Walking past the hot dog vendor waiting on a customer. The vendor placed two hot dogs on the counter. He turned away to get some drink.

'Ok then, Mister Hotshot Soul walker Man.' I edged my way closer to the hot dog cart. I had never stolen anything in my life. That was all about to change. I had learnt from Jezzie that although we were invisible to humans and couldn't touch them. 'Unless you touch their soul,' he told me. 'If you do that, they will feel you. You will feel them.' I didn't know what that meant. But I found out we could move or pick up inanimate objects. I had done that several times during these visits I had to the 'other' side. Now I was going to test his theory. While the customer was trying to decide what drink to order, I snatched the hot dogs. Hid them under my coat so no human could see them. Then quickly dashed off.

 Jezzie sat in the quiet parking lot on the hood of an old red Mustang. He moaned and groaned. Picking bits of dirt off the food he had found in some bin. He growled louder on seeing me standing in front of him. I held out one of the warm hot dogs wrapped in the foil. The hobo turned his back on me. Mumbling to himself. Something about youngsters and not following rules and other stuff.

 'I'll get him back,' I smirked to myself. Sitting near-by to my mentor, I un-wrapped one of the dogs. As loud as I could I began to munch on it. Wolfing it down. Savouring every last bite. I hadn't realised how hungry I was. It tasted great. I licked my lips. A piece of onion fell from my mouth to the ground. The smell drifted towards Jezzie. Stubbornly he still didn't move.

 'That is so good…best I have ever tasted.' I opened up the second one. But before I had a chance to bite into it, Jezzie spun around. He snatched it out of my hand. Gobbling it down like a man who had been stuck on a desert island for many years with only plants and seaweed to eat. The tramp closed his eyes as he ate. Cherishing every morsel.

'Was that ok Mister James?' I grinned as wide as my mouth could stretch.

The hobo didn't answer. I folded my arms. 'I've had better,' Jezzie finally muttered. A large slice of onion lodged in his beard.

'Why do you still do that?' I asked him. Jezzie grunted. 'Why eat from trash cans or off the floor? 'I enquired, 'when you can eat whatever you want?'

'Old habits die hard.' He rolled up the empty foil. 'And I don't like stealing from others.' He launched it towards a garbage can. It fell short. 'Hey kid, put your garbage in the trash.'

'What?'

'You heard me.'

I picked up the foil. Placing it in the bin.

'While you're on your feet kid' Jezzie added, 'go get me another one. This time put some mustard on it. Some ketchup. More onions. Some cheese.'

I skipped back towards the stadium. A huge smile on my face. 'And a can of Coke,' Jezzie's cry followed me.

By the time we left the football stadium, Jezzie had eaten four hot dogs and washed them down with three cans of Coke. I did feel sorry for the vendor who couldn't understand what was happening to the fresh hot-dogs he was making. I made myself a promise to pay him back one day.

Bellies full, we headed downtown. 'Where are we going?' I asked. We strolled through a series of narrow alleyways. 'To save more souls?'

Jezzie shook his head. 'Shut up and walk.'

We wandered underneath the railway arches. Even though it was daytime, the place looked dark. Smelt of damp. Loose bricks and other debris littered our path. It made walking extremely difficult.

'Aaaaaaarrrrrrgggggghhhhhh!' I shrieked like a girl when a large brown rat ran across my foot. Still shaking as the creature disappeared up a drain pipe. 'Did you see that? It was the size of a poodle.'

Jezzie didn't say a word. We moved on. Silently. Through an opening in the wall into the inside of an old rundown railway station. I grabbed hold of the old man's smelly jacket. Refusing to let go. Blankets lined the cold, damp floor. It wasn't until I looked closer that I saw people lying under most of them. A woman walked past pushing a shopping cart full of cans. A man, with a placard on his back proclaiming that God saved the world from all evil, drank from a bottle covered in a brown paper bag. The man yelled out. Throwing his hands to the sky. A pack of hungry dogs fought fiercely near the far wall.

'This is so gross.' I walked about in a trance.

Jezzie whacked me on top of my head. 'This is where I live.' He pointed to a doorway. 'Just there. That's my spot. Ten years. In all weather.' The tramp went quiet. 'There's my old dog,

Harry…come here boy.' The confused creature sniffed the ground near our feet. It whimpered. Circling around Jezzie's invisible legs.

'Who are they?' I had seen things like this on TV in far off countries like Africa. I never realized it went on so close to home. The saddest things I had ever witnessed. 'Why are they here?'

'These are the homeless. The hobos. Tramps. To people like you. The nobodies. To me, my best friends,' he answered with pride.

Unnoticed by any of the homeless living humans, we continued on our journey. Wandering through the series of out-buildings. With each step the place got darker. More depressing. The walls crumbling. Pools of muddy water lined the floor. Everywhere I looked people huddled under rags or cardboard boxes. Trying to keep warm.

We squeezed through a small hole in a red brick wall. Entering into a strangely cold area. Pitch black. We continued onwards.

'Hey Jezzie…how's it going?' someone spoke up from the darkness.

I squinted my eyes. Trying to make out where the words had come from. Unexpectedly an old person's head popped up through a pile of rags. The head belonged to an old man with no teeth. That didn't stop him from smiling as if he was having his photo taken on his wedding day.

'Hi Bert…still here?' Jezzie asked.

'Afraid so Jezz…unless you're here to take me with you,' the man quipped.

My mentor bit his lip. 'Not today Bert…maybe next time.'

'You always say that.' Bert pulled the blanket tighter around his body. 'Who's the kid Jezz? He looks like hard work.' They both sniggered.

'You're not far off Bert.' Jezzie passed the man a few cigarette stubs from deep inside his jacket.

'You're a gentleman Jezzie…a true gent.'

'Hang on.' I needed to understand something. 'Is he a priest as well?'

'Me…a priest?' Bert roared like a lion, 'I'm more of a sinner kid.' He laughed again, Jezzie joined him.

'But you said,' I glanced at Jezzie. Lowering my voice,' that the only people able to see us are special priests…or…or dead spirits.'

Jezzie tapped me on the head again with his cane. 'Yes! So, numbskull the answer is?'

The two men stared at me. I chewed the puzzle over in my mind. 'Because…he's he's…dead. He's just a spirit?' Now I was confused.

'At last. Give him a gold medal with bells on,' Jezzie mocked me. 'Of course, he's dead. Three years ago, last week. Heart attack wasn't it, Bert?'

Bert was too busy lighting up his cigarette stub to answer straight away. He took a long hard drag. Coughed loudly. Nodding his head.

I put my hand up to my face. 'But if he's dead, sorry a dead spirit... how is he still here?' I whispered.

Jezzie filled up with emotion. 'Because no one knows or cares that they are here. Not even the soul walkers. These are the lost souls. Some of them have been murdered. Some died in their sleep. Many killed themselves.'

I let my mentor's words sink in. We said our goodbyes to Bert and moved on. A few hundred yards further, near a semi-demolished factory we sat down on some old rusty chairs. Next to us, a roaring fire housed in a metal barrel. A woman wearing holey mittens handed us two mugs of coffee. I didn't like coffee but drank it anyway.

'Thanks Merrill...how's life?' Jezzie asked. Warming his hands against the flames.

'You are such a joker Jezzie...you know I've been dead for ten years,' she giggled. Jezzie smiled. 'But I still look good though, don't I.' she added. It was the first real smile I had seen on the tramp's face. To be fair he was quite a handsome man under the rough edges and layers of grime. I caught Jezzie checking her out. The tramp shot a glance at me. 'What you looking at kid?'

I shrugged. Unsuccessfully trying to conceal the smirk on my face. 'I was going to ask you the same thing,' I was dying to say. But I thought better of it. 'Nothing.'

'Well drink your coffee. Then shut up.'

I did what I was told. I sat watching the spirit of the homeless dead people carrying on with their daily lives as if it was normal. 'How many lost souls are still here?' I broke the silence. I watched two young dead kids playing a game using some coins against the wall.

'Probably a hundred or so,' Jezzie replied. He threw more wood into the flames.

'Wow.' I sipped the warm drink. 'That's unbelievable.'

Merrill appeared again. This time she carried several bottles filled with water under her arms. 'Yeah…but our numbers are decreasing every day.' She glared across at Jezzie. Pouring the water into the kettle spanning across the barrel. 'They took Old Donald Gray yesterday. You remember him Jezzie. The sailor who had his throat cut a few years ago.'

I stiffened up. 'Who took him?'

'The demons did. Picking us off they are. One by one if we wander outside.' She topped my mug up without asking. 'God only knows what would happen if they knew we were here.' She physically shivered.

'That's terrible.' I noticed Jezzie sitting there. A serious frown on his face.

She carried on. 'It is terrible, a crying shame. And even though I'm sick of living this life.' I tried not to laugh at the irony of her last sentence. I concentrated hard. She added. 'When I go. I wanna make my peace with God. Leave him decide my fate.' Sadness washed over her face. 'Instead of having them …them… demons deciding it for me.'

I jumped up. A bit too over excited. 'I know, Jezzie.' He glared at me. 'Sorry, Mister James, why don't we take them to one of the stations…it can't be that far.'

'Just drink your coffee I said.' The tramp didn't look up. I stared at him. No one said anything for several seconds.

'But Jezz…sorry Mister James…it would be…'

The tramps scrambled to his feet. 'No. These are my friends. I never want to see them hurt. At least here they can enjoy what life, or death, they have. Safe. Safe from those evil creatures.'

'But, together we could…'

Jezzie threw the mug into the fire. 'Together we can do what kid? Come on tell me? Me, a half cripple and you…you a…a useless excuse for a soul walker. It's too dangerous. There's too many of them. It would be a slaughter. The demons and the others would be waiting.' He hurried away without looking back or saying goodbye.

I felt hurt. I thanked Merrill. Chasing after my mentor. Back towards the lights of the city. Silently we walked on. A few blocks over, I had something else on my mind. I wanted to offload.

'Mister James, can I ask you something?'

'Look kid, I'm sorry for being so plain speaking…it's just…'

I stopped him. 'No, it's not that.'

'What?' the tramp kept on walking.

I stuttered. 'Why me? Why am I a soul walker?'

'Probably because they couldn't find anyone else.' His face serious. He spat onto the ground.

I laughed weakly. 'No, please…why me? Why am I here?' my voice dropped a few notches. 'I struggle to survive in the real world. Never mind in this one. I'm just a big loser.' I started to cry.

Jezzie shook his head. 'Look kid, dry your eyes…it will be ok.'

'No, it won't…I'm useless…I don't even know what it all means…I'm a loser.'

'Join the club, kid,' Jezzie raised his voice. 'I'm the biggest loser of all.'

I wiped my eyes. 'No, you're not. You're a hero. Even the weird guy in the library said so.'

'In this world. The spiritual world, maybe.' The tramp sat next to me 'But in the real world, I'm the biggest loser there is. Even bigger than you.' He forced a smile from his lips. 'And that takes some doing.'

'Don't say that Mister James. I saw you getting beaten up. That's not your fault.'

'Thanks, kid.' Jezzie twirled his cane through his fingers. 'Anyway, you can't be a loser…because you're a warrior.' I looked at him. Jezzie continued. 'I was told when I asked the same thing as you. I was told that this all-started thousands of years ago. God apparently needed help trying to protect people's souls from Lucifer and all the other kind of demons.'

'What? THEE God?'

Jezzie nodded, I listened intently. 'Yeah! Thee God. The one up there.' The tramp gestured to the sky. 'Apparently he instructed his archangels to hand pick the best warriors on Earth to assist.'

I bit my lip. Screwing up my features. 'What's that got to do with me?'

'Because numb-brain,' Jezzie sounded irritated. 'A long time ago, you must have been one of them brave warriors.' He looked me up and down. Muttering quietly. 'But I can't see it myself.'

'Me a warrior?' I blew my nose. 'Are you serious?'

Jezzie nodded. 'Yep…there' an old saying. Once a soul walker, always a soul walker. Doesn't matter what body you come back to Earth in.'

'Huh!'

Jezzie rolled his eyes. 'Look kid, I'm a tramp now but in the past, I've been a king. A pilot. Even an acrobat. And in all those bodies, I've always been a soul walker. It's probably been the same with you.'

It made sense in a nonsensical type of way. Maybe that would explain why I knew all about other countries. About history and that kind of stuff. 'Me, Leo Young, a brave warrior.' I couldn't wait to tell Josh. Beth. And definitely Ethan. See what he thinks.

'But you have to prove it yet kid. Prove you are a warrior. Not the loser you think you are.'

'So, if I can do this. I won't be a loser anymore. Kids will like me,' I nearly walked into a lamppost.

'Guess so.' The tramp's mood lightened a little. We strolled onwards. 'Hey Leo,' Jezzie said, 'How's the karate kid?'

I stopped in my track. It was the first and only time he had called me by my first name.

'How do you know I'm doing karate?'

'Maybe I've been snooping into your life as well.' The hobo grinned at me through yellow teeth. 'By the way kid. You call that music you made me listen to in the hospital. All that screaming and shouting. Who the hell is that anyway?'

I spoke quietly. 'Metallica, Mister James…they're a heavy metal band.'

'Metallica,' he repeated the name. 'What kind of name is that?' I shrugged. Staring down at my feet. Jezzie continued. 'Do you have any more albums by them?'

I looked up at him. 'What's an album?'

'You know…think you kids call it a CD.'

'Oh…yeah I do.'

'Good,' he replied 'Bring it the next time you come to see the living me in the hospital.' It was time for me to roll my eyes. 'And from now on you can call me…Jezzie.'

The tramp turned away. It took me several moments before I realized what I had just heard. More importantly, what it meant. I wanted to hug him. I ran up behind him. I suddenly felt cold. My head cloudy. Next thing I woke up on the floor in the hospital corridor, A lump the size of an egg on my head.

'Leo…are you ok?' Beth asked. A nurse stood over her shoulder.

'Fantastic…absolutely fantastic.' I lay on the floor smiling up at them.

9
'The black eye dude'

'Jezzie…behind you,' I screamed above the noise of the traffic.

The tramp spun around just in time to catch sight of a demon lunging at him. Its fangs showing. Hatred in its yellow eyes. Jezzie sidestepped out of its way. The tip of his elbow connected sweetly with the creature's jaw. The beast tumbled head first to the ground. It laid there. Twitching in pain.

I stood admiring my mentor's handywork. Suddenly a demon leaped on my back.

'Arrrggggggggggghhhhhhhhhh,' I shrieked. The force knocked both of us into the middle of the road. Another creature joined in. Pinning me to the asphalt.

'Get off me. Jezz…Jezz,' I shouted out.

The hobo hobbled to my rescue once again. He kicked one of the demons full-force in the ribs. I could hear the crack. The creature rolled off howling like a wounded dog. Jezzie picked up the other one by its head. His fingers lodged in its eye sockets. He whacked it hard on its nose. It yelped brashly before racing away. Tail firmly between its legs.

I leant against the wall. 'Tell Zotto, the boys are back in town,' I shouted after them. My heart beating fast. The adrenaline pumping through my veins. I stood fist clenched in a karate stance.

'Well done Rocky.' Jezzie mocked while searching around for his cane. 'Now tie that one up.' He pointed to the demon spitting its loose teeth onto the pavement. 'I want to ask it some questions.'

I followed my orders. Pulling the cord extra tight around the creature's wrists as I did it. 'Where are we taking him Jezz?' I felt good about myself. This was my fifth soul walking mission since the time we had taken Jezzie's thug attacker to the station. In those two weeks, we had taken six souls to various stations across the city. We had fought off at least fifteen demons. Ok, more like Jezzie had taken six souls to various stations across the city and fought off most of the fifteen demons. Truthfully, most of that time, I got beaten up until the tramp came and saved my skin. But I was getting better. More confident. Jezzie trusted me a little more.

'All done Jezz,' I beamed.

'W…w…where's…t…t…the clients?' Jezzie paced aimlessly about. His words struggling to fall out of his mouth. He seemed disorientated. Confused.

'We've delivered them already Jezz…remember.' I stared at him rather bemused. How could he have forgotten the rich couple killed in a hit-and-run? The spirits of that not nice couple who hadn't stopped complaining all the way to the station.

Something seemed off with him. I didn't know what. Then he staggered backwards, crashing into a lamppost. Sliding down onto the sidewalk. 'Where are we?' His hands trembled. He shook his head from side to side like he was trying to dislodge a small insect from his ear drum.

'What's wrong Jezz? Are you hurt?' I checked him for wounds.

The demon chuckled loudly.

The tramp sat on the curb. His head balancing in his rough hands. My eyes scanned the surroundings. I let out a muffled yell on seeing the hoodless Efil waiting on the opposite side of the street. It looked so evil. Menacing. Deadly. Much shorter than some of the others I'd encountered. Its shoulders rounded to the point of being hunched. I couldn't get over the size of its hands. Massive. Way out of proportion to the rest of its body. The Efil didn't move. Just stood examining the situation.

Jezzie sat crouched over on the curb. Hs worn-out socks poking through the holes in his boots.

'Get up Jezz?' I pulled at his arm. 'Please get up.' I kept glancing over at the Efil. Still motionless. Still staring.

'Just let me lie here for five minutes.' He slumped back on the concrete. His eyes closed. Hands by his side.

That was when something really strange happened. The tramp's face turned white. Then it began to go all blurry. Like interference on a television set in bad weather.

I rubbed my eyes to make sure I wasn't seeing things. 'Jezzie, what's happening?' I shook him

'He's going to die, boy,' the tortured demon hissed. 'Your mentor's going to croak. Then you are ours.' It snorted.

'Wake up, Jezz...wake up.' I didn't know what to do. I was scared. Helpless.

The demon grinned. It exposed his battle-worn mouth. 'And after you...it will be your family. Loser boy.'

Jezzie's breathing got more erratic. A strange wheezing noise rose up with each breath. I checked his pulse like they did on TV shows. I had no idea what I was supposed to be checking. In the end I gave up. I shook him gently again. 'Jezzie...Jezzie...don't you die on me.' Tears filled up my eyes. A large lump blocked my throat. I whispered in the tramp's ear. 'Please Jezz...please...get up...get up,' my words mingling with the clamour of the traffic. The sound of the street.

The Efil creature began to stride across the road towards us. I jumped up. I wanted to run. But didn't. I couldn't. I picked up a metal bar which one of the demons had dropped during the scrap. Gripping it like a baseball bat I glared at the deformed creature heading our way.

The creature got closer. Its teeth snarling. I stood hunched over. My hands shaking. Then unexpectedly the beast stopped. It turned. Strolled away without a backward glance

'Hey kid.' I peeped down to see Jezzie looking up at me. The tramp coughed hard. Lifting himself up on his elbows. His face back to its normal grubby grey colour. 'That was weird,' he murmured. 'Really weird.'

I was too scared to speak. I wiped tears from my eyes. The metal bar dropped on the sidewalk with a thump.

Jezzie continued muttering to himself. Trying to make sense of the situation. 'Bright. Bright lights. Bright people. Things grabbed my feet. I fell, fell down and down and then bang. I'm here again.' He pointed at my face. 'But at least I ain't going to have a shiner like that in the morning.'

I touched my eye. Wincing in pain. During all the commotion one of the demons must have caught me with a peach of a right hook. I checked my reflection in the mirror of a parked car. My eye almost closed. Turning several shades of purple.

'My first real badge of war,' I proclaimed with pride.

'Put some steak on that when you get back. It will bring out the swelling,' Jezzie still quite unsteady got to his feet.

'That will be nothing when Zotto catches up with you,' the demon, with half his teeth missing and blood tickling down his mouth, announced. 'You wait until you find out what he's got in store for you two.'

Jezzie's features turned to stone. Deadpan. He limped towards the creature. 'Got something to say, have you? You piece of crap.'

The demon spat in the tramp's face. Blood-stained phlegm tickled down Jezzie's cheek. He didn't bother to wipe it off. 'Bring him with us.' He picked up the metal bar. Hobbled off towards the river. We arrived at the side of the docks.

'Tie him to the lamppost,' Jezzie motioned to me. He started a fire in one of the trash cans.

The demon struggled. I secured him good and tight. At least I was getting good at something.

'How's Beth?' the creature teased in a strange psychotic voice.

'What did you say?' I asked.

'You heard me,' it sniggered.

I stood there in front of him. My fists clenched. 'You better not....not....'

'Move aside,' Jezzie appeared carrying the metal bar. The tip of the one end bright orange from where he had heated it up over the fire.

The demon thrashed about trying to free himself.

'What is Zotto up to?' Jezzie spoke slowly and concisely.

'You'll find out soon enough old man.' Its evil cackle sending a shiver down my spine.

Jezzie wasn't in the mood for games. He placed the hot metal on the creature's inner thigh. The demon screeched. The smell of burning flesh tickled my nostrils. 'One more time,' the tramp repeated the question.

The demon still refused to talk. Jezzie grabbed it by the throat. Pushing the hot bar into the creature's side. Green gunk flowed out. 'Ok…ok,' it shrieked loudly. 'I'll tell you…I'll tell you.'

The tramp pulled the bar out ever so slowly. Twisting it as he did.

'He intends to …to…send demons to destroy you both.' The anguish evident on its contorted face.

I chipped in. 'We'll beat you anywhere. Anytime.'

The demon stared at me. 'Not in this world, boy. In the living world.'

I froze. The hairs on my neck stood on end. 'How can he do that?' I faced the tramp.

'I'm not sure.' A concerned look appeared on Jezzie's face.

The demon crowed again. 'We'll see how tough you really are. By yourself. Without him.' He taunted me again. 'We're coming to get you this time.' Jezzie plunged the hot poker into the beast's chest. The creature's evil snicker instantly replaced by a horrendous scream.

'Well, you won't be there.' The tramp pulled the weapon back out. Before stabbing it in again. 'Throw that piece of dog dirt in the river,' he demanded.

We sat on the dockside in silence for the next hour. My mentor deep in thought. I knew him well enough by now to know when to keep quiet. I sat watching a ship out to sea getting further and further away. It finally disappeared beyond the horizon.

The next thing, I found myself on the carpeted floor. Back in the safety of my bedroom. Luckily, my parents didn't even know I had blacked out. I had been in my room by myself. Playing on my computer when I must have zoned out. I quickly washed my face. Climbed into bed. I felt exhausted and fell asleep in seconds.

∎∎

The next morning, I was woken up by my mother shouting up the stairs. 'Leo…Leo. Josh is here.'

'Send him up,' I grunted. Sleep stuck in the corner of my eyes.

Josh clambered up the stairs like an elephant in snow boots. He pushed open the door. A piece of toast balancing from his lips.

'Your mother gave me these for you.' He put the mug down on the dresser. And the plate with the rest of the toast on it. 'Hey who clipped you?' He pointed to my face.

'What?'

'The black eye dude…it's a beaut.'

I sprung out of bed. 'Oh no…I can't believe it.' I knew my mother and father would freak if they saw it. They definitely wouldn't let me go on the school field trip. 'What am I going to do?'

'Say you did it at karate.'

'I can't say that. I'm not supposed to be doing it remember. You faked the forms idiot?'

'Oh yeah.' Josh picked up the second piece of toast. 'Can I have this?' He rammed it into his mouth before I had chance to reply. 'Well how did you do it?' Josh mumbled.

'It's a long story…'

'I ain't going anywhere.' He slumped down on my bed. Guzzling down the last piece of toast in record time.

I wasn't sure how much I should tell him. But I needed to confide in someone. I had missed my chance with Beth. I checked to make sure there was no one outside my door. I then described in great detail my soul walking experiences. Josh didn't utter a single word. I finished telling the story. He looked around in silence. His face hadn't moved a muscle. 'So, when you go into one of your fits…you are really walking the souls of the dead?' His eyes intently focused me.

I nodded my head. Staring down at the carpet. Slightly embarrassed. I expected him to tell me to take a run and jump. But he didn't.

'Wow, that's totally rockin' dude.' Josh thought for a second. 'So do you walk through walls and stuff like that?'

'Not really.' I smiled. 'People and objects can sometimes walk through me…but apart from that…everything else is more or less the same as here.'

I could see him thinking again. The clogs in his brain ticking over. 'That's a shame…we could have had some fun''

'We…what do you mean we?'

Josh pulled a candy bar from his jacket. He talked as he unwrapped it. 'I don't know…I was just thinking that we could soul walk together. Walk the earth like a pair of zombies or werewolves or those lost tramp soul things?'

He talked and talked. Question after question. I regretted telling him now. His overactive mind was scaring me more than the demons did.

'Can I come next time?' Josh looked at his watch as if he was about to set it.

I laughed. 'I don't think so. You would have to be in a coma or having a fit or knocked out.'

Jumping up, Josh grabbed a baseball bat from the corner of the room. 'Go on…hit me.' He bent his head towards me.

'What?'

'Just hit me with it.' He pushed it into my hand. 'Come on, I wanna be a soul walker too…I hope I get to escort a rock star…Bon Jovi or Ozzy Osborne would be cool.'

I was tempted to strike him just to shut him up. 'It's more complicated than that. You need to have been a warrior in a past life. Well, that's what Jezzie said.'

'Hang on a minute,' he gulped. 'So, you are a warrior as well as a soul walker?' Josh asked wide eyed. 'Awesome. Does Beth know?'

'No,' I blushed. 'Why would I tell her?'

Josh put the bat back down on the bed. 'Because she's your girlfriend…duh!'

My face turned several shades of red. 'No, she's not. We're…we're just friends.'

'Yeah, and I'm a finely tuned athlete.' He sucked his stomach in.

'Ok, we've hung out a few times…but it's nothing serious.'

'That's not what I heard,' he beamed.

I shrugged my shoulders. 'Look Josh, I only told you. So don't tell anyone else.' I knew deep down he wouldn't.

Josh crossed his heart. 'And hope to die.' He laughed. 'And Leo, if I do die, I hope you will be my soul walker.' His voice sailed through the rest of the house. 'And you better not let me get eaten by demons or that monster thing.'

'Shhhhhh,' I hissed. 'My mother's snooping around. Let's get out of here.'

I got dressed. Josh stopped me as we crept down the stairs. 'I think we need to get some steak,' he whispered.

'Someone else told me that,' I looked at my black eye in the full-length mirror. 'They said it would help bring out the bruising.'

'Not for your eye, you idiot. For breakfast…I'm starving…let's go to Bob Evans.' He was serious.

We escaped out the back door into the yard.

******

Later that night, I stood in my bedroom packing my things in my backpack. Getting ready for the field trip to Teatown Lake in the morning. There was a gentle knock on my door. My parents entered. Sporting their infamous funeral faces. I stared into the computer so they couldn't see my swollen eye.

My mother, as usual, kicked off the conversation. 'Leo, your father and I have been talking. We don't think you should go on the school trip tomorrow.' They held each other's hands for moral support.

'What?' I got up. Putting my hat and gloves into my backpack. Very carefully keeping my un-bruised side of my face towards them.

My father took over like a verbal tag wrestler. 'Not in your condition. It's too risky. What if you have a…a…a.' My father left a space before saying the word "seizure". He always got tongue tied when it came to saying what was actually wrong with his son!!

'But I'll be fine,' I pleaded. 'I haven't had a seizure for ages.'

'What if you are down a cave. Or climbing. Or…or…in the water…and…and…and you know. There would be no medical assistance. It wouldn't be fair to your teachers.'

I threw my pack to the floor. I stared at both of them in quick succession.

'Leo, what's happened to your eye?' my mother rushed over to comfort me.

I pushed her off. 'It's nothing…why can't I go? Mister Hubbard said it would be ok.'

My mother chipped in again. 'We spoke to Mister Hubbard and he agrees with us.'

'When did you talk to him?'

My mother sat down on the bed. 'Your father called him up today. The good news is he said you can have the day off.' Her smile was as weak as a wet twig.

'I was thinking we could go fishing like we used to,' my dad tried to sound enthusiastic.

'No…I want to go on the trip with my friends,' I blurted out.

'Sorry son…maybe next time.' I could tell by their tone their minds had been made up.

'This is so unfair,' I ranted. They had been saying the same old thing to me all of my life. 'Maybe next time Leo…maybe next time.' I didn't want to spend my entire life waiting for the next time. I wanted to live it now.

My mother put her arm around my shoulders. I shrugged her off. 'Leave me alone…just get out.'

'But Leo…it's for your own good.'

'Get out!' I snapped at them. 'Get out…NOW'

Reluctantly they left. Closing the door behind them. I punched my pillow until my arms were tired and my tears had dried up.

10
who's the loser now?

The song blasting from the radio-alarm clock startled me awake. I slammed it with my fist. Knocking the device off the bedside table onto the floor. It made a strange groaning noise before grinding to a stop. It was the morning of the school trip. The trip I was banned from going on. Banned like some criminal not allowed to go into a bank or shop.

Why am I awake? Trust me to forget to turn off my alarm. I hated my life.

Outside the bright rays of the sun crept through a gap in the bedroom curtains.

'Great…just fantastic,' I pulled the sheets over my head. Wishing I was dead. Really dead. Not off soul walking dead. Dead. Dead.

I'd phoned Josh after my parents had left to tell him I couldn't go. Of course, my mate was disappointed. Knowing fully well it would be him alone who would have to put up with Ethan's uncalled for mental and physical torture. Beth barely said a word when I told her my bad news.

I lay in bed picturing the scene outside the school. Mister Hubbard dressed in some goofy safari clothes. Thinking he was Harrison Ford from Raiders of the Lost Ark. Ushering the kids onto the bus. Ethan, of course, loud and obnoxious. Rapping everyone on the head as they boarded the bus. Josh already in his seat. Head down. Ready to dive into the biggest lunch box in the entire world.

I wonder what Beth would be doing? What she would be wearing? More importantly, would she be missing me? Or did she really think I was just a karate kicking mammy's boy.

Eventually I rolled out of bed. Throwing on whatever clothes that were strewed over the floor from the night before, I trudged into the kitchen as if I was wading through quicksand.

'Do you want me to make you a nice breakfast?' my mother asked. A big fake smile on her face.

'I'm not hungry,' I grunted. Staring at her.

She tried again. 'How about a piece of toast and some juice?

'No, Mam,' I said, 'I'm not hungry!' I snapped back. My dad strolled in the back door. Full of smiles. Dressed in his fishing gear.

'Come on lazy bones; let's get going if we are going to catch some trout or a nice salmon.'

Ignoring him completely I wandered into the family room. Tumbling down on the settee, I turned on the TV. I felt so mad. Angry. Disappointed.

'Leo!' my father yelled. 'What's wrong now?'

'Leave him alone honey. Too much stress could trigger another…another….' I heard what she was saying about me. Before she had time to finish, I stormed back into the kitchen. 'A seizure…go on say it…a seizure…a big bloody seizure,' I hissed at them both in turn like an angry snake cornered under a rock. Slamming the front door behind me I left the house.

I meandered down the street. Kicking a plastic Coke bottle. 'I hate my life…hate it…hate it.'

Up in the sky, dark rain clouds appeared on the horizon. It felt like a storm brewing. I placed the out of shape plastic bottle in a garbage can. I waited on the curb for a car to pass before heading to the park. I walked head down. Feeling sorry for myself. I glanced over my shoulder. A police car, with blacked out windows, followed slowly behind.

I didn't think anything of it. Half expecting the vehicle to shoot past me at any moment. Drive off to solve some crime. It didn't. Instead, it just rolled menacingly behind. I hadn't done anything wrong but it still made me felt uneasy. I quickened my pace. The park gates getting nearer with each stride. I kept turning around. Unsure what I should do. The sudden revving noise of the car's engine made my mind up. Something didn't feel right. I ran. I ran into the park. Across the grass. Into a sparsely wooded area. The cop car following right behind me. Lights flashing. Near the water fountain I changed direction. Trying to ditch it. Running through a cluster of trees, I dived down into a bush near a park bench.

The patrol car drove around in a circle. It stopped about twenty yards from where I hid. I ducked down further. Holding my breath. Two uniformed policemen got out of the vehicle. Facing away from me. Guns in their hands. A bit over the top I thought.

'Where did he go?' One searched about before disappearing into the rest room.

'Hey kid,' the other office shouted out. 'Come out, we only want to ask you some questions,' His voice very deep. Sounded odd. As if it was fake. Mechanical. 'We only want to talk to you about the sighting of a suspect who was seen in these parts.'

'He's not in there.' Shaking his head, the other cop came out of the restroom. 'What should we do now?'

I leaned back against the base of a tree. My mind bouncing about wildly. 'Am I going crazy?' I gulped. 'I'm just paranoid. They are the police.' I began to stand up.

'Don't worry,' one of the copper's muttered, 'we'll tell Zotto he got away.'

I dropped back to the ground. Lying face down. My heart thumping loudly. Afraid to move. Almost afraid to breathe. Had I heard him correctly? Did he really mention Zotto? I crawled on my belly. A few feet away from them. Carefully I peeked out through the leaves of the bush. The officer turned to face me. I froze on seeing the copper's features. The face wasn't human; It was the face of a soul stealer. Burnt and repulsive.

'Leave him. Let's go. Zotto will be ok as long as we get the tramp. He's the main threat,' the other one sneered.

They climbed back into the patrol car. Wheels spinning, they raced out of the park like a couple of teenagers in a drag race.

Immediately my mind went into overdrive. 'Jezzie… I've got to help Jezzie.'

I galloped out into the street after the car. I 'borrowed' a push bike parked outside someone's garage. Peddling with all my might out onto the main drag I soon realised it would take forever to get to the hospital. I ditched the bicycle. Without thinking I stepped out into the middle of the road. Several cars drove around me. Horns blaring. Drivers screaming. A van skidded. Utter panic on the driver's face. I covered my eyes. The vehicle screeched to a stop. Missing me by a few inches.

'What the hell are you doing?' the man yelled out of the window.

'Quick, I need to get to the hospital. Phillip's Memorial,' I panted. 'It's my…my …my sister…she's sick…very sick.' Trying to sound genuine, I added, 'she's in a coma…and she's not going to make it.' I actually started to believe in my own made-up story.

The driver looked me up and down. 'Ok…jump in.' He pushed some empty fast-food boxes off the passenger's seat onto the already garbage filled floor.

I piled in. I didn't care what the van looked or smelt like. The driver slammed it into gear. Skidding around the bend. Weaving in and out of the on-coming traffic like a stock car racer on the last lap.

'What happened to her?' he asked.

'I don't want to talk about it.' I looked out of the window. An image of Jezzie getting mutilated in his sleep by the demon coppers rolled down in front of my eyes.

The van screeched to a halt. 'No way,' the driver grunted. A long line of cars jammed up the road in front of us. 'Must be an accident,' he said.

I could see a police car ahead. Also stuck in the jam. I prayed it was the car with the demons in. 'What are we going to do now?' I asked.

The driver popped a strip of gum in his mouth. 'Don't worry...I didn't win the best delivery driver for the last two years on the run for nothing.' He shifted it down into second gear. The car catapulted into a side street. 'I know all the short cuts.'

The car driver must have thought he was steering a racing car. I held on tightly to the passenger seat. He weaved in and out of side streets, missing cars by inches. Within no time, the van skidded to a stop outside the front of the hospital.

'Thank you!' I jumped out. Sweat dripping off my forehead.

'No problem. I hope she gets better,' the man replied. Speeding off around the bend.

I sprinted through the front entrance. Nearly knocking over a man coming the other way.

Six flights of stairs later, I burst into Jezzie's room. A man in a white coat leant over Jezzie's bed. Without thinking I soared like a salmon (well, maybe more like a goldfish) on his back. The both of us plus a water jug went crashing to the floor.

'Leave him alone!' I roared. Pinning him to the wet floor with my knees.

A mixture of shock and horror lined the young doctor's face. 'I'm only giving him his daily medication,' his voice shook. I gripped his throat. Glaring deep into his eyes.

He seemed genuine. His face looked human enough. No hint of demon. No smell either. 'Sorry…sorry,' I apologized. 'I thought you were…you were…. never mind,' I stood up. Freeing the young man from my grip.

'Who…who are you?' the doctor asked.

'I'm…I'm…. his cousin.' The doctor looked suspiciously at me, 'on my father's side.'

I cleaned up the mess while the shellshocked doctor finished giving Jezzie his medicine. Once alone, I looked up and down the corridor to make sure we were alone. I locked the door to the room behind me. I pulled a chair up to the bed. 'Jezzie, I think we're screwed,' the vulgarity sounded awkward coming out of my mouth. 'The demons. They are disguised as police. They are coming to get you.' I needed my mentor now more than ever. Jezzie just lay there. Eyes closed. The machine beeping noisily in the corner.

Footsteps approached. I searched around for something. Anything I could use as a weapon. I picked up the bedpan on the table next to the bed. I considered it for a minute until I pictured Zotto and his gang doubled over in laughter at the sight of me swinging it at them.

I noticed a heavy brass door stop just inside the door. 'This will do.' I gripped the door stop in my fist. I sat back down. Placing earphones over the tramp's ears. 'If they want you, they will have to get through me first.' The footsteps got louder. I braced myself. Whoever it was walked by.

Two hours past. Still no sign of any demons in disguise. The ward stood peaceful. The only sound, the ticking of the clock on the wall. I quietly unlocked the door. Again, I checked the hallway. Empty. No sound, other than the sound of me re-locking it.

'I have to go to the bathroom,' I told Jezzie. Even though he was in a coma I still thought it my duty to ask him for permission. I knew it was silly. 'But don't worry, I'll be back.' I chuckled at the reference to the Terminator film. 'I'll be back,' I mimicked Arnie's voice. For some reason, I even did robotic actions as I walked across the room.

I left the door open. Unzipped the fly of my jeans.

The shudder rocked my body. Like a jolt of electricity travelling through every muscle. I stiffened up like an ironing board.

'Oh no, not again.' The twitching started in my legs. I knew what was coming next. I did my best to overcome it. 'Not now…please.' My head spun. My mouth dry. I staggered back out into the room. I looked at Jezzie. Praying he would wake up. Wake up and save me. Too late. I toppled over. Landing face down on the edge of the bed.

My entire body shot forward. My eyes reopened. It took me a full minute to realise I was sitting next to Josh on the school bus. I stared at the sight of my best friend's face. 'What the hell is going on now?' I muttered. Just before something bounced off Josh's head. It landed at his feet. There was a bout of laughter from the back.

'Thanks for coming Leo,' Josh muttered to no one in particular.

'Josh, Josh, I'm here.' Trying to tap the side of his head.

'Hey fatty,' Ethan shouted. 'Wonder what your mate, the coward, is doing? Probably having his brain tested.' He laughed at his own joke. Of course, his cronies followed suit.

Beth turned around in her seat, 'At least he's got a brain, you numb skull,' her words shot out like daggers. Sticking into Ethan's thick skin.

Everyone fell silent. The bully looked fiercely at her. I could see him struggling to find the right reply. 'You better shut your mouth girl…or I'll come down there and…and…'

Mister Hubbard turned around in his seat. He pointed at the boy. Ethan growled and slumped down in his own seat at the back.

In temper, he punched Johnny James, the boy next to him, as an alternative.

'She really does like me,' a wide grin spread across my face. 'She likes the karate kicking mammy's boy.'

Next to me, Josh bit into a giant chocolate bar. I'm assuming he had hidden it in his jacket the night before in case of emergencies. His face looked glum. His head leaning against the window. Looking out at the trees and the mountains shooting past.

I glanced around the rest of the bus to see what else was going on. Mister Hubbard sat near the front. On his head, a stupid army hat. Sharon Bell sat in the seat in front of us putting on lipstick. Most of the other kids sat quietly listening to music on their IPods. I assumed all mobile phones had been banned from the trip. They usually were. At the back Ethan had come back to life. On his feet again. Barking orders at his gang of hangers-on.

I grinned to myself. 'Ok, Mister Ethan Jackson…it's revenge time.' I headed down the aisle to the back row. 'Hey tough guy, look it's me…the coward boy,' Plonking myself in front of Ethan. Bravely I flicked out at his nose. Of course, he couldn't feel it. But it still made me feel good. 'You can't see me, can you? You can't see me, you, big ugly monkey,' I mocked Ethan and his gang. Pity no one could see what I was doing. I really wished Beth could see me. She would be so proud. I think!!

I repeated my taunts several more times. For once I was enjoying myself. A smile on my face. Just then a reality bullet hit me right between the eyes. A big powerful reality bullet. 'They can't see me.' My hand slapped my forehead.

Racing up and down the aisle, I howled out. 'Quick, quick…something is going to happen. We have got to get off.'

Just at that moment, the roar of thunder filled the sky. Followed quickly by bolts of lightning. Several girls screamed. Seconds later, the entire sky turned a dark grey colour. Huge raindrops spat onto the windows.

I made my way to the front. The driver, an old grey-haired man in a chequered shirt and Red Sock's hat, sat concentrating hard. Trying his best to keep control of the vehicle. He switched the wipers onto high speed.

'Stop the bus…stop!' I screamed in the man's face.

I tried to grab the steering wheel. No use. The driver looked straight ahead at the windshield. His face just blank. I tried to pull his foot off the accelerator. Again, no good. My hand just went through his skin and bone.

'Slow down!' I bellowed in his face.

The bus skidded violently around a bend. On the narrow winding road, the hanging branches of a tree scraped up against the windows. I looked down the aisle of the bus. All of the kids sat quietly. Their faces staring ahead. Hands gripping the seat in front of them for dear life. Thunder echoing all around us. Mister Hubbard rose up from his seat.

'Thank God,' I thought. He'll be able to talk to the driver.

The teacher stood in the aisle. 'Mister McAleer,' he said politely, 'are you sure you should be going this fast?' Another sharp tug of the steering wheel sent the bus veering up on one set of wheels. Mister Hubbard staggering towards the back of the vehicle. Trying to grab the seat to stop his fall. He failed. His head smashed on the floor of the bus. He lay there out cold.

None of the kids on the bus laughed. Not even Ethan. There was a sense of dread.

I rushed back towards Josh. 'Josh…Josh…' I screamed as loud as I could. I tried to slap his face. 'You've got to stop the bus Josh. It's going to crash and you are all going to d…d…d,' I couldn't say the words.

The heavier the rain came down, the faster the bus sped along the road. Beth crouched up in the seat across from Josh. Her knees curled up to her chin. I slid in next to her. 'I won't let you…d…d…. down,' I whispered in her ear.

Up towards the front, an Efil appeared out of nowhere. It filled the aisle with its broad shoulders and massive frame. Even though the bus rocked left and right, the creature stood rock-like. Its white piercing eyes glowed against the rainy grey background of the windshield.

I stood up slowly to face it. 'Not now,' the words dripping from my mouth.

The Efil's eyes looked straight at me. Its large mouth wide open. Saliva dripped onto the floor. The Efil and me, the soul walker, stood facing each other. The bus rambling on. Faster and faster. Sharon Bell shrieked out in a near frenzy. Her screams filled every inch of the bus. Drilling like a six-inch nail into everyone's brain.

'Shut up…shut up,' Beth yelled at her.

Blood pumped around the veins in my body. My neck throbbed. I stared at the Efil. 'Leave my friends alone,' I struggled to keep my footing. The creature turned towards where Sharon Bell sat. Totally unaware of the danger, she sat there screaming hysterically. The beast let go of an even louder roar. The noise deafening. Drowning out the cries of the frightened teenagers.

I knew it was up to me to do something. Without thinking of the consequences, I took a deep breath. Closing my eyes, head down I ran at the creature standing at the front of the bus. We collided. I bounced off it. I ended up on my back in the aisle. Its size and strength shocked me. It felt like running into a brick wall. I got back up. Rushed it again. This time ducking down low so I could tackle the creature. We both toppled backwards. Crashing into the windshield.

The driver didn't move a muscle. His nose inches from the steering wheel. We fell into the stairwell near the main door. The creature rolled over on top of me. Its enormous hands wrapped around my throat.

It was the first time I had been up this close to one of these monsters. It was hideous. The skin on its face like an old dinosaur.

It's white, lifeless eyes sunk deep into its head. Glowing like light bulbs.

I thrashed about trying to move. The Efil lay on top of me. Reaching up with its huge fingers, it pressed the big red button. The pneumatic door hissed. It opened up. I glanced over my shoulder. The blackness of the road inches from my head. The rain lashed at my face. The noise of the tires on the surface of the road echoed in my brain. The backdraft almost sucked me out. The creature's grip tightened around my neck. Choking me. In desperation I stretched up. Digging my nails into the creature's eye sockets. I squeezed as hard as I could. The Efil's grip loosened slightly. It allowed me to place my leg on the pit of the monster's stomach. Summoning up all my self-defence training, I judo threw it over my head. The creature landed on its back on the open road. It rolled down a muddy bank. It was gone. The danger was gone.

I lay upside down in the recess for several moments. Trying to catch my breath. To clear my head. I pressed the button for the door. It closed behind me. Locking the rain and the evil thing outside. Again, I wished my classmates could have seen me in action. I nailed it.

Gingerly I crawled back out of the stairwell. Most of the kids were still screaming. Mister Hubbard still out cold on the floor.

'Bravo…bravo,' someone piped up next to me. 'I'm impressed.'

I turned to see the driver standing up. He had let go of the steering wheel. Staring at me. Clapping his hands.

'What are you doing?' my cry short lived. One large yellow eye and an empty socket where the driver's face should have been glared back to me.

'Zotto!' I mouthed its name.

The demon possessed driver sneered. 'Yessss…guess what? All your friends are going to die, boy…die.'

11

just another shipment of souls

In absolute astonishment I watched the deformed figure of Zotto emerging from the driver's body. Like some kind of hideous rebirth. Once complete, the demon scurried across the floor. Perching itself up on the front seat.

'So,' Zotto began to count the kids on the bus, 'that's 14 new souls for me…and none for you.' It laughed. Puffing out its chest. While leaping from seat to seat in excitement.

The now demon-free driver looked around. Confused stamped on his features. 'Oh my God!' he glanced out of the window. Reaching over to grab the steering wheel. He scrambled to get back into his seat. The leg of his pants caught in the gear stick. He struggled to get free. Too late. The bus careened off the road. Crashing through a wooden barrier. Over an area of long grass. Before plunging off the edge of a small cliff. The vehicle sailed through the air in slow motion for what seemed like an eternity. It nosed diving into the freezing cold water. An insane rush of noise and movement followed.

The initial splash sent me and the others sailing over several seats. I landed upside down surrounded by a pile of other kids. It went all quiet for a while. Then a concert of cries and moans began to leak upwards. Dirty cold water began to seep into every crack of the bus. Josh wandered down the aisle of the vehicle. Dazed. Bleeding from his nose. Within minutes the water reached knee height. Continuing to rise rapidly.

'Josh! Where's Beth?' I grabbed out at the front of his shirt with both fists. But to no avail. I waded down the aisle in search of her. No sign. I assumed she was trapped under the ever-rising water line. I took a deep breath. Counting to three I ducked down into its murky depths. It was pitch black. Couldn't see a thing. I felt my way forward.

Something big blocked my path. A body. I panicked. Swallowing a gut full of water. The corpse floated up to the surface. I didn't want to look. But I did. The bruised and bloodied lifeless face of Johnny James, Ethan's best friend and partner in bullying crime, bobbed up in front of me.

I didn't have time to feel sorry for the poor boy. I needed to find Beth. I kept on searching. The natural light from the windows got sparser. The bus sank leisurely down into the water. Filling my lungs up with a big gulp of air, I dived back under for a second time. Near the back, I saw a figure. Kicking and writhing about. It was

Beth. Trapped in her seat. The belt from her jacket wrapped around a metal bar.

'Hold on Beth!' I swallowed more dirty water. My effort to tug the belt free proved futile. I swam back up to the surface. 'Help! Someone Help!' The bus was almost submerged. Almost in complete darkness. I spied Josh struggling to keep his head above water near one of the last few remaining windows. Just above the water line.

'Josh…Beth is stuck…down there!' I pleaded. Again, I tried to grab Josh's face with both hands. My cold fingers went straight through. 'She's going to die. Please Josh. Do something.' I almost resigned myself to defeat. 'And it's all my fault.' My mate didn't look good.

I peered over. Mister Hubbard was now fully conscious. With both hands, he pried open the emergency doors. Some of the kids swam out of the door into the lake itself. The teacher held his nose. He sunk down into the darkness. Moments later, the brave teacher reappeared with Beth in his arms. Maybe he was dressed like Indiana Jones for a reason. What a hero!

'Josh! Quick…this way,' the teacher yelled. Water filled up every inch of the remaining space of the vehicle. I looked around for anyone else stuck in the doomed machine.

Within seconds, the bus lost all of its colour. Just blackness. Black as night. I heard an eerie creaking noise. The bus rocked back and forth. It glided downwards. Gently bumping on to the bottom of the lagoon. I swam through the door. Swam up towards the morning daylight that glistened above me. Mister Hubbard and the driver stood waist high in the lake. They stood dragging teenage bodies onto the bank. Gasping for air, I clambered up the muddy verge. My lungs full of dirty water. I coughed and sputtered. Scanning the tragic scene unfolding in front of me. I let out a cry. Beth and Josh lay motionless in the damp grass. Just lying there. Side by side. Eyes closed. Not breathing. Statures.

'No...No!' I fell to my knees next to them. I banged the ground with my bare hands.

'That's life, kid.' I looked up. Jezzie stood next to me. He held out his hand. 'Come on we've got work to do.'

I refused his hand up. I remained rooted on the ground. Crying. 'Why Jezz...Why? They didn't harm anyone.'

The tramp plonked himself down beside me. He put his arm around my shoulders. I buried my head into the old man's chest. 'I know kid. Life is unfair. But we need to...'

'No, Jezz...I've had enough...I can't do this anymore.'

'AAAAAAHHHHHHH!' A shrilled shriek pierced the air.

I turned to see the spirit of Sharon Bell. She stood staring down at her dead body on the ground. Shivering. Her ghostly fingers pointing at her corpse. She screamed again. This time louder.

Beth's spirit popped up next. Followed by the essence of Johnny James in the water. He swam to the shore. His body still floating faced down in the lake. Colin and Yvonne appeared soon after. Then Josh's spirit appeared. Because of the muddy bank, he slipped. Almost falling back into the water.

'It's time, kid,' Jezzie reminded me of my duties.

'No.'

'It's got to be done. Leo it's your purpose. Your soul purpose.'

I knew he was right but I didn't want to accept it. My worst nightmare. Tears streamed down my face. I trudged towards the spirits of my dead class mates. Wondering how I was going to break the bad news to them. On the river bank, Mister Hubbard, on his knees, banged on Ethan's chest. Everyone else looked on. He bent over the boy. Giving him the kiss of life.

'Breathe Ethan…breathe,' I reached over to hold Beth's hand. She looked at me. Mystified. 'I'll explain later,' I whispered to her.

'What's happened to me?' Sharon Bell kept repeating the question. Glaring down at her own dead body.

Everyone ignored her. We all stood watching Mister Hubbard. Willing him on. Willing him to save the boy who had made my life hell.

'He's going to make it,' I said hopefully. Jezzie shook his head. 'He is Jezz…he's going to make…' My face dropped at the sight of Ethan's spirit rising up from his body. Rising up through my teacher to stand with the rest of the dead souls.

'What you all looking at?' the bully boy grunted.

I turned away to face the trees behind us. Not because of Ethan's stare. I was trying my best to stop more tears racing down my cheeks. I was lost for words.

'Hi Leo.' Someone tapped me on the shoulder.

Josh stood in front of me. I threw my arms around my friend's neck. Gripping around him tightly as I could. Josh struggled free. He looked me up and down. 'So does this mean I'm…I'm,' he found it difficult to say.

I nodded my head. 'If you mean dead…yes…I'm afraid so.'

'I can't believe it.' Josh snapped the stick he was holding in two. He threw the bits to the floor.

I continued, 'I know it sucks Josh, but there's nothing you can do now.'

'It's not just that.' He stomped about. Obviously upset. 'I've been on a diet for two weeks, and tomorrow for a treat, my mam's making us her special lasagna…with, wait for it…with homemade garlic bread.'

I hugged him again. 'You're nuts.'

Meanwhile, Jezzie stood alone scanning the surrounding area. I could tell what he was thinking. I knew he felt uneasy with the whole situation. 'Leo,' He pulled me to one side. 'You need to concentrate. You need to forget that they are your friends.'

'But they are my friends.'

Jezzie looked into his eyes. 'Look they're just another shipment of souls. Another shipment we need to deliver and quickly.'

'NO…I can't…you take them.'

Jezzie dropped his cane. He grabbed my shoulders. 'Listen kid…this is your mission…not mine…I'm here to support this time. And this is going to be a tough assignment. If you get this right, you will be signed off….and a qualified soul walker….no more mentor…no more me.'

I stepped back. 'No, Jezzie…I can't do it…I can't do…'

'Colin,' Beth screamed out. 'It's got Colin.'

I spun around. Colin Bird's head was already in the mouth of an Efil which had sprung up out of the water. The boy kicked and thrashed about. The creature's jaws way too powerful to let go. Too determined. The fishlike Efil sank back into the water. Pulling the boy's spiritual body down with it.

On the bank, none of the dead teenagers said a word. They all stood silent. They all turned to face me.

'What was that?' Ethan backed up. Falling over a stump of a tree.

'Something you need to stay clear of,' Jezzie muttered casually. He picked up his cane. 'Come on Leo, let's get moving.' He hobbled off towards the bank of trees.

No one else moved. Stunned. Scared. In the background, two ambulances screeched to a stop near the river bank. Several paramedics jumped out and raced across the grass. Rushing towards the bodies of the teenagers. Mister Hubbard sat crying all alone. His head in his hands. The driver's face as white as a ghost. Shaking his head. Wondering what the heck had happened.

'Looks guys,' I tried to herd my class mates up the hill. Away from the water's edge. 'I need to tell you something.' I know it was against the soul walker's rules but I thought it would be best to explain some of the situation they were now in.

The spirits of the teenagers stood in silence until I finished my explanation of what had happened to them.

'I can't be dead,' Sharon protested. On the verge of another screaming fit. 'I was nominated for prom queen and the prom is next week and I've already got my dress!'

Beth tutted. 'Typical.'

Ethan pushed me hard in the chest. 'That's the stupidest thing I've ever heard coward. I ain't dead.'

'It's true,' Josh jumped to my defense. 'Leo is a soul walker. He told me last week.'

Beth turned sharply. 'You told him? Why didn't you tell me?' She folded her arms waiting for a response.

Ignoring our conversation, Jezzie began unrolling the map.

'Sorry Beth,' I said, 'I did try…honest.'

Jezzie pointed towards the range of mountains in the distance. 'There's a station about ten miles that way. A place called Tarrytown.'

'What's that smelly old tramp talking about?' Ethan hollered.

I saw the anger brewing up in Jezzie's face. I quickly moved in before he exploded. 'Please trust us, Ethan. We need to get out of here before…'

From across the other side of the riverbank, the manic cry from the Efil creature rang out. 'Before that thing comes back.' I pointed.

Not even Ethan argued. We struggled up the muddy grass bank. Slipping and sliding. Near the top, Sharon, in her expensive and unpractical boots, lost her footing. She tumbled all the way back down to the bottom of the hill. She stood up covered in mud. Bits of grass in her hair. Tears gushing from her eyes. No one laughed. Everyone was too scared.

'Something ain't right,' Jezzie cast his experienced eyes over the undergrowth. 'It's too quiet. Keep your eyes peeled.'

In one long line our gang headed south. I led from the front. Jezzie took up the rear. We walked for about a mile. It wasn't easy. The terrain was difficult. Plus, I noticed the Efil following us. I kept it to myself.

'I'm tired.' Sharon caked in mud uttered. 'Can we stop for a while?' she asked Jezzie.

'Of course, my dear,' he replied. 'If you want to get eaten by demons.' He hobbled past her. Humming some tune. I was sure it was a Metallica song.

'Demons!' she thrilled, 'What demons?'

The rest of the group turned to face her. 'He said we are all going to get eaten by demons.' She pointed at Jezzie, 'or devil things.'

'You said that thing that ate Colin was an elf…or whatever?' Ethan piped up.

This time they all turned to face me. 'It's called an Efil not an elf. And he's just exaggerating,' I lied. I didn't want them panicking any more than they already were. 'There's no demons.' I marched on. Muttering under my breath, 'around here…I hope.'

Another hour into the journey, we reached a clearing in the trees. An old derelict wooden shack with boarded up windows stood all alone. Jezzie motioned for me to check it out.

'Me?' I mouthed the word back at the tramp.

Jezzie nodded his head.

Reluctantly I picked up a stick. Creeping up onto the porch. Peeking in through a crack in the window. Inside it was dark. It looked empty except for a broken chair tipped on its side. I opened the door very slowly. 'Aaaarrrrrggghhhhhhhhhhh!' Something plowed into my legs. Knocking me to the ground. I rolled onto my side. Covering up my face with my arms. 'Help.'

A loud bout of laughter was the last thing I expected to hear. Opening my eyes to see the behind of a small pig running away into the woods.

'Told you he was a coward,' Ethan screeched. 'Scared by a little bitty piggy. This little coward went wee wee wee…you chicken.' The bully slapped his leg. Beth was also grinning.

Jezzie tapped me on the head. 'Get up. Let's rest.'

A while later, most of us sat on the porch in a small circle. I fell silent. Contemplating the long journey ahead. More importantly what was going to happen to my classmates when we arrived. Other than sitting here with the spirits of my parents, this was the worst dead walking assignment I could have ever imagined.

'I'm starving.' Josh checked his pockets for morsels of food. 'Leo…I need food.'

'You could eat Johnny's ear wax,' Beth joked. 'There's more than enough for all of us in there.' She rubbed her stomach.

Johnny frowned. Checking his ears with a damp finger.

Jezzie winked at me. He rolled a small log over with his boot. Several large red beetles scurried about as if they were being chased by a large beetle-eating creature. The tramp grabbed two. 'Try one of these.' He popped one of them in his mouth.

'Oh my god. how gross was that?' Sharon Bell put her hand up to her face. 'Major gross. Did you see what that…that…that old man did?'

'Best fast food around,' Jezzie offered the other one to Josh. Josh looked at it cautiously. 'Go on…it tastes exactly like fried chicken.' The tramp licked his lips.

Josh stared at it. His brain ticking over. He couldn't resist. He snatched it out of Jezzie's hand. 'Give me it…I'll have a taste.'

The others watched on in horror. I had a weird kind of admiration as I observed Josh chewing on the insect. His inquisitive face changed to a look of utter disgust. He spat the half-eaten insect out on the ground. He raced behind a tree. Five minutes later he ambled back wiping vomit from his mouth. His face a terrible sickly shade of green. 'That doesn't taste anything like chicken.'

Jezzie open the palm of his hand. The beetle he had supposed to have eaten crawled up his arm. He placed it back down gently onto the ground. 'Sorry Josh, my mistake. It's not these ones that taste of chicken…it's the other type. Sorry.'

We all burst out laughing. Josh spewed up again.

'What next?' I asked Jezzie.

The tramp shrugged. 'You're in charge kid. This is your show.' He nodded to me. 'You must take control.'

Hesitantly I got to my feet. 'Excuse me everyone. I think…it's time to get going.' I reached down to help Beth up. From behind me, someone shoved me hard in the back. I stumbled. Just managing to keep my balance.

'I'm sick of all this nonsense,' Ethan crowed. 'I ain't listening to an old hobo and a yellow- bellied coward.'

Striding towards the bully, Jezzie gripped his cane in both hands. I stepped between them for the second time. 'Ethan, please…we've got to go,' I pleaded.

'I'm not going.' Ethan stuck his face up close to mine. This time I stood my ground.

'Ethan, don't do this.'

The bully reached out to shove me again. I moved out of the way. Causing him to push out at fresh air. He almost tripped over. Everyone stood opened mouthed.

'Come on everyone…let's go,' I turned my back to head off.

Ethan picked up a thick piece of branch. He aimed it at the back of my head. In the flash of an eye, the bully boy lay flat out on the floor. Foot swept by Jezzie's cane. The tramp stood over him. His stick positioned menacingly near the boy's nose.

'Leave him, Jezz' I pulled the tramp away. 'Get up.' I held out my hand to help the bully up.

Ethan dismissed it. He scrambled to his feet. 'I'm going this way.' He looked around at the others. 'Who's coming?'

Most of the others stared down at the ground. 'Thought so…bunch of dorks…come on Johnny, let's get outta here,' he instructed his only ally.

Johnny started to protest but chickened out. 'Ok.'

'Ethan, we need to stay together. In one big group,' I begged. 'You don't know what's out there.'

My warning fell on deaf ears. The bully boy stormed away. Followed reluctantly by Johnny. The rest of the gang watched them disappear out of sight into the thick, dark forest.

'Let them go,' Josh piped up. But only after he knew Ethan was out of ear shot.

'I agree,' Beth added. 'He's nothing but trouble.'

Jezzie pulled me to one side. 'He's a pain. A big pain. But you need to go and bring him back.'

'Me?'

'No…Elvis Presley!'

'What?'

'Of course, you, boy.'

'But…He's a…a…'

Jezzie gripped me by the collar. 'One of the rules of soul walking. Don't make it personal. Remember? I agree he is a pratt. But they will be dead meat if you don't go and bring them back.' I looked towards the forest 'I'll stay here with the others until you get back.' He tapped me on the head with his cane. 'But be careful, boy. Very careful.

A big part of me wanted to just let them go. I was sick of being bullied. I didn't care if the demons picked Ethan's bones clean. Yet deep down I knew the vagabond was right. I couldn't let it happen. Especially after I had witnessed Jezzie dutifully walking the spirit of the gangster thug. The thug, who had beaten him into a coma, to the station, unscathed.

I picked up a heavy piece of wood and followed them.

'I'll come with you.' Someone yelled. I turned around. Beth stood by my side. 'Don't argue Goth boy,' she whispered. 'I'm coming.'

I wasn't going to. I had a feeling I would need all the help I could get. We scaled down the embankment into the trees shouting the boys' names.

.

12

'that's for Johnny'

Beth and I wandered through the dense forest. Every step seemed to be fraught with danger. She held my hand tight. Well, maybe it was me holding her hand tight. The thick branches of the trees overhead blocked out large amounts of the daylight. The surroundings eerily moody. Dark. Menacing. It was quiet. Too quiet.

'We've lost them.' My eyes searching around the gloominess for a clue.

'Look. Footsteps.' Beth pointed at the ground. Two sets of prints in the mud 'They're heading that way.' She began to follow them.

'Hang on… they could be anyone's or anything's.' I said curiously.

Jokingly Beth placed her hands to her face. 'What? Like some big foot or something?'

At first, I didn't realise she was mocking me. 'Funny! You know what I'm…m…mean?' I stuttered. 'You never know.'

'You're right,' she injected, 'I'm not sure if Big Foot and his Misses would be wearing sneakers and eating sour cream and onion chips.' She picked up the wrapper from the ground.

Crack.

The abrupt sound of a branch snapping somewhere off to our left immediately halted her teasing. 'What's that?' She clutched onto me even tighter. Her fingers crushing mine with her strong grip.

'Ouch.' I released her grasp.

Crack! Crack! Crack!

The noise got louder. Nearer.

'Get ready to run,' I whispered quietly into Beth's ear. We stepped backwards a few paces.

'Where to?'

'Back to the others. I'll stay and fight it off,' I bravely replied. Deep down hoping that whatever it was would just run the other way.

'Yeah right…I'm not leaving.' She squeezed my arm.

I didn't argue. I was too damn scared too. I clutched the piece of wood with both hands. The bushes shook back and forth. 'Come on,' I yelled, 'I'm not afraid,' My voice didn't sound convincing. I knew it. She knew it. Whatever was in the bushes probably did as well.

The rustling stopped. Nothing stirred. I inhaled. Beth went to say something. Suddenly whatever it was came bounding through the greenery straight towards us.

'Run!' I bellowed. Dragging her along with me in the opposite direction.

We sprinted. Not sure where we were heading. I didn't care. Just needed to get away. After galloping down a small ravine, Beth slipped onto the ground. I stopped to help her to her feet. My nerves in shreds. Once up we ran again. Glancing over her shoulder, Beth stopped dead. 'Look,' she said.

Turning back, I caught sight of the magnificent stag standing in the clearing. Sniffing the air. It stood well over five feet tall. Antlers making it appear twice its size.

'It's only a deer,' Beth tried to catch her breath.

'Shhhhhhh. Maybe something spooked it.' My body still tense.

'Yeah…us.' She poked me in the ribs.

The deer looked around before trotting off back into the safety of the forest. Nothing else stirred. When my nerves stopped quivering, we continued on our journey.

'By the way,' Beth looked at me. 'What happened to, I'll stand and fight it?' You are a bit of a coward, ain't you,' she giggled. 'Wait until I tell the others.'

'I was going to… but….' I noticed her smirking. 'Oh, shut up.' I gently punched her in the arm. I loved the way she knew how to make me smile though.

Our journey got a little easier the less dense and populated the forest became. I wasn't sure how long we should keep going.

We'd been walking another thirty minutes or so. Still no sign of our classmates.

'Wow, look at these!' Beth pointed to a huge set of deformed footprints in the dirt. The prints headed off in the same direction we were going. 'Now that does look like it belongs to big foot...or big feet.' She put her own foot inside one of the prints in the dirt. It was nearly three times the size of hers.

'An Efil,' my response was concise. 'Let's go.'

Stepping out through the last remaining line of trees, we found ourselves high up on the side of a steep mountain. A dodgy looking rope bridge spanned the gap of the valley to the mountain on the other side. I guess the crossing was well over 800 feet long. Down below a fast-flowing river sat at the bottom of the valley. A long, long way down.

'There they are,' Beth pointed at the two boys climbing up the steep hill on the other side of the bridge.

'Ethan...Johnny!' I used my hands as a make-shift megaphone.

Johnny spun around. Ethan shoved him in the back. 'Keep moving Johnny,' he demanded. The two boys fastened their pace.

'Look,' Beth shook her head, 'they're running now? What a pair of idiots.'

I wasn't really listening. More concerned with the rope bridge laid out in front of us. I hated heights. Nearly as much as I detested spiders. And recently, I had a very strong disliking for demons and Efil creatures.

Beth stood at the bridge opening. 'Come on Leo.' It was only wide enough for one person.

I gulped. I really didn't want to cross it. It didn't look safe. Several slats were missing. Many others damaged beyond repair.

'Leo…Leo…look.' Beth motioned down to the river bed below.

An Efil waded through the water. It's eight legs extended, It took only a matter of seconds before it was out and ascending up the steep rock face on the other side. Scrambling up towards our class mates.

'You stay here,' I ordered Beth. 'I'll go alone.

'Oh Ok,' with hands on hips she voiced. 'I'll just wait here for Tarantula man's younger brother to show up.' She pushed me in the back. 'I'm coming.'

I took a deep breath. 'Ok.' I stepped on the first rung. Holding onto both sides of the rope handrail for dear life. Slowly I inched my way across. Treading deliberately. The archaic bridge creaked. Swayed. Swung. It felt like being on the scariest ride in the fair…ever!

'Where's it gone?' She noticed the man-spider creature had disappeared out of sight.

I was afraid to look anywhere other than straight ahead. 'Aaaaarrrrrrgggggghhhhhh!' A rotten wooden slat crumbled under my weight. I dropped. My left leg disappearing through the gap. Frantically I reached up. Trying to grab hold of whatever I could. A small pebble fell from the bridge. It seemed to take an age before it splashed into the stream below.

'Help... help me,' I shrieked.

Beth got onto her stomach. Crawling towards me. Her hand outstretched. 'Leo...grab it,' she commanded.

I extended my arm as far as I could. Locking my fingers into hers. Her fingers felt so soft. I started to pull myself up. Beth's face showed the strain. Another section of wood gave way, I dropped again. This time my entire body fell through the gap. Luckily, I managed to clutch onto the rope which had once held the slats in place. My feet dangled in fresh air over the valley down below.

'Leo,' Beth poked her head through the missing slats. 'Oh no.'

'What?'

'Nothing.' She replied. I could tell she was lying. Still hanging there, I turned and looked behind me. I quickly found out what she didn't want me to see. The Efil creature from the river hung upside down underneath the bridge. Hung absolutely still. Just hanging there. Staring at me. About 100 feet away from us.

Trust my luck. Not only was I dangling from a rope bridge for dear life, a huge man-spider beast was eyeing me up for lunch. Panic set in. I swung my legs back and forth. Gaining enough momentum to reach the remaining bridge slats with my feet. I missed my target. Tried again. Missed again. One eye on the creature. I swung a third time. I made it, Holding on desperately. Using my feet and elbows, I pulled myself back up onto the bridge. I lay on the slats. My entire body covered in a ball of sweat. Beth sat near me shaking uncontrollably. Tears flowing down her face. Fear etched into her eyes.

'Hurry,' I said. Helping her up.

It was too late to go back. We treaded onwards. The Efil deliberately shuffled itself up from the underside of the bridge in front of us. Its hairy legs tangled around the ropes. The side of the beast's face covered in cuts and bruises. Only when it stared at me with its piercing eyes did I recognize it. It looked like the beast I had fought on the school bus. Its large barrel chest expanded and fell slowly with each breath. A green colored gas escaped from its mouth.

The creature dropped onto the slats without causing a ripple. A loud growl escaped from its throat.

'Leave us alone,' I cried.

It stood stationary. No expression on its face.

Beth yanked on my tee-shirt. Her voice quivering. 'Let's go back. Its freaking me out.' I nodded in agreement.

Yet before we had chance to move, the creature crawled up on one of the supporting ropes of the old bridge. It balanced upside down for a moment. Its eyes looked stranger than ever. Saliva dripped from its mouth onto the wooden slats.

I stepped in front of Beth. My eyes never leaving the Efil that hung a few feet away. All of a sudden, the creature came at us. As fast as lightening.

'Run Beth…run.'

This time I stood my ground. The Efil rushed forward. Sweeping me to one side without breaking stride. It almost knocked me clean off the bridge. With mouth open wide, it leapt straight onto Beth.

She screamed. Falling onto the slats. The Efil landed on top of her. Her legs kicked and thrashed about. Trying to escape its grip. 'Leo…it's going to bite me.' The creature's mouth inches from swallowing her whole.

I dived on its back. Wrapping my arms around its neck. Holding it in a head brace. The creature rocked its head back and forth violently. I held on for dear life. The bridge swung frantically. I squeezed harder. Closing my eyes. Hanging on. I could sense the Efil buckling under the pressure.

'I've got you. I've got you…' I muttered.

One of its powerful legs smashed me in the ribs. I fell backwards. Beth kicked and flailed at it. Breaking free from its grip, she scurried backwards. On her backside, she moved out of reach of the creature's deadly grip.

The snarling Efil turned back around to face me. It wrapped its legs around my head. It squeezed. I felt dizzy. Digging my fingernails into its eyes like I had done on the bus. The Efil wasn't going to get caught a second time. It embraced harder.

The life started to drain from me. My body going limp. The beast pulled me in closer. Picking me up above its head. I looked down at the river below. Behind us, Beth pulled one of the slats from the bridge. Using all her strength, she whacked the creature on the back. The piece of wood snapped in two.

'Get off him…leave him alone,' her cries bellowed out around the valley.

The Efil dropped me. I moved away from its outstretched arms. Trying to clear my head. In one movement the beast smacked the wooden slat out of Bath's hands. It seized her by the ankle. Pulling her towards it like a giant spider dragging in a fly.

I scrambled to my feet. Picking up one half of the discarded piece of wood I jammed the sharp edge of it right into the white eye of the beast. 'Take that you, ugly git!' I hollered in its face.

The noise that escaped from the beast's mouth was sickening. Its cries reverberated around the valley. Sending hundreds of birds flying out of the trees. It staggered to his knees. Trying frantically to dislodge the stick from its face. I grab hold of its legs. Heaving it up and throwing it over the side of the bridge. I watched the creature spinning around several times before splattering on the rocks below.

'Quick, let's get off this thing,' I grabbed Beth's hand.

Once across, I peeped down. Expecting to see the crumbled body of the Efil in the water. There was nothing there. It had gone. I sunk to my knees. Beth sat on a tree stump.

'Why was that thing after me?' Beth's entire body trembled. 'It didn't want you. It wanted me. Why?'

I hadn't told her or the others the real reason the creatures were after them. 'It's after your soul.'

She clutched my face. 'What?'

'Your soul.' Before I had a chance to explain, a loud stomach-turning screech rose up from high in the mountainside. We looked at each other. Fear evident on both our features. 'Ethan,' I rushed up the slope towards the cries. Without considering the danger, Beth followed close behind.

The climb up the rock-laded mountain proved to be tougher than it looked. The back of my calves ached. I could hardly catch my breath on reaching the large flat area cut into the rock. Several small abandoned wooden cabins were dotted around. To me it looked like some kind of old gold mining town in one of those old Western movies. I sniffed the thin air. My body stiffened up at the strong scent drafting up my nostrils. I recognized the smell straight away. The scent of demon. Lots of them.

Sticking close together we checked out the three outhouses. Luckily, we found the buildings empty.

'Ethan!' I shouted out the bully boy's name. 'Johnny!'

'There!' Beth signaled towards the entrance to the mine cut into the side of the mountain. The words 'Zetec Ponill 21' painted in black letters over the top of it. Wooden planks hammered across the opening had the words 'Keep Out…Danger' written in red. Several planks had been displaced. Leaving enough room for a single person to climb inside.

'HELP…HELP!' the terrifying scream echoed from way inside the darkness of the mine.

'Stay close to me,' I told Beth. My mind racing about like a greyhound chasing a rabbit across a field.

'Thanks,' another hint of sarcasm in her voice. 'I thought you were going to tell me to hang out here again….by myself.'

I was too scared to argue. We quietly stepped inside. Treading over a pile of rocks. My eyes took time to adjust to the greyness of the interior. The place smelled old. Damp. Water dripped from the ceilings. Small puddles lined the uneven floor.

'Get away from me!' the petrified yells rebounded again from somewhere deep inside the dark space. The pitiful cries mingled in with a string of weird high-pitched shrieks. It sounded like a rabid pack of hungry hyenas on a daytrip to a slaughterhouse.

My legs turned to jelly. I wanted to turn and run. Grab Beth and run as fast as we could. But I knew I had no choice. I had come here to do a job and I needed to try.

'You, ok?' I asked Beth.

'Not really,' honesty in her reply.

Following the noise, we wandered into the heart of the tunnels. The darkness crept on us with each step we took. Around a sharp bend, a homemade lit torch swung wildly in the blackness. Its flame causing weird shadows to dance off the walls.

'Leave me alone!' The cry came from Ethan. Situated up against a wall. Surrounded by four or five soul stealers. He kept them at bay by swinging the fire torch at them. The flame fading with each swung. The creatures getting nearer and nearer. One lunged at Ethan. He hit it away with his fist. The demon rolled over. But instantly jumped back onto its feet. Nose bleeding.

'Shhhhhhh,' I placed my hand over Beth's mouth. The creatures hadn't spied us yet. I picked up an old pick resting against a rock. 'Wait here.' I pushed her gently into a small recess in the rock. 'And don't argue.'

This time she didn't even try.

Ethan's eyes lit up on seeing me over the shoulders of his attackers.

The colour and the size of the demons shocked me. Much different than the ones that roamed the streets of New York. These were smaller. Dark red eyes. Covered in some kind of luminous white substance from head to toe. I could see their veins through their thin translucent skin.

Inside my head, I counted to ten. 'Yeeeeeeeeerrrrrrrrrrrrrrrrrr,' I charged at them. Swinging the pick above my head. I connected sweetly with one demon that hadn't seen me coming. It rolled about on the ground. Blood oozing from its wounds. I split another one's head open wide. Knocking it out cold. Another creature turned to me. Rushing in the darkness. Red eyes shining. I swung at it wildly. Missing my intended target. I tripped onto the floor instead. The demon dived on top of me. Its sharp yellow teeth two inches from my earlobe. Its fingernails scratching at my cheek.

In a complete panic, I held the creature's face with both hands. Full up with rage I tossed it into the wall. The demon cried out in agony. Limping off holding its dazed head.

The bigger demon nearest to Ethan roared out at the top of its voice. The cry filled the cave. It was so loud I thought it would cause some kind of rock fall. I looked across at Beth standing in the shadows. The beast licked its lips as if it was tasting a plate of gravy-covered meatloaf. It swaggered towards her. Completely ignoring me. I turned to help but another stealer vaulted onto my back. Knocking me back down. I caught my ribs on a sharp rock. It took the wind out of my sails.

'Ethan…quick, help Beth,' I managed to call out. While wrestling with the beast at the same time.

Beth trapped herself further into the corner of the recess. The demon scurried towards her. Smirking sadistically. Cracking its knuckles. Beth screamed. I had to help her. With several sharp blows using a loose stone, I bashed the demon I had been wrestling with in its face. It fell to the ground.

I sprang to my feet. Across the cave, the other demon closed in on Beth.

'Ethan!' I roared. He didn't move. Or more like he couldn't move. Stood cowering in the corner. His body shaking from head to toe. I couldn't believe it. This was the boy who bullied me for most of my schooling. 'And he calls me the coward,' I thought. 'The torch…throw her the torch, Ethan…the torch,' I shouted.

He stood shaking his head. I needed to act fast. Grabbing the lit torch out of his hand I raced to towards her. 'Beth!' I threw the flaming torch. It landed at her feet. The large demon lunged at her. In one movement she bent down, picked it up and rammed it into the creature's face. It shrieked. Its head on fire. Racing around in the darkness. Beating its face with its hand. It staggered passed me. Sticking its head into a small puddle. Its face hissed. The entire mine filled with the smell of burnt flesh.

'Quick.' I motioned to my two classmates. 'We've got to get out before they regroup.'

In the dark we made our way as best as we could through the tunnels. Heading towards the light of the entrance. Ethan barged his way to the front.

'Keep running, don't look back,' I insisted. A dozen sets of red eyes sparkled from way back in the shadows.

Near an old tram line, Beth fell over. Banging her head on the stony ground. I reached down to pick her up. Unknowingly escaping the clutches of a demon that flew over my head. It smashed into a wall.

We carried on towards the light. Ethan reached the entrance first. I could see his large frame squeezing through the missing slats. Out into the sunlight. Beth and I weren't far behind.

'Everyone ok?' I asked. The knees of my jeans covered in dirt.

Beth nodded. Ethan stared blankly ahead. Unable to talk.

'Which way?' Beth said. Hands on her knees. Breathing heavy.

Before I could answer, the wooden planks boarding up the entrance exploded outwards into hundreds of tiny pieces. Several white coloured demons appeared. Several more rushed out from behind them. They all stopped in their tracks. Shielding their eyes from the sun light.

'Down…down.' I pointed to the bridge.

Darting down the hillside, tripping and slipping on the wet grass. I fell. Skidding down a small embankment. I quickly clambered up. Meanwhile the demons had readjusted to the light. Regrouped. Refocused. They chased after us. Not far behind. A rock hit me on the shoulder. Sending an electric shock down my arm to my fingertips. One side of my body went numb. I continued zigzagging back and forth using the trees for cover. The rocks sailed past my head.

Half way down to the bridge, I bumped into Ethan. He stood perfectly still. Looking up at a tree. Beth positioned next to him. Her hands covering her mouth to stop the scream from escaping.

'What's wrong?' I asked. 'Keep going.'

Ethan raised his finger. Pointing. Johnny James hung upside down from the branches of the tree. His stomach ripped apart. His eyes wide open.

'Quick…we've got to go,' I demanded.

'But Johnny.' Ethan's words dribbled out of his mouth.

'It's too late for him now.' I didn't mean for it to sound so cold. But I could see the fastest of the demons sprinting through the trees about twenty yards from us.

'Quick.'

We fled downwards. The demon hot on our tails.

'Keep going,' I tried my best to encourage the others. I stopped to face the danger. The nearest demon flew through the air at me. Luckily, I moved to one side just in time. The creature flew straight into a tree. A branch stuck through its body. Impaling it.

'That's for Johnny,' I muttered. Another six demons appeared over the hill top

Down below Beth and Ethan had already begun scampering across the bridge. I reached it seconds later. I too started crossing the swinging bridge.

Boosh.

A banging noise caused me to turn back the way we had come.

Boosh.

A demon with a large axe chopped away at one of the two ropes attaching the bridge to the rock. The other creatures egged it on to cut the rope faster.

I caught up with the others. We still had over half way to go to reach the other end. The sound of the axe echoed throughout the valley. Without warning the one side of the bridge jerked violently. The support rope gave way. Throwing us off balance. Tipping us on to the wooden slats. Getting up, I helped the others.

'Come on,' I urged. The demon with the axe had already starting on the last remaining rope support. 'It's not that far,' I lied.

With every blow of the axe, my heart missed a beat. I looked down at the river way below.

Boosh.

The bridge swayed. It tilted on one side. The single rope now holding the one side of the bridge up groaned under the strain. The axe chopping stopped for a split second. Another demon took over. The banging continued. Faster than ever. The mass of white coloured demons bounced and hollered around excitedly on the mountainside.

From out of nowhere, the man-spider creature appeared. It sprinted at the demons. Scattering them in all directions. The one with the axe swung it at the Efil. The man-spider creature snatched the weapon out of its grip. It threw the axe and then the demon over the edge of the cliff.

'Aarrrrrrrgggggggggghhhhhhhhhhhhh!' the demon cried for an age before smashing into the rocks below.

Beth and Ethan clambered off the bridge onto the opposite mountain. I followed quickly behind. On the other side, the Efil creature banged its chest. Its huge eyes shining bright. It stepped forward. Striding faster and faster towards us. I felt too weak to fight it. It got closer and closer. I knew our days were numbered. The end of the road. The last strands of the support rope unraveled. The one side of the bridge fell away from the mountain.

The earth-shattering roar from the Efil sailed down the valley as it fell spiraling to its death.

13

they can't run from me

The three of us tiptoed cautiously towards the wooden shack. I prayed that the others would be waiting inside. Safe and sound. The newly arrived moon up in the evening sky cast eerie shadows throughout the forest.

'Jezz...' Beth called out the tramp's name.

'No,' I placed my hand over her mouth.

She freed herself from my palm. 'What's wrong?'

I looked around. 'Too quiet,' I whispered. 'Could be a trap.' A faint trace of demon in the air. Nothing as strong as the disgusting odor at the mine. But there was definitely a scent.

Without talking I signaled to Ethan to check around the back of the shack. He refused to budge. 'Ethan,' I hissed. 'Go...now!'

He shook his head in violent disagreement. 'No, dude...no way.' It was the first words he had spoken since we had got off the bridge.

Beth sighed. She picked up a large stick from the ground. 'Ok you, big sissy…I'll do it.' She disappeared around the corner of the building.

I turned to face Ethan. I wanted so badly to grab him by the collar of his jacket. Shake him hard. I chickened out. He was still much bigger than me. 'Anything happens to her and I'll…I'll kill you.' It was a stupid thing to say to a dead spirit, but I didn't care. 'Now go with her,' I snapped.

Surprisingly Ethan did what he was told. Heading off behind the shack.

I waited a few seconds before inching forward towards the front of the building. As quiet as possible I treaded carefully up the short set of wooden stairs leading up to the porch. A step at a time. The dead body of a soul stealer lay slumped over a section of broken railing. Its head bashed in.

'Another notch on Jezzie's walking stick,' I stepped past the corpse. Pausing briefly outside the door. I stared at the timber structure. My legs shaking nearly as much as my hands. My lips parched. The veins pulsing in my neck. I hadn't really considered my next move. I knew it wouldn't involve knocking and waiting for someone, or something to answer. I reached out very slowly. Gripping the rusty old handle. In one swift movement the wooden door shot open wide. A hand came out. Yanking me inside. It happened so fast I had no time to cry out or fight back. I found myself flat on my back on the dusty old floor. Facing up towards the ceiling.

The light from the moon projecting through a small hole in the roof. It illuminated the manic figure of Jezzie. Looming ominously over me. A chair above his head. Ready to bring it down on mine.

'Oh, it's you.' The tramp threw the chair down. Landing on its side with a bang. 'Where the hell have you been… on a picnic?' He slammed the door shut.

'I'm glad to see you too.' I got to my feet. Brushing myself down.

The rest of the gang sat huddled in the far corner. Petrified looks on their faces.

'You, ok?' I asked.

He motioned his eyes to the far corner of the room. Two demons lay stationary near the fireplace. One on top of the other. At the other end, near the window, another creature lay faced down. Blood from its head formed a dark red pool on the floor.

Sharon sat tied to a chair. A strip of silver duct tape covering her mouth. Black mascara streamed down her face.

'What's going on?' I asked.

Josh nodded towards Jezzie. 'He did it,' he whispered.

I ripped the tape off Sharon's mouth. Untying her hands.

'Outrageous.' Sharon stood up in a rage. 'Not only have I been attacked by devils…lots of them…but that horrible…horrible man taped my mouth up…'

'Sharon shut up,' Josh interrupted the girl's rant. 'He had to do something…you wouldn't stop screaming,' his voice reduced to a whisper, 'Leo…that Jezzie guy is fantastic. He's like a ninja. A ninja tramp.'

Inwardly, I chuckled to myself at Josh's description of my mentor. Jezzie stood oblivious to the entire conversation. Or knowing him, just choosing to ignore us. He remained guarding the door. Cane held firmly in his hand. His eyes darting back and forth into the darkness.

Suddenly, a head poked through the smashed window,

'DEVILS!' Sharon screamed.

Jezzie spun around on a dime. His cane ready to smash the intruder's skull into next week.

'It's ok, Jezz.' I seized the stick from continuing its downward journey. 'It's Beth and Ethan.' I opened up the window fully. The pair climbed in.

Once inside Beth, arms folded, glared at me. 'Thanks for forgetting about me.'

'What?'

'You heard me.'

'But…but.'

Jezzie puffed out his cheeks. 'This is not the time or the place for a lover's quarrel!'

'We are not…lo…lov…. lovers.' I stuttered.

'ARRGGHHHHHH.' Ethan raced towards me. A chair positioned above his head. His eyes wild. He swung it in my direction. I just stood there. The chair missed me by inches.

Thankfully I wasn't the target of his attack. Instead, the chair crashed down on the head of one of the injured demons who was about to take a bite out of my ankle. The creature slumped back down unconscious.

Ethan stood holding the last remaining leg of the chair in his hand. His eyes focused on the small monster. 'Don't mess with my friend,' he gestured.

'Thanks mate.' We exchanged an awkward fist bump.

Everyone else in the room looked at us in amazement. Not about the demon attack but that the bully boy and the coward had somehow become friends. Fist bumping muckers/ Josh shrugged his shoulders at me.

'It's a long story,' I replied. Kicking the demon in the side just to make sure it wasn't acting.

Jezzie broke the silence. 'Let's get out of here. We haven't got much time.' He walked outside.

'I'm not going out there.' Sharon protested. Backing up to the old fireplace.

I could see by the look on the faces of the others that she wasn't alone. I tried to calm their fears. 'Look, there's a station not far. Maybe a mile or two.' It was further. Much further. But they didn't need to know that at that moment.

No one moved. Something suddenly scampered across the rooftop. Everyone's eyes traced the movements of whatever it was. It went quiet again. Then the noise again. Like footsteps scuffling along. The sounds quickly changed the teenager's minds. They all trudged down the steps. Unaware that the noise had been a couple of stones thrown by Jezzie. He winked at me. I winked back. I still had a lot to learn from my mentor.

Back in the woods, we formed another long line. Josh walked alongside me. 'What happened out there?' he asked, 'Did Ethan see a ghost?'

'Something like that,' My trainers splashing through a small stream. The shallow water came up to my ankles. The others followed without question.

Josh tried again. 'Where's Johnny?'

I purposely ignored his question. The image of the boy ripped apart hanging from the tree shot into my mind. 'Just hurry up Josh.'

The way he looked at me before taking up his position near the back of the line, I could tell he had a good idea what had happened to poor old Johnny.

Although it was already quite dark, it soon got even darker. The clouds wrapped themselves around the light of the moon. Progress was slow. We meandered through the bank of trees. Then through the wild undergrowth which snatched out at our feet. No one uttered a word. We moved onwards by all holding onto the person in front.

Jezzie hobbled up to me. 'How you feeling, kid?' he asked. A hint of concern in his voice.

'Not bad...my arm's a bit sore.' I winced as I moved it. 'A demon caught me with a rock.'

'Not just that. How are you feeling? Ok?'

I stopped walking. I'd known him long enough now to know when there was something on his mind. 'What are you getting at Jezz?

The sound of a truck off in the distance broke our conversation. Its headlights came into view through the cluster of trees.

'It's a truck,' Sharon yelled out. 'There must be a road.' She raced off. The rest of the gang sprinted after her. Running towards the long grey strip of tarmac. Jezzie and I strolled behind like two parents watching their children racing across the sand to swim in the sea.

'What's wrong Jezz?'

'Nothing.'

'Jezz.'

'Ok...ok.' He touched my arm. 'It's just that you've been on this assignment for a long time...too long.'

'So have you.'

'Yeah, but I'm in a coma. Remember. You're not. I've got medical equipment helping me survive. You haven't. You've blacked out somewhere.' He turned me around to face him. His fingernails digging into my arms. 'Look Leo, you're in danger...you have to go back. Don't worry about your friends...I'll get them all to the station, I promise.' The tramp looked deep into my eyes. I let his words sink into my brain. He added, 'When we get up to the road, stare at the headlights of any of the vehicles.;

'Why?'

'That may be the trigger you need to get you back.'

'No.'

'Yes.'

'No. These are my friends. My assignment. My soul walk…remember?'

The tramp grunted. 'Well at this rate, it could be your last.' He passed the map to me. Storming off obviously upset.

I checked the map again. The town wasn't far away. About an inch at the most. I caught up with the gang trekking along the side of the road in a much better spirit. Pardon the pun. It was really late. From time to time a car or truck sped past. Headlights unknowingly lighting us all up. I kept my eyes down. Purposely avoiding eye contact with the beam. Jezzie's grave warning spinning around in my head.

'No! It's your turn.' A barrage of shouting near the back of the line caught my attention. Josh and Ethan stood facing up to each other. Chest to chest.

I shook my head. Sick to death of their bickering. I had more important things on my mind. I marched towards them.

'No…I'm not going last,' Josh stood his ground. Looking up angrily at the taller boy.

'It's your turn fatty.' Ethan tried barging his way in front of him.

Josh blocked his path.

'I've had enough,' Jezzie hobbled towards them. His knuckles white around his cane. 'I'll sort this out.'

'Stop calling me fatty…Frankenstein head.' Josh pushed Ethan hard in the chest. He tumbled backwards Landing on his backside into the middle of the road.

He jumped up. Looking for revenge. Snarl on his face 'I'm going to…' Suddenly the headlights of a police car came into view. Blue lights flashing wildly. They lit up Ethen's entire body.

'Watch out,' Beth covered her eyes.

Ethan stood frozen in the glare of the vehicle. His mouth wide open. Sharon's piercing scream rang out in the night. Several feet from impact the car swerved to miss the boy. It carried on down the open road. The bully boy stood still in the road. 'Am I alright?' Patting his spiritual body from head to toe.

Josh raced over to him. 'I'm sorry…I didn't mean to push you…I'm so sorry…I'm so sorry.'

Ethan grabbed him by the throat. 'You nearly got me killed you idiot.'

'I said I'm sorry. Ok…ok…I will go to the back,' Josh gave in.

'That was odd,' I spoke out loud. 'Why did the driver of the car swerve? Did he see him?' I was trying to work out the answer when the brake lights on the police car lit up. I shot a glance at Jezzie. He stood close-by sniffing the air. The tramp's face confirmed my worst fear. All of a sudden, the police car propelled itself backwards.

'Run!' I cried out. 'Quick…into the field!'

They all stared at me. Then at the speeding cop car.

'What's wrong?' Beth enquired.

'Demons…I think. Demons…in the police car.'

One by one the gang scrambled down the bank into the corn field. Dashing off towards the woods at the far end. I waited until everyone had raced away. The cop car pulled up alongside. The darkened window on the driver's side rolled slowly down. A face stared directly at me. The face wasn't human.

'Hello boy,' Zotto grinned. His tongue licked his rotten teeth. His empty eye socket covered by a patch decorated with skull and crossbones. 'They can't run from me boy.' He spat. Its green phlegm landed on my cheek. 'I'm looking forward to the hunt.'

Too shocked to reply I wiped the gooey substance off. Then legged it as fast as I could in the same direction as the others. I soon caught up with Jezzie. He was struggling to keep up with the more youthful spirits. 'Come on Jezz.' He slowed to almost a walk. I looked back. More cop cars arrived.

'I'm ok…you go.'

'No.'

'Yes.'

Ethan trotted back towards us. 'Can I help?' he asked.

I nodded. 'Yeah…let's carry him.'

'I don't need your help…I'm fine!' the tramp argued.

We ignored Jezzie's instructions. Positioning ourselves under his arms, we picked him up. He was surprisingly heavy. But to be honest, his coat by itself must have weighed about a ton. We struggled on. Hard work. Eventually we reached the wooded area. Plonking him down on a tree stump. In front of us, a wide river. Probably around 80 feet from bank to bank. It looked deep as well with a strong current.

'What are we going to do?' someone asked.

'Look!' Beth pointed. Near the edge, a homemade wooden raft bobbed in the water. Big enough for all of us. 'We could use that.'

The gang looked at the raft and then at the fast-flowing river. I could sense their apprehension.

'That doesn't look safe,' Sharon muttered. For a change others nodded in agreement.

'Everyone ok?' I asked. Catching my breath.

A few nods. Most were too exhausted to reply. Sharon Bell looked like she'd been dragged through a hedge backwards and then dragged frontwards again. Yvonne stood shaking all over. Her bottom lip quivered uncontrollably. The others sat quiet. Staring out like zombies in a trance.

'What's next Leo?' asked Josh.

Up on the road, more police cars arrived. I looked across at Jezzie for guidance. The tramp could hardly breathe. Never mind speak. His chest wheezed like an old harmonica. 'I'll go and see if they are following us' I headed back to the edge of the woods. Up on the roadside in the light of the moon several torches heading our way. I raced back to the gang. 'We've got to go.'

'Are the coming,' Beth asked. I nodded my head.

Jezzie finally spoke. 'Leo... I'm too tired and too old to run.'

'What are we going to do?' I didn't really want to know his answer.

'Fight.'

'Sounds good to me,' Ethan punched his palm.

Suddenly the noise of barking made everyone's hair stand on end.

'What in god's name was that?' Josh piped up. Inching closer to Jezzie.

The tramp's face changed. As if he'd eaten a protein bar, he staggered to his feet 'Let's go...quick...quick.' Beth passed him his cane. 'In the river...in the river now.'

'Thought we were fighting them?' Ethan disappointedly asked.

'No...no...we can't fight them...not with...not with the ...the ... dogs.'

It was Josh who spoke up this time. 'But dogs can't hurt us.'

'He's right Jezz. They won't be able to see us.' I recalled the time under the railway arches when Jezzie's dog couldn't see me or him.

Jezzie snapped a branch off a tree. He started to sharpen the end of it into a point with a penknife.

'What is it Jezz?' I stood waiting for an explanation.

The tramp continued to work on the branch. 'That ain't the bark of any normal dog. That ain't no human dog.'

We all moved in closer to him. The barking grew louder. He looked at each of us in turn. 'That's the bark of....' he left a pause, '…..demon dogs.'

'Demon dogs?' everyone mouthed the words in unison.

Sharon's voice rose up above the others. 'Oh my god…we've got devil dogs after us now?'

This time no one bothered to tell her to shut up. All eyes focused on Jezzie then quickly turned towards the sound of the barking. Josh snapped a branch for himself. His hands shaking like a leaf.

'Right…water …raft…now,' I commanded.

14

this is personal now

Too late. The sudden rustling of branches, mixed with a deep low growling noise, startled us.

'Look!' Beth's tight grip nearly crushed my hand.

'Oh my god,' Sharon shrieked. A large demon dog sat perched up on the low hanging branch of a tree. It looked like a Rottweiler. But much scarier. Clumps of fur covering its oversized head. A body of black bones inside transparent thin veined skin.

'No sudden movements,' the tramp hissed. 'And no screaming.' He shot Sharon a glance.

The creature glared at us with its two large dog eyes. While another two cat-shaped eyeballs just below its ears stared into the woods. Each eye dark purple in colour. The demon dog arched its back. Another strange noise escaped from its throat. It sent a cold chill racing through my body.

Without thinking, I stepped in front of Beth. Jezzie edged forward to protect the others. The demon dog rose up on its hind legs. Howling into the dark sky. It was followed by a chorus of dog barks ringing off in the distance.

'There's more of them,' Jezzie muttered trying not to move his lips. 'We need to be quick. They will be here soon.'

The dog's eyes changed to an orange fiery glow.

'Listen up,' Jezzie murmured. 'Walk slowly to the river...keep together.'

'Not the water again,' Sharon protested. 'I'd rather...

'Listen girl,' the tramp shushed her through clenched teeth. 'Do exactly what I say. Get on the raft and shut the hell up.'

Jezzie handed me the pointed stick. The dog leapt on to the ground several feet away. Standing frozen. Like a statue. Its 4 eyes stalking our every move.

Inch by inch our group treaded backwards. Moving as one. 'Good...good,' Jezzie encouraged. 'Keep moving... keep moving.'

'I'm scared,' the words shivered out of Yvonne's lips. 'I'm scared of dogs.'

'Keep going,' Beth grabbed her mate's hand.

'I can't... I'm...I'm.....' Yvonne broke free from her grip. She rushed towards the river.

'Yvonne, no,' I shouted.

'No one else move,' Jezzie barked out his instructions. 'No one.'

The dog's head moved sharply towards the fleeing girl. It seemed to almost grin to itself. Then like a large grasshopper, it leapt into action. It glided effortlessly across the grass after her. Its speed shocked me. Within seconds, Yvonne lay pinned to the ground. The creature's powerful jaws bit into her arm. Shaking her about like a rag doll.

Yvonne's pitiful screams stabbed their way into my brain. Into the gang's brains.

'Help her,' Beth looked at me.

I stepped forward but hesitated. Not sure what I could do to help. Ethan bravely raced past me. He booted the dog in the side. It rolled off her. Turning sharply back towards him. Snapping at his ankles. Anger in its evil eyes. Ethan swung his boot again. It missed. I took several deep breaths. I dashed forward. Smashing the stick across the thing's back. The branch broke in half. Ethan kicked it squarely in the ribs. It snarled fiercely. Its mouth opened wide. The colour of its eyes now Jet black. Black like little balls of onyx. It looked viler than ever.

To be fair, Ethan didn't take a backward step. He kicked out at it again. 'Come on punk…I'll tear you up,' he yelled at it.

The dog turned away from me and snapped at him. This gave me an opening. I stabbed the remaining half of the stick into the dog's side. The make-shift weapon went straight through its body. Sticking the beast to the ground. A black gooey substance flowed from the wound. The dog howled in pain. It went for Yvonne for the second time. Ethan kicked it again.

'Leave her alone,' I spat out my words.

The beast spun around and around trying to dislodge the stick from its body. Beth helped Yvonne to her feet. Blood oozing from the bite mark on her arm, Beth led her back to safety. By the river, Jezzie untied the homemade boat. All the teenagers climbed on board.

'Run!' I yelled at Ethan.

'No…let's finish this mutt off.' Ethan swung his boot. The hurt dog swayed out of reach. Kicking fresh air, Ethan slipped over. The evil canine came at him again. Snapping out with its sharp fangs.

Why didn't we just run? I thought. Now instead, here I was jumping on its tail. It yelped. Jerking its head around. Its dead eyes boring into me.

'Run!' Ethan screamed out in panic. I looked around to see three other demon dogs charging through the trees.

'Oh no,' I gulped.

Both of us sprinted towards the river.

'Come on Leo,' Beth yelled. 'Quick, quick.'

Out in the middle of the river, the raft had already begun to drift downstream. Ethan swam towards it. Fighting against the current. I reached the river's edge. A sudden injection of pain shoot through my lower leg. One of the demon dogs latched onto my shin bone. I tried desperately to shake it off.

'Help him. Help Leo,' Beth pleaded.

Ethan was already climbing up onto the raft.

Wincing in agony, I waded through the water. The dog still attached to my leg. I punched out at the beast. Hurting my hand. The other devil mutts paced the edge of the river bank. Barking and howling feverishly. Two of them started to fight with each other.

The demon dog hung heavy on my leg, Weighing me down. Making each stride hard work. I tried to open up its jaw with my bare hands. No use. The creature's grip was way too powerful. I fell into the water onto my backside. Both me and the dog submerged for a few seconds. Water filled my mouth. We reappeared. The dog looked scared. Its eyes shifted about frantically. It's tail splashing about.

'You don't like water huh?' I muttered. Finding new inner strength. I dropped to my knees. Placing my hand on the dog's large head, I pushed down with all my might. The mutt went under. Fully immersed. The beast thrashed about violently.

'Die! Die!' I positioned my knee on its head and shoulders. Every muscle in my body ached. I kept pushing down.

The other dogs on the bank barked and yapped. One of the beasts raced into the cold water. It reached up to its stomach. Snarling aggressively but it turned and rushed back to dry land.

In the water, the beast's bony tail smacked me in the face. Gashing my lip open. I continued to hold it under the water. It was tough. Struggling. I felt the dog releasing its grip on my leg. It went limp in my arms. I held it under for a full minute. I wasn't taking any chances. I let go. The hound bobbed to the surface. Upside down. Dead. Its lifeless body floated off downstream. My mates on the raft cheered and clapped. I felt as if I had scored the winning touchdown for the school instead of killing a spirit-eating creature.

On the bank, the other beasts growled. They stood still. Their eyes burning into me.

Knackered, I swam out to the makeshift boat. With some help from the others, I clambered up on board. A wry smile on my face.

Ethan held out his hand. 'The 'A' team, dude.'

'Yeah, the A team.' I shook it.

Josh pointed towards the bank. 'Look.'

A gang of demons appeared through the trees. They raced along the river bank. Throwing rocks at the raft. Luckily, we were out of range.

'Kiss this,' Josh flashed his backside at them.

The demons and their creatures disappeared back into the trees. The river got wider. The current much stronger. It gave us all time to breathe. I checked the map. 'Tarrytown is ahead.' I slumped to my knees. Exhausted.

Beth ripped a strip of material from her t-shirt. Tying it tightly around the bite marks on my leg. 'That should keep you alive.' She grinned at me. Her eyes looked puffy. I assumed she'd been crying. I assumed she had been crying because she thought I had been in danger. It made me feel kind of chuffed.

I smiled back at her. Placing my head on the rough wooden slats. Relaxing. Watching the clouds overhead swirl in the blue sky. I closed my eyes. Drifting off to sleep.

'Leo, wake up...wake up,' a faint voice echoed in my head.

I opened my eyes. I found myself in a dark room with no doors or windows. Above me a fluorescent light flickered on and off.

'Leo? The voice echoed around me again.

'Beth?' I struggled to speak. My mouth felt like cotton. 'Is that you?'

I positioned myself up onto my elbow. The whiff of disinfectant tickled my nostrils

'Leo,' the woman said again. *'Can you hear me?'*

Her voice seeping through the walls. I put my ear up against the concrete.

'We need to get him down to the third floor urgently...I'll get a gurney,' a man interjected. I could hear footsteps racing away.

'Ok...Leo...Le...o,' the woman's voice started to fade away.

What the heck was going on. *'Hello? Can anyone hear me?'* I banged on the walls until my hands hurt.

All of a sudden, the room started to rumble. To shake. I struggled to keep my balance. Grabbing out to hold on to the bed. The walls moved in around me. Sucking the air out of the chamber. I climbed back onto the bed. Rolling myself up into a ball. My knees tight to my chest. Hands covering my face.

'Leo...Leo...Leo.' Someone shook me violently.

'Help…help.' I thrashed out with both feet.

'LEO! Wake up! Jezzie needs your help!'

'Josh…is that you?' I fought hard to open my eyes. Josh stood above me. A look of sheer terror on his face.

'Leo! The Efil!' He pointed.

The raft rocked ferociously. Water splashed all around. Beth huddled in the corner. Dripping wet. Doing her best to stay on board. In the water, Ethan and Yvonne thrashed about.

I grappled to my feet. 'What's happening?'

'An Efil thing in the water. It attacked us.'

I could see the outline of the creature about twenty feet away. Massive. Scary. It disappeared. I stared over the edge into the murky waves.

'Get me out of here,' Ethan cried. Trying to get back onto the raft.

I took hold of the boy's arm. Yanking him back onto the homemade boat.

'What about me?' Yvonne screamed. Frantically scrambling to get onboard. She kept slipping back in.

'Grab hold…' I bent towards her. My hand outreached.

WOOOOOOSSSSSSHHHHHH.

The Efil surfaced again. Inches from the raft. I jumped back. Nearly falling off the other side. In one swoop, the creature pulled Yvonne under with it.

'Yvonne!' Beth screamed out.

The raft stopped rocking. The water went still. Sharon stood up. Her body shaking violently. Everything else quiet. Beth embraced Sharon. Trying to stop her from shivering. I glanced at Jezzie. He stood hunched over on one side. Looking into the still water. His cane positioned like a spear.

There was no sign of the poor girl. Or the creature.

'Look.' Josh pointed. There were a few houses dotted along the river bank.

'The town must be close,' Jezzie hissed, 'Thank God...we've no time to waste.' He took control. 'This has gone on long enough. Josh, Leo, get on that side of the boat and start paddling. Beth, Sharon, Ethan that side.' We did what we were told. Jezzie kneeled down behind Josh. With his cane he began to help propel the boat to shore.

Tired. Sore. Upset. We docked the raft. Sitting in silence for a few minutes before heading up the steep road towards the buildings. The line of shops and restaurants just begun to open for business. A few cars drove past. At the far end of the town, the steeple of the church projected into the sky. I took a slow deliberate breath before heading towards it.

'Leo.' Josh pulled on my sleeve. 'Can I talk to you?' We walked past the bank.

I didn't really want to speak to anyone. 'Not now Josh...later.' It wouldn't be long until I would be saying goodbye to him. Goodbye to him and the others for good. I was trying to push the thought to the back of my mind. I continued onwards.

The station of discovery stood only a few blocks away. Two stone gargoyle effigies decorated the top of the old building.

Josh didn't take no for an answer. Pushing me into a doorway. Away from the others. 'Leo…. I remember you telling me what happens to the spirits when they get to the church,' he lowered his voice. 'We are all going to explode…aren't we? There will be no later…right? Just like that thug kid you told me about.'

I stared at the ground. 'It won't be like that for you…I promise. It won't…you…you will be fine.'

'Leo, stop lying, it doesn't suit you.' Josh stared into my eyes. 'I just want to ask you one last thing…one last favour for old-time sake.'

'Anything Josh…anything.' Feeling the emotion building up during my reply.

Josh bit his bottom lip. 'Can…can…can we grab something to eat first?'

'What?'

'Please…I'm starving.' His face somber. 'Call it our last supper.'

I nodded and hugged him tightly. My voice shaking. 'You big idiot.'

'Hey…less of the big,' Josh joked. Licking his lips.

We joined back up with the others. I approached my mentor. 'Jezzie,' I spoke softly, 'Can I have a quick word with you.'

'After.'

'Jezz,' I put on my best innocent face. 'One favour…for me…please.'

'You've got to be joking,' Jezzie replied, when I told him what I wanted to do. 'This ain't a picnic. We ain't going to the beach.'

'But they deserve it…before… before…' I couldn't say it.

He shrugged. 'Ok… Ok… Bloody teenagers. Always thinking of food.' Reluctantly Jezzie followed the gang into McDonalds. The restaurant was relatively empty. A couple of old men sat in the corner. Drinking coffee and talking about the Yankees game. The food chutes piled high with burgers. Ready for the breakfast rush I assumed. We sat around the corner. Out of the way of human eyes.

'Egg McMuffins with sausage and hash browns all the way around?' I asked.

'Hold the sausage on mine,' Sharon interjected. 'I'm a vegetarian.'

'That figures. Weirdo,' Ethan muttered under his breath.

'Get some BBQ sauce, and honey mustard,' Josh chipped in. 'Can't have hash browns without BBQ sauce.' His smile as wide as the river they had just travelled down.

Using my coat to hide the stolen food from the humans in the restaurant, Beth and I brought back the stash to the gang. Everyone dived in.

'I could eat a scabby horse,' Josh plastered his food in as many different sauces as he could get his hands on.

I sat back grinning to myself. For an instant I completely forgot why we were there. Jezzie sat next to Ethan. Munching eagerly on the breakfast he didn't want. The old man telling the boy tales of previous battles with the soul stealers. Beth and Sharon talked about American Idol. They even discussed fashion. Josh shook his head, complaining about the size of his portion. He sneaked back to the counter for a second helping. A few minutes later, sauntering back to the table carrying the biggest burger anyone had ever set eyes on.

'My very own creation. A mega Josh-burger with special sauce. Fried it up myself.'

'Josh, there's enough cheese on that for six burgers,' Sharon protested. 'You'll have a heart attack and die if you carry on.'

We all burst out laughing.

Ignoring her, and the rest of us, he sat at a table by himself. Not bothering to look up again until it was completely demolished. It didn't take very long.

'Can I sit here?' Beth slid into the plastic seat next to me.

'Of course.' My cheeks getting redder by the second.

We sipped on diet Cokes. Watching the normal 'living' people getting on with their daily lives through the windows.

'What's going to happen to us?' she asked.

'When?'

'You know when. When we get to the church Leo…I won't ever see you again will I?'

I finished the drink. 'Don't talk stupid…of course you will.'

She stared at me. Waiting. I hesitated. Searching for the right words to say.

'Leo,' Jezzie nodded towards the street. A police car cruised by. Menacingly. Gun shy, I instinctively ducked down until the car drove past.

'It's time we left,' Jezzie placed his tray neatly on the tray rack. I didn't argue. 'Everyone, we need to get to the church,' he added.

Josh moaned. 'But I haven't had an apple pie yet.'

I glared at him. 'Now Josh, now.'

Halfheartedly everyone left their seats and headed for the door. Outside a fire engine screeched past the window. Lights flashing. Sirens blaring. It drove on around the corner and out of sight. A young mother with a baby in her arms wandered into the restaurant. Another small child wrapped around her leg.

'Hi Julia…what's going on out there?' The girl at the counter greeted her. The other customers peered out of the window. Trying to see what the commotion was all about.

'There's a fire,' the mother replied. 'Over in the church. It's a big one too.'

I peered at Jezzie. He was already half way towards the door.

'Quick,' I ushered the others. 'Let's go.'

As I placed my trash in the garbage can, the young mother stepped in my path, grabbing my arm. She grinned oddly at me. How can she see me? How can she grab me? Picking up a plastic knife, she slowly moving it across her throat. 'There's no escape boy…no escape for you or your friends. Ha Ha Ha Ha Ha Ha…' a deep laugh escaped from her red lips. Reverberating through my brain. Everyone in the room stared at her as if she was losing her mind.

I jerked my arm free. Scampering out into the street. The others were already a block ahead. I raced among the living. Most of them heading towards the smoke bellowing up high into the morning sky. I turned the corner. My heart sank on seeing the flames engulfing the entire building. Fire crews fought heroically to get it under control. A section of the roof collapsed to the ground with a deafening crash.

Jezzie stood by my side. 'We need to get to the priest. He will help,' he panted. Wiping smoke from his eyes.

Two paramedics appeared from one section of the building. Walking past us, carrying someone on a stretcher. Automatically, I moved aside to let them pass. A sick feeling bubbled up in my stomach. On the stretcher, the charred face of a man. A man wearing a priest's collar.

Beth looked away. Jezzie swore under his breath. I made the sign of the cross. A loud explosion in the church brought another part of the wall tumbling down.

Near-by, the town's fire chief talked loudly to one of his officers. 'What do you think caused it Bill?'

The officer held up an empty gas canister. It's screw top missing. 'I think it may have been arson.'

'Arson…in Tarrytown?' The fire chief's words came out sluggishly. Deliberate. 'Arson…in the church. Who would do such a thing?'

Josh stood directly in front of me. 'Can I ask you something?' He purposely avoided the charred features of the dead priest.

'Josh, don't mention food.' I wasn't in the mood.

He sulked away. Muttering quietly. 'I was only going to say that if the priest has just died…his spirit soul body must be around here somewhere.'

My mate's words finally registering in my brain. 'Josh…you're right.' I kissed Josh on the head. Racing off to search for the holy soul. Around the back I climbed over the wall of the small graveyard in the back of the old 19th century building. A whimpering noise, coming from near one of the large tomb stones caught my attention. I picked up a large stone. Tiptoeing over through the gravestones. Sometimes over the top of the graves themselves. A large stone gargoyle beast stood bent over. Licking the face of the spirit body of the priest. The man had already been ripped apart. His chest bone crushed. I stepped in closer. Smoothing the creature's head, I reached down to close the priest's eyes.

'Hey boy,' someone hollered.

I turned sharply. Several soul stealers sat on the wall. Demon dogs on the ground Growling. Snarling. Zotto appeared. Holding up a pulsing soul. 'Looking for this boy?' He bit into it. Blood ran down his chin. He laughed. The rest snickered with him.

The gargoyle lunged forward. 'Stay boy.' I fought to hold it back.

'That priest didn't do anything to you, Zotto,' I quipped.

The evil demon swaggered closer. His deformed face inches from me. He lifted up his eye patch. 'This is personal now boy. No one stops me getting what I want. I'm going to rip every one of your friends to shreds in front of your very eyes...and then.' He poked me in the chest. I could almost taste his bad breath. In my mouth 'I'm having you...you boy. Should give me plenty of souls to earn a seat at Satan's table.'

Zotto's laugh was filled with pure wickedness. 'Come on boys...lets go. I'm quite enjoying this game of cat and mouse. This is going to get worse, boy...a lot worse.' The demon turned away. Disappearing with the others over the church wall.

Stopping myself from shaking, I sprinted back to the others. The stone gargoyle by my side.

15
living on a prayer

Jezzie refused to leave until we buried the spirit body of the dead priest. We stood around the grave. Heads bowed. Listening to him muttering some words of condolences. Eventually we headed out of town. The remains of the old wooden church still smoldering in the background.

'Where now?' Beth whispered.

I didn't answer. Still too stunned to think straight. The image of the dead priest fixed in my mind's eye.

'The Bronx,' Jezzie announced. Briskly hobbling past. The stone gargoyle panting along by his side. 'We're heading to the Bronx,' he repeated.

'What?' His words snapped me out of my daze.

'You heard me.' He rummaged around in his coat. Pulling out a small bar of chocolate he fed it to the humanoid. 'Here you go boy.' The beast and the hobo had taken an instant liking to each other. Maybe they were two of a kind. Two lost souls looking for company. Or two lost souls looking for demons to bash!!

I opened out the map; New York City wasn't even on it. 'Why the Bronx Jezz?' I asked.

The tramp patted the creature on the head. 'There's a small station there…a special place. It's not your usual kind of church.'

'Isn't the Bronx dangerous?' Sharon chipped in.

'Only if you're a demon or a spoiled little mammy's girl.' He winked at her sarcastically.

'But what if that church is burned down too? And the priest murdered? What then?' Beth asked.

Jezzie's horse laugh boomed out. 'I'd like to see them try. The priest is an old friend. A Vet.'

'What? He works with animals?' Sharon spoke up.

'No, a Vietnam army vet.' His face serious. 'One mean mother. I'll tell you now. No demon would go anywhere near the place. Unless they want to get their butt kicked.'

'That's a long way, Jezz.' I looked at the line of trees and mountains in front of us. 'At least ten miles,'

We better stop talking then and start walking.' He tapped me on the head with his cane. 'Lead the way Mister Young.'

We walked on a few miles. The sun beat down on our heads. It was unusually warm for mid-May. The heat waves shimmered on the horizon. A blue jeep drove past. Disappearing out of sight.

Followed shortly after by a convertible. Its top down. Loud music blaring.

'I'm thirsty,' Josh wiped sweat from his brow. 'Can't we hitch a lift?' he asked. 'I'm going to collapse soon.' I could see he was really struggling, not only from the heat, but from the exercise. They all were.

I sighed. 'How Idiot? No one can see us…remember?'

'Unless it's a patrol car jammed packed with demons in cop's bodies,' Ethan wasn't trying to be funny.

'I'm just saying.' Josh sulked away. Kicking out at tree stump, he stubbed his toe in the process. I couldn't help but smile.

We soldiered onward. The heat getting more intense with every stride. Even Jezzie rolled up the sleeves on his jacket. Josh came bounding back to me. An enormous grin covering his face. 'I know…I know,' his words rushing out of his mouth. 'Put something in the road.'

'I'll put you in the road in a minute,' Ethan threatened.

'For what?' I was more than a little annoyed with Josh's interruptions.

Josh folded his arms smugly. 'So, we can make the cars stop. Stupid. Then we can grab ourselves a ride.'

Jezzie placed his finger on his chin. 'Hey…that ain't a bad idea kid.' He stopped walking.

'I told you.' Josh poked his tongue out at me and Ethan. He then danced a little jig in front of us all. Pointing to his feet, he added, 'Down there for dancing.'

'What?' I asked.

'Down there for dancing. Up here for thinking.' He tapped his head.

Jezzie pointed to an old tree stump on side of the road. 'That.'

It took us ages and a lot of elbow grease to move it. Josh stood to the side directing operations. 'Well, it was my idea,' he announced when challenged by the rest of the team.

Working together the rest of us pulled the heavy tree stump into the middle of the road. Ducking out of the way, we hid down the small banking. Jezzie by me gently stroking the gargoyle's stony fur.

'Keep down,' I said

After five fruitless minutes, Beth hissed, 'Leo.'

'What?'

'Can anyone see us?'

'What?'

'I said can anyone see us?'

'No…you know they can't.'

She stood up. 'So why are we hiding then?'

The others looked at each other. Before bursting out laughing. Well, everyone did except for Jezzie. He sat there, rolling his eyes. Old habits die hard I thought, Minutes later, a large light-grey semi-truck with a broad red stripe on the side appeared. The driver's features quickly changed on seeing the object blocking his path. His vehicle skidded to a halt. Its air brakes shrieked. The back-end swung out like the tail of a large grass snake. The smell of burning rubber filled the air.

The heavy-set driver not so much leapt out of his cab, but clambered leisurely out like an old man climbing down a ladder. Sweating profusely. Swearing freely. He kicked the log. As if it was going to roll away. He pulled it. He pushed it. Desperately trying to move it so he could carry on his journey. He looked at it. Hands on hips.

'Hurry up…hurry up,' Jezzie opened up the back doors. He glanced inside. 'Perfect.' He started snickering. 'Just perfect.'

Ethan gripped the door but stopped before climbing inside. 'No way. I'm not going in there.'

A grinning Jezzie opened the door wider. Standing on the tarmac we stared in at about 50 frozen dead cows hanging from the roof on shiny metal hooks.

'Yes, way.' Jezzie pushed Ethan inside. 'They won't bite you.'

'It's freezing in here,' came back the hollow sounding reply

Jezzie ignored him. He struggled to lift Josh in next. 'Hey Josh…save some of them for McDonalds.' He joked. This time everyone else laughed except Josh.

Back at the front, the truck driver, smoking a cigarette, stood looking at the stump. Scratching his head with his grease-stained fingers.

After Josh disappeared inside the truck, Beth clenched my hand. Her face white with fear. 'Leo, I can't go in there.'

'What?' I looked at her. 'Why?'

'I'm claustrophobic.'

'It will be alright,' I said reassuringly. 'I'm with you.'

She rolled her eyes. 'No, you don't understand…I had an experience when I was a small child.' She began to hyperventilate. The panic evident on her pretty features.

'Jezzie,' I called out. 'We'll ride up in the front with the driver. Ok?'

The tramp frowned. But carried on.

'Why does she get to ride up front?' Sharon grunted.

Jezzie pushed her into the back with the others. 'Cause I said. Now all aboard.'

I closed the door behind them. Beth and I walked past the driver, who still hadn't moved the obstacle. He was on already on his second ciggy. We climbed up in the cab. Beth sat by the window. Fidgeting. Watching the driver struggle. 'Are you going to give him a hand, or are we going to sit here all day? She looked at me.

It was my turn to make a face. 'Ok.' I jumped down. To the great amusement of Beth, I struggled alongside the unaware trucker as the tree stump slowly moved it enough for the truck to get passed.

He must have thought he had turned into superman. I'm positive I did all of the moving.

'You took your time, tomato face,' she mocked the color of my cheeks when I climbed back into the cab.

'Well, he wasn't much help.' We watched the driver emptying his bladder on the wheel of his cab. Wiping his hands in his jeans, he scrambled back on board. Once ready, the driver shifted the rig in to gear. The truck eased into motion. Some terrible country and western tune blared out of the radio speakers. The cab smelled of stale sweat and cigarette smoke. It got even worse when the driver farted. We both held our noses in disgust. Although we did find the sunny side of the situation. Giggling to each other like two school kids who had heard someone say a naughty word.

'Breaker one-nine...breaker one-nine...this here's Green Snake...I'm on route 446...watch out for falling trees...over,' the driver talked into his CB radio/

'Thank you, Green Snake. This is Teddy Bear Bill, over.'

Beth nudged me. Dying to laugh. 'How the heck do they come up with these names?' she whispered.

'Weird childhood, I'm guessing,' I replied. 'Quick duck,' I squeezed Beth's hand. Trying to push her head down below the dashboard.

The police car drove towards us from the opposite direction. It powered past. I released my grip.

'Is it always like this?' She looked annoyed at me.

'Is what always like this?'

She kicked her shoes off. Placing her feet up on the massive dashboard. 'You know. Soul walking. Is it always as crazy and dangerous as this?'

I shook my head. 'Only when I have to deal with the horrendous smell of some Goth girl's feet in the cab of a big already smelly rig.'

She poked me in the ribs with her elbow. 'Very funny.'

'Just kidding,' I laughed. With time to spare and to stop us thinking of the terrible smell coming from the driver, I proceeded to tell her in detail all about my experiences so far. The suicide girl. The rock star. The rich couple and of course the demons. She listened intently. Her eyes alive. 'Anyway, that's enough of me and my weird hobby…what about you and confined spaces?'

'Oh that,' she sighed. 'That's my mad aunty from Philly's fault.'

I looked over at her. 'And?'

'She locked me in a closet when I was young. I've never been the same since. That's also why I hate spiders. The cupboard was full of them.'

'That sounds terrible.'

'It was.'

The siren from the same police car crept up from behind. Two cop motorcycles in convoy. The truck driver stopped picking his nose. He stared into the rear-view mirror.

'What now?' he sounded peeved.

The patrol car pulled up alongside. I sank down deeper in the seat. Pulling Beth down with me again.

The cop motioned with his finger for the driver to pull over. I crawled across to steal a peak out of the window. The evil face of Zotto tucked neatly inside the brown-haired cop's head, glared back up. By his side, another demon-possessed policeman held a large knife in its hands. In the back seat, two demon dogs. Their noses lodged into the crack in the window. Salvia dripping from their mouths. Growled. Barking.

'It's Zotto,' I gasped.

Zotto motioned for the driver to stop for a second time. On seeing a pull-in area up ahead, the driver indicated.

'What we're going to do?' Beth nervously inquired. 'They'll kill us if we stop.'

I tried to put my foot on the accelerator. The driver's boot was in the way. The truck began to slow down. I glanced uneasily out the window at Zotto. Then back at the driver. 'How does he take control of them?'

'Who?' Beth asked.

I muttered to myself more than asking a question 'Zotto. First the bus driver. Now the police man. I wonder.'

'Wonder what?' Beth replied.

'Wonder if I can do it to.' I took my jacket off. Handing it to her. 'Hold this.' I rolled up my shirt sleeves.

'What are you doing?' Beth demanded to know.

'I have an idea.' I took a deep breath. Kissed her on the cheek, before proceeding to squeeze myself into the body of the truck driver.

'No.' Beth tried to pull me back. I released her grip on my arm. A few second later I slid myself completely inside the man's overweight frame.

It felt strange. Dark. Pitch black. It smelt of stale cigarette smoke. I rummaged about in the obscurity with my hands. Trying to feel my way around the inside of the man's body. Then I saw it. Red. Glowing. The man's soul. I'm not sure why but I reached over and grabbed it in my hands. I recalled the time Jezzie told me the only way to touch a human was by handling their soul. 'So, this is the trick, is it.'

'Oh, what's going on?' the truck driver shook his head. A puzzled expression on his face. 'I feel…I feel...' He stopped talking mid-flight. Stopped completely as if he'd fallen fast asleep.

'Leo…come out…you're scaring me,' Beth's voice echoed from outside.

'I can…I can control him…yessss.' My own voice echoed in the darkness. I pushed my head up into the man's head. After a bit of work. I managed to align my own eyes up with the drivers. Wow. I could see the road in front of me. See my hands. Well, the other man's hands. 'Now, come on Zotto,' I pushed my arms into the man's arms. My legs into his legs. It felt as if I was putting on an ill-fitting jumpsuit.

Now the important part. I concentrated as hard as I could. Trying to move the man's tattooed left hand. It wouldn't shift. 'Come on…move…move,' I scowled at it. The fingers still wouldn't budge. I tried again. Willing it on. Another go. Then another. Still no good. The truck was still slowing down. Then as if by magic, the driver's fingers started to twitch. I focused even harder. The entire hand, and then the arm moved up. I stimulated the driver's thick fingers to scratch his ear lobe.

'Yesssss,' I cheered. Turning the driver's head towards Beth, I made him smile. Her face frozen in fear. Hugging her knees up into her chest, she moved as far away from the driver as possible.

I focused my efforts back toward the road. Putting the driver's foot down hard on the accelerator. The truck shot forward. Leaving the cop car in its slip stream. I imagined Zotto's roaring out in anger. Seconds later, the cop car pulled back up alongside the bigger vehicle. I gripped the wheel securely. Counted to three before swerving the truck into the side of the car.

Zotto's swerved the car away. Just in time to avoid an on-coming gas truck.

'Take that, freak!' I screamed out. 'Come on! Who's the daddy?'

Beth looked across. 'Leo…is that you?'

'Yep!' I rammed the car again. Sparks flew as metal came in contact with metal. Using the size of the truck to take up every inch of the road, Forcing the patrol car up onto the grassy bank. Zotto spun the steering wheel. But lost control. The vehicle travelled down the bank. Bouncing up and down before crashing into a ditch. The demon-cop passenger shot through the windshield. Smashing into a tree. Zotto sat angrily in the car. Smoked bellowed out from the radiator. The leader of the demons yelled out at the top of his voice. Punching the airbag.

'Home run baby!' I blew the horn with the driver's hand. The deafening noise filled the cab. 'Down there for dancing,' I mimicked Josh.

Beth looked over at the driver. Studying him as if he was an alien. I pointed at the green sign ahead. New York, 5 miles. I pushed Green Snake's foot down hard on the gas pedal. 'There's no stopping us now.' A voice broke over the CB radio. 'Green snake…this is Teddy Bear Bill. Any more sign of trouble, over.'

I picked up the device. 'Teddy Bear Bill, Green Snake is currently unavailable…this is,' I hesitated for a few seconds. 'This is Le…Le…This is soul walker. I'm on a mission. Over and out.'

'Leo is that really you?' Beth sounded apprehensive.

I nodded. Fiddling with the dial of the radio.

'Whooah we're halfway there…living on a prayer…..take my hand and we'll make it I swear… Whooah…living on a prayer.'

I turned the music up. Singing along at the top of my voice. Well, the driver's voice. I held the driver's hand out to Beth. She hesitated before reaching out to take it.

'New York, here we come,' I smiled.

KKKKKKSSSSSSSSSHHHHHH!

The driver's side window shattered. Sending glass splinters all over the side of the driver's face. A demon clambered up onto the cab. Its face hanging through the window. Down below on the road, another one drove the motorcycle. The creature's hand gripped the driver around the neck. Another demon smashed the passenger side window. Pulling Beth by the hair through the opening. She hung halfway in and halfway out of the cab.

The other demon's fingers locked into the driver's eye sockets. The truck swayed left then right. The creature sank his fangs into the neck of the driver. The blood spouted out like a hot spring. I could actually feel it even though I was inside the driver's body.

I needed to act. And fast. I strained as if to pull my head out of his head. It wasn't working. I let go of the driver's soul. Squeezing myself back out of the trucker's body as fast and as carefully as I could. All of a sudden, POP. Like a champagne cork, I was out. I fell back on the leather seat. Facing the road. My head cloudy. Chaos all around me. I regained my bearings. Scurrying across the seat I tugged at Beth's legs. Trying to free her from the demon's strong grip. No use. I reached over and opened the passenger's door. Trying to get at the creature. Beth screamed. She held on to the swinging door for dear life. Her body more out of the cab than in.

I climbed down onto the foot step. Trapping the creature between the open door and the hood. I pushed hard. Squashing the creature until it eventually let go of Beth. She scrambled back into the cab. Giving me enough space to smack the door into the demon's body. Smacking it into its ugly head again and again. It let go of the door. Rolling off onto the grass. I climbed back inside. Slamming the door closed.

'What the hell is going on?' the driver swerved the truck back into the correct lane.

I clambered over the top of the man's body. Beating at the beast still hanging on to the trucker's neck. The demon lost its grip. Falling from the window. Rolling over and over and over on the ground. The motorcycle following behind cut the creature in half. The bike flipped forward. Sending the cop demon driver down the banking. The motorbike exploding into flames.

Beth caught around me tightly. 'It's ok,' I whispered. 'We're safe now.'

'Oh no!' the driver yelled. The on-coming truck headed straight at us. He twisted the steering wheel sharply. Clipping the backend of the vehicle. The truck flipped on its side. Skidding across the tarmac. Sending a shower of sparks across the road. Beth buried her head into my chest. I glared out of the window. The truck headed towards a bank of trees.

BANG

Everything went black.

I lay there motionless. My body ached. The soft sound of music forced me to open my eyes. The whiteness of the room was a sudden shock to my system. I looked around for Beth. A television set sitting in the corner of a hospital room instead. On the screen, a talking St. Bernard tried to convince pet owners that Max's Dog food was nutritious and delicious.

'Hey you,' someone hissed.

I glanced over at an old man lying in a hospital bed. 'I thought you were never going to come back.' He grinned though a mouth of missing teeth.

'What? What did you say?'

'You must have been having some nightmare. You were making some weird noises,' the man added.

'Where am I?' I inquired. Getting up onto my elbows.

'In bed,' the man quipped.

Another man, opposite us, laughed out loud. 'Very funny George. In bed. Like he didn't know that.'

'No,' I snapped. 'Where am I?'

'St Luke's Hospital.' Both men looked oddly at me.

I tried to get up. The tube in my arm held me back. 'I need to go back. I need to go back to save my friends.' I purposely toppled off the bed. Whacking my head on the hard tiled floor.

16

the queen of the prom

I opened my eyes. Somone moaning. Someone next to me. I was back inside the cab of the truck. Face pressed up against the windshield. By my side, the truck driver laid groaning and groggy. Blood gushing from a very deep cut over his eye and from the bite marks on his neck.

The rest of the cab was empty, Beth had gone. Still in pain, I scrambled out through the broken window. Falling into the ditch where the truck now rested. Its back wheels spinning.

Up on the road several cars had stopped. A few people cautiously made their way down the muddy embankment to help.

'Beth,' I called out her name. 'Betttttthhhhhhhhh!'

Bang! Bang! Bang!

The thumping noise came from the back of the truck. I ran towards the sound. Beth stood desperately trying to open up the back doors of the trailer.

'Leo.' She flung her arms around me. Hugging me super firmly. 'Where did you go?'

I looked at her confused. 'I was in the cab,' I replied.

She shook her head very, very slowly. 'No, you weren't Leo…you disappeared. Disappeared into thin air.'

An image of the hospital flashed back into my mind. It was quickly replaced by the banging and muffled cries from inside of the truck. Beth and I frantically dug away at the earth with our hands. Two human men passed by helping the dazed trucker up towards the road.

'What happened to your neck man?' one of the men asked. 'Looks like you had a tumble with a vampire.'

The driver stumbled on still in a daze. 'Beats me…I must have blacked out.'

They helped him up the hill.

I dug harder and faster. Sweat pumping out of me. 'Pass me that.' I pointed to a large round rock lodged in the ditch.

Beth picked it up. 'This feels strange,' she said, 'rubbery and quite light… Oh my god,' she shrieked on realizing it wasn't a rock but the head of the demon that had been run over by the motorbike.

The creature's eyes popped open.

'Aaaarrrrggghhhhhhhhhhh!' She dropped it back on to the ground.

'What's wrong?'

'Look.' A look of terror on her face.

Without a second thought, I kicked the skull as hard as I could down the hill. It landed with a splash in a small stream. 'One, nil.' I held my hands above my head.

'Leo,' Beth brought me back down to earth. 'Our friends are in there.'

I searched about for something else to use. I know. I raced back to the cab. Minutes later returning. A crow bar in my hands. After a few attempts, I released the lock and pried open the doors, Jezzie scrambled out. Shielding his eyes from the light. Inside the truck it looked as if a bomb had gone off. Dead carcasses scattered everywhere.

'Thought you were supposed to be watching the driver!' Ethan poked his head up from between the hind legs of a cow.

'You have no idea.' I called back.

The rest of the teenagers clambered out. Smelling of raw meat, they stood about trying to warm themselves up in the sun.

'Where's Sharon?' Beth held her nose.

I glanced back at the pile of carcasses spewed all over the inside of the truck. 'Oh no!' I scuttled in. Followed closely by Ethan. We both waded through the mountain of corpses. Listening for any sounds. Any movement.

'Help…help,' a small muffled cry rose up from near the back.

'These things are freezing.' I heaved one of the carcasses out of the way.

Ethan stopped moving the large slab of meat. He glared at me. 'Lucky no one was locked in here early then,' he said sarcastically.

'Sorry,' I muttered. Moving another slab out of the way.

Sharon's blonde hair stood out amongst the dead bodies. Her face squashed into the backend of a cow.

'Are you ok?' Out of breath and panting, I shifted the last dead animal off the girl.

Sharon staggered to her feet. Spitting and sputtering towards the back door. 'I'm a vegetarian, so what do you think?'

Ethan looked at me before bursting out laughing. 'Hey Leo,' he asked. Clambering over the corpses to the exit. 'Do dead cows have Soul Walkers?'

I stopped to look back. 'Guess so.' I leapt back out into the sunshine. 'But I'm not hanging around to find out.' I laughed.

Patiently we waited around in some nearby bushes until Sharon had stopped crying. Then on foot we continued the mile and a half into the city. We entered one of the vast suburbs surrounding New York. Still stiflingly hot. A large section of wasteland stretched out in front of us. The place seemed to be littered with derelict factories encircled by damaged fences. Garbage, metal piping and loose bricks covered the entire area.

'Ain't you hot in that coat?' a bare-chested Ethan asked Jezzie.

'Never mind about my coat. Keep your eyes peeled.' Jezzie held up his right hand.

The line stopped. Near the back, Josh bumped into me. Nearly knocking me over. 'Sorry,' he stuttered, 'but I smell nachos.'

'Josh…you are supposed to be the look out.' I regained my balance. 'And not just for Taco Bell.' I wandered up to the front to find out what the problem was.

'What's up Jezz?' I watched a couple of small human children using the hood of an old rusty car as a makeshift trampoline.

The tramp sniffed the air.

'Demons?' I whispered.

Jezzie shrugged. 'I'm not sure.' Holding his cane like a sword, he took the lead again. His eyes scanning all directions at the same time. We strolled alongside the gutted shell of a building. From the broken sign hanging on the wall, I could see it once manufactured rubber components.

Nervously we wandered past a deserted gatehouse. Walking out onto the open stretch of land between the buildings. The gargoyle trotted restlessly alongside Jezzie. Its teeth grinding with every stride.

Jezzie smoothed its coat. 'It's ok boy…take it easy.'

'What's that?' Josh gulped. A weird noise came from our left. It sounded like someone running their fingers over a chalkboard; Beth grabbed hold of my hand. The noise drilling straight through our bodies.

'Shhhhhhhhh.' Jezzie motioned to the others. I'm sure he was hoping the sound wasn't what we both thought it was. He gripped his cane. I said a quiet prayer.

The racket grew louder and louder. Echoing around us from all directions.

'What is it Jezz?' Josh's voice trembling

'Just keep walking,' the tramp demanded. His pace quickening. 'And whatever happens…stick together.'

Something moved to my right. Something moving in the long-overgrown grass. About thirty yards away. 'Did you see that?' I asked Beth.

'See what?'

'Nothing. It was nothing.' I could tell she was scared. I was scared. We all were.

Something moved again. Small and black. Then another. And another. Whatever it was, there were lots of them. I carried on. Not wanting to worry the others.

'RATS!' Josh hollered from the back of the line.

I twisted almost 180 degrees. Goosepimples covered every inch of my body on seeing hundreds of the rodents scurrying towards us like a huge black furry wave.

'RUN!' I think we all cried out at the same time.

It was no use. The rats surrounded us. The rats looked different to normal rodents. Then it hit me why? These rats were dead. These too were spirits. We crowded together. The gargoyle snapped one of the rats in its mouth. The rodent's high-pitched squeal pierced my eardrums. Two others ran straight at me. I kicked them away. Unaware the human children, were still jumping up and down on the abandoned car.

'Stick together,' Jezzie stamped on one of the creatures. Snapping its backbone under the weight.

The vermin kept coming. Wave after wave. Sharon screamed frantically. One of the gnawers stuck in her hair. Nibbling on her ear. She panicked. Trying to pull it off. She split from the rest of the group. Running away. Disappearing into one of the buildings.

'Sharon come back.' I chased after her. My path blocked by a thick black carpet of vermin. One bit my leg. Ripping the skin with its sharp teeth.

'OWWWW!' I yelped out in pain. Ethan kicked it away with his boot. Then stamped the beast into the ground.

Forming into a tight circle, we moved slowly backwards. The gargoyle racing around us outside the ring. Fighting courageously with the small black brutes. The rats backed away from it. Hissing loudly at the larger creature. Meanwhile, Jezzie poked at the rodents with his stick. Stabbing one in the side. He threw it over the roof of the abandoned car.

Still the black wave came at us. The gargoyle began to tire. The rats edged closer. Waiting to pounce. Several of the larger rats rushed the stone creature. Overpowering it. With the path clear, the others swamped us. Teeth glaring. Biting into me and the spirits of the teenagers at will. Beth tripped onto the ground. Within seconds her body was completely covered. I sank to my knees. Pulling as many as I could off her. An extra-large rodent scurried up Josh's back towards his face. He just managed to grab it by the throat before it latched onto his nose.

Somehow, we held them off. I knew it would be short lived. There were too many of them. At least 50 to every one of us. What a weird way to die,' I thought to myself as I held a rat about two inches from my face. Its eyes boring into me.

All of a sudden, a high-pitched whistling stopped the attack. The vermin retreated. On-mass they rushed back to the emptiness of the buildings and the overgrown grass. All except for one still tangled by its legs in Beth's hair. I grabbed it by the tail. Launching the pest high into the sky. It landed on its back.

'Where are they going?' Josh doubled over trying to catch his breath. Grazes all over his arms.

'I'm not su…,' I stopped.

'Hey Soul Walker,' Zotto strolled from out of the shadows of the building of the abandoned rubber company. By his side, a band of demons and a few demon dogs. A massive black rat sat on Zotto's shoulder. The demon clicked his fingers. A demon disappeared into the doorway. It reappeared dragging Sharon out by her hair. Several rats positioned all over her body.

'Look who I found, boy' Zotto grunted.

The pack of demons sniggered and hollered. One of the creatures gnawed on Sharon's ear. She screamed out in agony.

'Enough,' Zotto clicked his fingers. The biting stopped.

'Let her go Zotto!' Jezzie yelled at him.

The demon laughed. Of course, the others followed. 'Ok…I will let her go…to hell.' He snapped his fingers again. This time his pack of soul stealers set about her in a wild feeding frenzy. Tearing her to small pieces. Sharon's pitiful cries ceased. She lay motionless on the ground. Zotto rammed his fist into her chest. Pulling out her soul. The other demons danced around her body. The demon dogs howled.

The gargoyle lunged towards them. Jezzie held it back.

'She's all yours now.' Zotto spat on her limp body.

'Let's take them Zotto,' a demon hissed. 'Let's rip them all apart.'

'Not yet,' Zotto glared at me. 'I have a plan.' He snapped his fingers yet again. The demons departed. Leaving the battered and bruised spirit body of Sharon Bell stretched out on the ground.

'Let's bury her and get going,' Jezzie's voice lacked any kind of emotion

'But…' Ethan piped up.

I stopped him. 'He's right Ethan. She's gone. It's too late for her.'

Using pieces of wood and metal can lids we dug a shallow grave. When it was filled back in, Beth placed a plastic silver children's crown she found on top of the mound of earth.

'Sharon,' she piped up, 'you are...sorry, you were...the queen of the prom and by far the prettiest girl in the school.'

We said our goodbyes and strolled on quietly. Head down I walked by myself. Feeling racked with guilt. Beating myself up inside for letting this happen. Wondering if there was anything I could have done to prevent Sharon's second death.

'Leo,' Beth cried out. 'It's Jezzie.'

The tramp lay flat out on the ground. His body convulsing in spasms. The gargoyle whimpering softly by his side. 'Jezzie,' I bent down. Unbuttoning my mentor's shirt. The others crowded around.

'Give him some air,' I commanded.

The tramp stopped shaking. His body jolted upwards several times. The four of us teenagers watched helpless. The gargoyle pawed at the old man's sleeve.

'Jezzieeeeeeeeeeee,' The tramp started to fade away. Fade away in front of us. In an instant, he'd disappeared completely in front of our very eyes. Where his body had been I patted the ground with my hands.

'That's what happened to you.'

'What?' I looked at Beth.

'In the cab of the truck when we crashed...you disappeared just like that.'

I stood up. Off in the distances, I could see the hospital building. 'Let's go.'

17

I've almost been run over by a train

I burst in through the door into the hospital room. Several nurses surrounded the bed. A doctor, holding two silver paddles, hovered over the top of a lifeless Jezzie. The rest of my spiritual gang rushed in behind me.

By the window, a huge Efil loomed. His eyes focusing on the activities taking place on the bed. It didn't bother to look at us at all. Its hood down off its face. Exposing its hideous features.

'Leave him alone you freak!' I shouted in rage.

The Efil stepped closer to the bed. Oblivious to anyone but Jezzie.

'AARRRRRRGGGGHHHHH.' I sprinted towards the beast. Plowing into it with all my might. The Efil stumbled backwards. Pulling me with it. We both crashed into the window. Splinters of glass exploded into thousands of pieces.

'What the…?' the doctor turned towards the commotion.

One of the nurses screamed. Her head blooded from a stray piece of glass.

'Must have been a bird,' another nurse chipped in. She bent down to pick up the debris.

'Never mind,' the doctor looked down at Jezzie. 'let's sort him out first.'

What they couldn't see was me and the Efil hanging half way out of the window. The road below a long way down. One of the creature's strong hands held on to the window frame. The other hand locking itself around my throat. I struggled to breathe. Beth and Ethan punched out at the creature. Trying their best to get it off me. It only seemed to make it madder. Its thick fingers clasped sterner around my throat. I bit down hard into its vile tasting digits holding on to the wooden frame. The Efil lost its grip. Toppling backwards. Six stories it plummeted. Landing on the hood of a parked car. I dangled upside down. Saved only by the cord of the blinds wrapped around my leg.

Down below I could see the beast rolling off the vehicle. It gazed up momentarily before disappearing back in through the main doors of the hospital. 'Oh no,' I thought. 'I can't kill it. It's must be the spiritual terminator.'

'Help!'

Ethan and Josh rushed over pulling me up to safety.

'That was close,' Josh sighed. I slumped on the floor next to him. Body shaking. Mind doing cartwheels.

During the commotion, unaware the hospital staff were still trying to save my mentor's life. The doctor turned back to face the unresponsive tramp. The paddles still in his grasp. 'Stand back,' he ordered the nurses.

BAM.

Several hundred volts of electricity shot through Jezzie's body. Sending his thick limp frame several inches off the bed. It flopped back down again. Absolutely still.

My gang stood watching in silence. The doctor barked more instructions to the nurses. The older nurse, who had taken special interest in Jezzie, rushed around the bed. An injection in her hand. Tears streaming down her face.

'Don't go Jezz,' Ethan started the rally cry. He repeated it again. Only louder. We all joined in. Even the gargoyle whimpered along.

I could barely look. Putting my hands over my face. 'Come on Jezz for me…please…I wanna see you again,' I muttered quietly.

'Ouch,' Josh moaned. The bathroom door swung open. Whacking him on the shoulder. The spirit body of the tramp strolled out of the small cubicle.

'Jezzie?' my mouth dropped.

'I haven't had a proper pee for ages,' he announced. Wiping his hands in his trousers. 'What are you lot staring at?'

'Jezzie…you're a…a…live…' Beth stopped in mid-flow. 'You're dead.'

'Give that girl a gold star.' He twirled around to face me. 'You took your time. I've already done half of your job for you.' He pointed into the bathroom. Two demons lay unconscious inside. One's head stuffed down in the toilet bowl. The other hung there with the light cord wrapped around its neck. Its face a strange pale blue color.

The tramp bent down patting the gargoyle's head. 'I'm so glad to see you.' The creature licked Jezzie's face like an excited puppy. 'Now let's get out of here before I start getting all emotional,' Jezzie picked up his walking stick. Tapping me lightly on top of my head, he hobbled out.

We left the doctor still trying his best to save the human Jezzie. We rode down in the elevator in silence. The old tramp broke wind. Loudly. He grinned to himself.

'Gross dude...rotting eggs,' Josh held his nose.

'You can talk Josh,' I piped up, 'yours are twice as bad.'

Everyone else tried not to breath in. Even the stony creature looked distressed at the smell filling up the compact room.

The moment the lift doors opened, we all rushed out. Gasping for air. Coughing. Spluttering.

'Well Leo my boy.' A smiling Jezzie stepped out into the sunshine. 'It's up to you now. I'm not your mentor anymore. I'm just your client.' Looking up to the heavens, he made the sign of the cross.

I stopped dead in my tracks. Ignoring the others bounding across the busy road. Completely ignoring the threat of the traffic. I took a sharp intake of breath. Puffing out my cheeks. Beads of sweat traveled from the top of my neck down to my toes. 'Yeah, but you need to help me?' I chased after the tramp.

'It's your show now Leo… you're the top dog.'

His words shook me to my core. Nervous. Still in a bit of a daze, I led the gang through the people-packed streets towards the station of discovery. At a crossroads, I recognized the entrance to the railway arches where all the homeless souls hung out. 'Let's go this way,' I yelled out. 'It will be quicker.'

The gang turned as one. All except Jezzie. He stood frozen to the spot. 'Leo…can I have a word with you?' He pulled at my sleeve.

The others stopped to listen. Trying their best not to show what they were doing. 'Wait for us up ahead,' I motioned to them. Waiting until they were out of ear shot before, I continued. 'What's up Jezz?'

The tramp raised his head. His grubby hand pointing in the opposite direction to the arches. 'I'm sure it's quicker down Donald Avenue.'

I looked at him with a frown. 'I don't think so Jezz, it's much quicker the other way. And you can say hi to Merrill and the others. I bet she would love to see you.' I winked at him knowingly.

Jezzie looked perturbed. 'Please Leo…not that way…not today.'

It was the first time I had ever heard him say the P word.

'I'm confused Jezz?' A train rumbled on noisily over our heads. It quickly disappeared out of sight into a tunnel.

Jezzie didn't look at me. He hesitated before he spoke. 'I don't want them to see me like this.'

'Like what?' I was still baffled.

The hobo quickly added, 'Look Leo, you know I promised them I would take them all to the station of discovery one day…and now I've let them all down,' his voice quivered. He purposely turned away.

I shrugged. 'I don't think so. You're their hero. They all love you.'

'Not anymore.' He sulked. His shoulders slumped forward in his big heavy jacket. 'Not like this.'

I jumped down some steps after him. 'But…but…what if…'

Jezzie kicked out at a can on the ground. 'Just take me to the station Leo…you know the rules.' He stomped away.

'I can't win.' I waved the others back over. 'Change of plan…we're going this way.'

'I thought you said it was quicker…' Josh stood munching on an enormous bag of chips he had stolen from a convenience store.

'Josh…do as I say,' I barked. Ethan stood at the back, opening a pack of cigarettes.

'I didn't know you smoked,' I grunted.

'I don't. Just thought I may as well try it before…' He stopped in mid-sentence. 'Look,' he pointed.

A police car drove leisurely past. A demon dog crouched down in the back. To our left another cop car pulled out in the adjacent road. I looked around for another way to go. 'The subway.' I yelled on seeing the sign at the end of the street.

Beth tensed up. 'Can't we just walk?' her voice quivering. 'I don't do subways.'

Over near a shopping mall, several demons jumped out of one of the cop cars. They marched about. Looking through the windows of the shops. 'Don't worry Beth I'll look after you. Let's go,' I barked the orders to the others.

Our gang raced down the first set of concrete stairs. Snaking our way down further on the long escalator. It was slow. Took forever. I scanned every living human with suspicion. The low deep rumble of the subway trains below the ground formed a wall of noise. The lower we travelled the darker and gloomier the subway became. Paint peeling off the dirty graffiti walls next to ripped posters advertising lipstick and other products.

The platform was more or less deserted except for a few teenagers playing soccer with a Coke can. Until their metal ball got lost on the track. A blindman in dark glasses played a saxophone for money near a vending machine. His mellow tune floating around in the confined space. Beth held my hand. 'Don't let go,' she declared.

'I won't, I promise,' I smiled nervously back at her.

The headlight of the approaching train danced excitedly on the dark walls. I wiped the sweat from my brow. Glancing back nervously towards the moving stairs. Half expecting some creature to be heading towards them.

The train pulled up alongside the platform. Its brakes screeched. The carriages shuddered to a grinding halt. The strip lights above flickered off and on several times.

'Is this ours?' Josh piped up. Still eating the chips.

'No,' I replied.

The coke kicking teenagers piled onto the train. Jostling and pushing their way inside. A strong familiar smell made the hairs on the back of my neck stand on end.

'Jezzie…demons,' I yelled across.

The doors of the train began to close. A gang of soul stealers sauntered out of the carriage. Lining themselves up on to the other end of the platform like soldiers. In their arms an array of weapons. Chains. Knives. Metal bars. And other dangerous looking items. They all wore a uniform. Like baseball players. They stood staring at us. I was waiting for Zotto to appear. But this seemed to be a different gang of stealers. A real ugly one with a scar running down his face stepped out from the back. A sizeable smirk on its purple face. 'It's show time,' his words sailed around the train station.

'This way.' I turned to the escalators. However, any thoughts of a quick escape disappeared when five more demons blocked the exit to the street.

'We're trapped…again,' muttered Josh.

'Fight!' Ethan stood his ground. Chest puffed out. Staring back at them.

The subway train demon gang edged towards us.

'What shall we do?' Josh asked me. They all stood waiting for my instructions. I looked across at Jezzie. 'Your call,' the tramp gestured, 'but I'm sick of running.'

I thought for a few seconds. Picking up a glass bottle from a trash can, I yelled. 'Ok…grab a weapon. Let's fight them.'

Another train left the station. Sending the lights above our heads into a flickering fit again. Beth stole an umbrella from a woman's bag. Ethan armed himself with an entire trash can. Jezzie reached into his jacket and slipped on a set of brass knuckles.

'Don't have a spare machine gun in there as well?' Josh anxiously asked the tramp.

'Ready.' My throat felt dry, I couldn't hardly get my words out. 'When I shout attack…we attack.'

'Are you sure?' grunted Josh. Still searching around for a weapon.

'Positive.' I remember listening to a football coach once saying after a Super Bowl game that attack was the best form of defense. I hoped he was right.

Everyone clutched their weapons in their hands.

'Attack!' I commanded.

We rushed at the gang of demons. Our actions took them by surprise. I think. I whacked the biggest of the creatures squarely on the chin with the bottle. The demon collapsed down like a pack of cards. Jezzie ducked to avoid getting hit by a chain swung at his head. Sadly, he wasn't so lucky with the baseball bat from another. Catching him in the ribs. The tramp rocked backwards from the heavy blow. Regaining his footing, he aimed a kick at the creature's kneecap. Breaking its leg in several places. A swift uppercut sent it crashing into the wall near the saxophone playing musician.

'Watch out,' Ethan shouted at me. Ducking down, I just managed to avoid a small plump demon flying over several people's heads. Missing me, its intended target, it landed on the railway tracks. To add to the creature's misery, the departing train unknowingly scooped it up and dragged it along through the tunnel.

'Thanks Ethan,' I responded. He gave me a salute. Two more demons lay at Ethan's feet.

Near the escalator, the gargoyle snapped at the heels of a few demon dogs. Josh bear hugged another demon until it couldn't breathe. Still in panic-mode, he drove the creature backwards. Both crashing into the vending machine. The glass of the machine shattered, exposing all the goodies snacks inside. With the demon out cold, Josh proceeded to strip the vending machine bare of all its chocolates.

The bodies of demons spewed out all over the platform. A human old couple walked through the platform completely unaware of the savage battle taking place. I stood with my back to the wall. Trying to control my breathing. I spotted the stealer with the scar sauntering out of the shadows towards Josh. In its grubby hand, a bike chain.

Whack!

The bike chain connected with my best mate's back. Josh fell to the ground. Yelling out in agony. I ripped a dangerous looking homemade spear out of the grasp of a dead demon. Rushing over to help, I stood a few feet away from Zotto's exposed back. Gripping the spear, I stood there shaking. Trying to muster all the courage I had to end its life. Willing myself on to stick it in the leader of the demons. I held it above my head.

'Hhhhheeeeellllllllllllllllllpppp,' the sound of Beth's screaming turned my attention immediately away from my target. She lay near the rail tracks. Struggling to hold off a stealer. Its teeth inches from her neck.

Ethan and Jezzie were up near the escalator. Fighting off several creatures tooled up with chains and bats. Beth screamed again. I looked back at her. By the time I'd turned around, the demon with the scar stood in front of me.

'You should have killed me when you had your chance, boy.' He booted me in the groin. I collapsed to my knee. The demon disappeared into the shadows.

I hobbled over to where Beth was still holding off a demon. Ramming the spear into the stealer's gut. The creature shrieked.

Blood dripped from its mouth. The spear impaled in its body. I chucked the demon kebab to one side. Reaching down to help her up off the cold floor

'You took your time Bruce Lee,' she whispered. The headlights of another train came in to view around the bend.

I caught around her. Holding her close. 'Told you I would look after y...' my words got cut short. The hard push in my back sent me sprawling on to the railway tracks. My chin smacked on the metal rail. Dazed, I could see a demon standing by Beth. I tried to scramble back up. The on-coming train only a few feet away. I rolled myself up into a ball. Covering up my head with my hands. The train grinding to a halt. Inches from where I lay. I couldn't believe how lucky I was. I lay there for a while looking up at the front of the train. Finally, I stood up. My body shaking with fear. My head throbbing from the contact with the ground. Jezzie had saved Beth from the demon's grasp.

'Get up here.' Jezzie lifted me back on to the platform by the collar of my jacket. The tramp's face covered with sweat and blood.

'That was close, I nearly got squashed by that train,' I clicked my battered and bruised body back into shape. Stretching my arms out as far as I could.

In the background, the bloodied and battered demon leader and its gang scurried towards the exit.

'That's not funny...not funny at all,' Jezzie slapped my face.

'What?'

'When will you learn kid? Never get involved with the clients. Never get personal.' Through the anger, I could see the relief in Jezzie's eyes. 'Your role is to take us all to the station...not just your girlfriend...understand...never get personal.'

I stared at the floor. Rather sheepishly. I hated being treated like a small kid. But deep down I knew my ex-mentor was right. Yet again.

Beth ran over to hug me. I purposely turned my back on her, Jezzie's words ringing out in my head. She looked upset. Confused. Josh joined us. His mouth full of the bars of chocolate from the vending machine.

It was time for me to take control again. To save their lives. No, to save their souls. They depended on me. 'Ok...next we're going to...' Before I had time to finish my sentence, two huge hairy spider-like arms appeared from out of the railway car. The arms seized Jezzie around the neck. Dragging him in. The doors automatically shut.

'Next stop...Queens Central,' a voice rang out.

'Help me, Ethan.' We tried to pry the doors open. It proved impossible. I looked through the glass. Straight into the eyes of the Efil. Its huge hands holding Jezzie up by the throat. The hobo's feet dangled off the ground. His eyes bulging in his head. He stared at me. His mouth trying to say something. I banged the window.

'Leave him alone...leave him alone.'

Glancing up, the creature opened its mouth. It eyeballed me, before swallowing my old mentor up with one bite.

I slumped to my knees. The train pulled away. The lights in the ceiling flickered off and on. I really didn't know what the heck I was going to do next.

18

anymore bright ideas?

Back up on the streets, the gargoyle slumped down on the pavement. Licking the deep wound on its hind leg. I sat next to Beth on the steps. Behind us a series of souvenir shops.

'Leo.' She put her arm around my shoulder. 'You did everything you could.'

I stared down at the ground. Tears, mixed with snot from my runny nose, flowed down my face. Dripping onto the sidewalk. I hadn't cried so much in my entire life. 'He knew I would let him down. He knew I would mess it all up. I'm useless,' I blurted out. The image of Jezzie's last moments fixed in my brain. Fixed in my brain for the rest of my life. The Efil gobbling him down. A hint of satisfaction evident on the creature's face.

Near the bus stop, Josh and Ethan started pushing each other. Voices raised.

'Not again,' I thought. 'Not now.'

'I did hold my own.' Josh wagged his finger at the bigger boy.

'Yeah…hiding behind the vending machine.' Ethan mocked. Swatting his finger away from his face.

Beth pulled my attention back towards her. 'Stop feeling sorry for yourself. Move on. Jezzie would have.'

'But I'm useless.' I got up. 'I was supposed to be a soul walker. Supposed to look after him. I screwed up. Screwed up big time.'

A man walking a small dog stopped to let the hairy mutt do its business on the pavement. The gargoyle looked disgusted as the man bent down to place the mess in a plastic bag.

'See. The world goes on,' Beth quipped. 'For the living and for the dead.'

'Not for Jezzie, it doesn't,' I banged a shop window with my open hands.

Ethan and Josh stopped arguing. They both looked across.

Beth marched over. Turning me around to face her. 'Stop feeling sorry for yourself I said…you did your best.'

An elderly woman unknowingly stepped in between us. She lit a cigarette. The smoke drafted into my face. 'But I let him down.' I glanced at my reflection in one of the shop windows. Inside the shop, the dummies, dressed in the latest fashions, reminded me of a series of zombies. Cold. Lifeless. One of them lay in a sleeping bag. outside a make-shift tent. 'I let him…' I stopped blabbering. A smile spread across my face. I grabbed Beth's arm. 'I know...I know what I can do for him.' Without asking, I planted a big wet kiss on her lips. 'Sorry...sorry.' I moved away from her. I think she was more shocked than me. She stood frozen for a good minute and a half. I rushed into the store.

Finally, she muttered. 'Grow up,' to Josh and Ethan who stood there giggling like two naughty kids.

I had a mission to complete. I came bounding back out of the store. Under my jacket, some torches and an small axe. 'Come on...I need your help.' I headed towards the underpass at such a fast pace the others struggled to keep up.

We arrived at the railway arches just as the greyness of the evening arrived. 'Hi Leo,' it was Bert, shouting out from under his blanket. 'Where's the old moaner tonight? Staying in to wash his hair?' His laughter lightened up the gloom.

I swallowed hard. Ignoring the old man's question, I instructed, 'Get your stuff together Bert.' I helped him to his feet. Trying my best not to stare at the red raw seeping bed sores on his legs.

'Where we going, kid? Coney Island?' Bert joked. 'I haven't been on the big wheel since I was knee high to a grasshopper.'

'No! To the station.' I piped up. 'My friends and I are taking you and the rest of the lost souls to find out your true destiny.'

Bert's face lit up. He caught Beth around the waist. Waltzing her around the piles of rubbish and old mattress scattered on the ground. 'We're going to the station. The wonderful, wonderful station.' Making up some tuneless song to accompany the dance.

I climbed up on to a rusty metal stanchion. Rolling up a discarded newspaper to use as a make-shift megaphone. 'Hi everyone...listen up,' bellowing it out a few more times.

Many of the lost spirits appeared. Emerging from out of every nook and cranny. Others rose up from the mounds of blankets and cardboard lining the floor. They crowded around.

'Dude, it's the night of the living dead,' Josh whispered. Stepping closer to Ethan.

I felt energized. Full of life. I shouted louder. 'Hey everyone...we're going to the station in about five minutes.' There was a loud gasp followed by a series of muttering. 'Now get ready. We have no time to waste.'

'What about our belongings?' a shriveled up old bag lady pushing a shopping trolley asked.

'No need to bring anything. Just yourselves. Now hurry.' I felt proud of myself for taking the bull by the horns. Proud for the first time in my life. I had made a decision. I was doing the right thing. Saving souls.

Josh crept up alongside. He whispered, 'Leo, who are all these people?'

'They are Jezzie's friends. He promised them one day he would take them all to the station.'

Josh started to count them. But gave up. 'There's loads of them.'

I smiled proudly. 'Yeah…and now we're going to take them. Rescue them. Every single one of them.'

Ethan picked up a flat metal plate. Tapping it into the palm of his hand several times. 'Awesome.' He spat on the ground.

About ten minutes later, a long line of homeless spirits assembled in front of us.

'We're going that way.' I pointed towards the top of a medium sized office building off in the distance. 'That's where the station is.'

Bert spoke up. 'That looks far kid,' His head motioned towards the boils on his legs.

'Come on Bert…it's only a mile as the crow flies,' Merrill chipped up. Catching firmly around my arm. 'The exercise will do you good,' she joked.

'This is for you Jezz, the best mentor ever,' I whispered, looking up at the sky.

We headed off towards the station in one long and very disorganized procession. The hobos. The tramps. The misfits. The gargoyle. Small children in bare feet. The teenagers from my school.

Progress was incredibly sluggish. Stopping every hundred yards or so for the rest of the slow pokes to catch up. Most of the homeless hadn't ventured out from under their dark and hidden bridge for a very long time. They looked scared. Yet excited.

I guided the gang through Walmart's huge parking lot. Looking back down the line to make sure everything was alright. Ethan carried a cute little blond-haired girl on his back. Another small child under his arm. Beth walked leisurely with Bert and several other old hobos. Laughing loudly while listening to all the jokes and stories the old guys told her. Josh located at the back with the last of the stragglers. His lack of fitness and his poor diet taking its toll. To be honest, he was probably the one slowing everything up.

Merrill waddled next to me. Her arm still wrapped around mine. Walking along like boyfriend and girlfriend. 'Hey handsome, will Jezzie be there. I bet he will. This was his idea wasn't it...I love him,' she beamed. 'I can't wait to see him. He's such a handsome man.'

I didn't have the heart to tell her the truth. The reality that Jezzie, her hero, was no more. Dead. Dead for good. Dead and gone. And it was my fault. There was no need to upset her. 'How did you guess?' I played along instead.

The old bag lady talked non-stop throughout the journey. If it wasn't about Jezzie, and how wonderful he was, it was how pretty she used to look in her teenage years.

'How old are you, Merrill?' I enquired. Checking the inside of a parked car as we passed.

'Not quite eighteen,' she laughed loudly. Squeezing my arm again. 'I've been eighteen for the last sixty-one years.'

Our trek continued a few more blocks. Constantly looking about for any unusual signs or abnormally huge figures lurking in the shadows.

'Have we got far now?' Merrill asked. Her breathing getting heavier.

'Not far.' I sniffed the air. My nostrils straining to pick up any unusual scents.

'Caught a cold, have you?' Merrill pulled a handkerchief from her sleeve. 'Have a good blow into this.'

I stared at the grubby stained cotton material which had long seen better days. Not wanting to hurt her feelings I did what I was told. 'Thanks.' Handing it back.

She placed it back in her sleeve without a second thought. 'Did I tell you about my third husband,' She clutched me again. 'Or was it my fourth?'

We continued. Around the next bend, a low wall of noise surrounded us.

'What's that?' Merrill asked.

It sounded like chanting. Banging. Getting louder and louder as we ambled on.

I looked back at Beth. She shrugged her shoulders. Halfway down the next street, I stopped in my tracks. My mouth dropped open. Up on the overpass bridge that straddled the road, fifty or so demons banged on the plastic windows covering the walkway.

'Souls...souls...souls...' the creatures bellowed out raucously. Loathing mixed with desire entrenched on their evil faces.

Zotto stood directly in the centre of them all. The large tattoo of a dragon on the left side of his face now colored in. The ink creature flowed down his shoulders. Its tail disappeared around his back.

'Oh no...we're going to get slaughtered,' Merrill shrieked out. The other lost souls began to panic. Some turned to hobble away.

Beth appeared by my side. 'I'm scared,' she whispered under her breath.

'Me too,' I replied honestly. Where was Jezzie when I really needed him? And maybe an army. With tanks and planes.

'Me three,' Ethan chimed in. 'Shall we go back?'

I shook my head. I knew it would be no use. We would never outrun the demons. Across the street stood a small strange looking church building. Sandwiched in between a row of rundown houses. A wooden cross and several vicious looking stone gargoyles decorated the roof. Just above the wooden door a bright, blue neon sign stated that it was 'The Church of the Lost Souls'.

'That's the place Jezzie mentioned, wasn't it?' I muttered

'An omen,' Ethan uttered. 'That name's an omen.'

'What?' Beth asked.

'Keep them moving. Head for the church. Stick together,' I demanded. Sounding a bit like my old mentor I took control.

The gang of spirits scrambled forward as fast as they physically could. Heads bent low. Afraid to glance up. They hurried past. I could see, and feel, the fear in their eyes. The fear running through their bodies. In their ever movement. The older ones and the handicapped struggled to keep up. 'Go…go…,' I muttered. More to myself than the others.

It suddenly went eerily silent. The chanting. The banging. Stopped.

'Hey boy,' Zotto called out. 'Thanks…my plan worked. Perfectly. You brought me enough souls to get me a place on the top table. Enough souls for me to sit next to the devil himself. I tried for that old smelly tramp to bring them to me but he had more sense than you, boy.' His cackling stopped abruptly. An evil look covered his face. He motioned with his finger.

The pack of demons swaggered down the steps of the bridge. Pushing each other to get to the front. The chanting started up again. Louder and louder.

'Not far Bert…just past the children's playground,' Beth egged the poor old man on.

He hobbled frantically towards the church. The sores on his legs bleeding. But he had a determined frown on his face.

From a side street another bunch of other demons appeared. At the front, the stealer with the car from the railway station. Many of them holding demon dogs on lengths of chains. Their teeth showing. The lost souls were now surrounded on three sides. I turned to face the advancing soul stealers, Ethan and Josh stood by my side. Forming a thin line of protection between the spirits and the demons that paced menacingly onwards.

Zotto held up his scabby arm. 'Attack.' He lowered it like a race-car starter. The rest of the demons rushed forward. Screaming. Hollering.

One of the lost souls reached the church. Opening the doors up wide. Beth helped some of them up the stairs. A demon dog bounded past me. I watched in horror as it jumped on the back of an old woman. It dragged her away. Dragged it back to Zotto.

We tried to fight the oncoming creatures. Ethan and even Josh stood their ground. But the attack was endless. More and more demons and their evil dogs dashing past. Catching up with the fleeing spirits. Some of the homeless, the younger ones, fought back. Most were powerless to resist. Bert hobbled along. A demon on his back. The bite to the old man's exposed neck buckled his knees. He fell onto the plastic seat of a swing. Two other demons devoured him in seconds. Ripping his soul out from a gaping hole in his back.

'No, Bert!' I roared out in frustration. I whacked one beast right in the mouth.

Merrill cowered next to a parked car. Josh ran over to help. A demon, with only arm, hunched on the roof of the vehicle. Ready to pounce. Merrill screamed. The creature leapt. To his credit, Josh smashed the creature with a plank of wood. Sending it toppling into a wall. In fear Merrill fell to the floor, Josh tried to pick her up. He struggled. Soldering on despite a demon dog planting its teeth firmly into his leg. He helped her up the steps to the church, Beth raced down the stairs to help some of the others. Off in the background, Zotto stood admiring the massacre playing out in front of him. Like a four-star general observing a battle playing out down in the valley. He clicked his fingers. Pointed. Several of his cronies sprinted towards Beth.

I wrestled with another one in the road. Knocking it out with a single blow to its face. I took a deep breath. Then froze. Ten demons, clutching baseball bats with six inches nails sticking out of the end, stood in front of me. They edged forward. Grins on their evil faces. I wanted to run. But there was nowhere to run to. Instead, I clenched my knuckles. Stepping backwards. Bumping into Ethan. He too was surrounded by an equal number of vile creatures. 'Anymore bright ideas?' he grunted.

'Yeah,' I replied. 'Fight…a little harder.'

Ethan half smiled. Nodding his head. Back-to-back we waited for the assault. My hands trembling. Heart beating. Mouth dry. The screams from the lost souls getting torn apart filled the air. There was nothing we could do. Nothing I could do. It was all my fault. Jezzie had warned me. But I hadn't listened. The demons closed in. Beating their bats on the ground.

Thud. Thud. Thud.

I gulped. We were doomed. No escape.

The sudden noise of gun fire halted the creature's advance. A handful of them exploded into tiny pieces. I looked over my shoulder. A man wearing a priest's collar and a red, white and blue bandana around his head stood on the top step of the church. In his hands, a large black and yellow machine gun. Bursts of green laser beams blasted out of the barrel. The man with the gun whistled loudly. A dozen gargoyles, wearing studded dog collars, came to life. The creatures leapt from the roof. Bounding towards the park. The gargoyles raced at the demon dogs. Chasing them away. One of the evil mutts savagely ripped apart by one of the stony beasts.

The man, who I assumed was the priest that Jezzie had mentioned, splattered his shots in all directions.

'Sit on this you ugly imps,' the priest cried out.

The demon creatures quickly retreated across the street. Taking shelter behind parked cars. Or in doorways.

Ethan hugged me 'We're totally bashed them dude.' The others cheered.

I sank to my knees. Exhausted. Blood trickled onto my chin from a cut on my lip. Suddenly a demon lying on the ground grabbed out at my leg. Before I could react, its head blew up like a burst balloon. On the porch, the priest smiled. Yellow smoke bellowed from the gun.

'Leo…Leo,' Josh waved his arms manically.

'What?' I got back up. Pain shot through every last inch of my body.

'Beth…it's Beth.' Josh pointed towards the houses at the far end of the park. 'Zotto's got her.'

My heart sank to the pit of my stomach. The demon leader stood on the hood of a car. Beth on her knees next to him. Her hands tied. Her mouth gagged, Zotto's arm around her neck. He pointed. 'It's your turn to chase me now boy.'

A beaten-up, old-style police car screeched around the corner. The vehicle pulled up alongside the demon. He threw his captive into the back seat. It shot off down the street with the rest of the demons. Followed by their dog beasts racing away in the same direction.

I started to run but stopped. It was no good. I felt defeated. Deflated. Angry. I look down at the demon with its leg half blown off below the knee. Crawling away.

I raced over to it. Picking its head up violently. 'Where's he taking her?' I yelled

The creature spat in my face. I snatched the strange looking firearm off the priest. Pointing it at the creature. I repeated the question. It ignored me again. It carried on dragging itself across the grass. I poked the nozzle in its face.

'Zotto told us you haven't got it in you. You're a baby.' It grinned.

Shaking with rage, I squeezed the trigger. The barrel clicked. The weapon jammed. I banged the gun with my hand. I went to squeeze the trigger for the second time.

'Ok…ok…' The creature pleaded. 'He's in the Dakota building in the city.'

'What room?'

It shook its head. I was sick of messing about. I fired the gun just past the demon's head. I placed the barrel in its mouth. 'I won't ask again.'

'The penthouse suite…the penthouse suite,' it muttered.

I handed the weapon back to the man of the cloth. On foot. I began walking towards the city. The bang from the gun didn't even faze me. I knew the demon was dead. Good riddance. I had more important things to do. The priest stepped in my path. 'Hey slow down…I need to show you something first.'

He led me up the stairs. Into the four walls of the small cold church.

19

reservoir demons

'Is this place weird or what?' Josh whispered. We stood inside the poorly light church. A collection of badly painted images lined the walls. 'They look like a six-year-olds painted them,' he added. 'Look at that!' On the small alter a tacky plastic crucifix surrounded by red lights took center stage. Next to it a photo of several soldiers. Wading waist high through muddy water in the jungle. Guns above their heads.

The priest stomped down off the altar. Wearing faded blue jeans and flip flops. Smoking a cigar.

Dotted amongst the pews, many of the homeless spirits that had survived the onslaught slumped down in the wooden seats. Others flat on their backs. Staring vacantly at the ceiling. Their cries and moans filled the church. Josh knelt down next to our gargoyle lying on its side. Its head resting on the cold wooden floor.

'I don't think it's going to make it,' Josh empathized. 'It's breathing funny.'

'Let me try.' The priest made the sign of the cross on the gargoyle's forehead. Within seconds the creature staggered to its feet. As bright as a button.

'Amazing,' Josh responded.

I turned to face the priest. 'Look father, I've got to get going.'

He grabbed my arm. 'Follow me first.' We walked past the single confessional box located in the far corner. Moved into the back room. The priest opened up a metal cabinet. It was packed full of weird-looking weapons. He sized me up. Then handed me a small compact machine gun.

'Perfect,' the priest muttered. Tying a leather belt around my waist.

'What are these?' I pulled one of the small metal pineapples from one of the pouches.

'Hand-grenades, man,' the holy man calmly announced. 'Blow a hole in the side of a tank.'

Very slowly I eased the explosive back into the pouch. 'Oh,' I gulped hard.

'Don't worry maaaan. They are made from pure holy water. The bullets for the gun are too. They will do you no harm. But deadly for those beasts of Satan.' He poured himself a shot of whiskey. Swigging it down in one go.

I covered the belt up with my shirt.

'Where's mine?' Ethan stood blocking the doorway.

'No Ethan, it's safer if you stay…the demons can't get you here,' I replied.

The teenager stormed into the room. Slamming the door behind him. 'Look Leo…I've been fighting all my life, but never anything worth really fighting for. This is my chance to do something good for once with my life.'

'But you are already…dea…dea…dea…never mind,' I didn't bother going there.

'Good soldier.' The priest threw Ethan two revolvers with shiny brown handles. Long silver barrels. And a holster. 'Those beauties will splatter a demon from two hundred yards.'

'Awesome.' Ethan twirled them around his finger like a gunslinger in a cowboy movie.

Back in the church, we headed towards the door. 'You ok Josh?' I asked. His leg looked badly bitten.

Josh shrugged. 'I'll live. Where are you going? I wanna come.'

'Josh, I think it's better if you stay here with Father…Father…' I glanced over at the priest.

'It's Dacey…Father Dacey…but you can call me Father D. Everyone does.'

'Josh…you stay with Father D and help get the people into the box.' I glanced back at the confessional box standing alone in the dark corner.

Disappointment covered Josh's face. But he nodded without putting up too much of a fight. Out on the steps, Ethan looked off towards the city. 'How are we going to get there, dude?'

The priest kind of smirked. The inside of his bottom lip bulging with substance. 'Oh, I almost forgot.' He pulled out a can of tobacco. 'Do you want some?' he put some more into his mouth.

We both declined his offer. The priest laughed again. 'Youngsters!!! Anyway, one last thing…this way.' He led us up an alleyway to the back of the building. Once there, he feverously tossed aside pieces of scrap wood and old bits of roofing leaning against the brick wall.

'Enjoying yourselves?' he grunted. More than a hint of sarcasm in his voice.

Ethan and I jumped in to help. Tossing more planks and stuff over onto the grass. It was hard work. Eventually a dirty old garage door became evident. We heaved it open. Inside stood an old rusty black motorbike with an even older looking rickety sidecar attached.

Ethan nudged me. 'I thought it was going to be an Aston Martin or something.'

'You wait, James Bond.' The priest handed us a helmet each. We looked over at each other. Then back at the bike.

'Bagsy me driving.' Ethan jumped onto the seat before I could say anything. Kick-starting the machine. It coughed. It spluttered. I slid into the sidecar. Strapping myself in. Ethan guided the machine slowly out of its garage prison.

'Are you sure about this Father?' Ethan queried.

Father D nodded. A smug knowing look on his features. Stepping forward he pushed the red button on the side of the gas tank. The machine rose up several inches off the ground. Hovering like a flying saucer. An inflatable driver also appeared.

'Well, it would look kinda strange a motorbike with no one driving it bombing around New York City, wouldn't it,' he said.

Ethan twisted the throttle a little more.

'Good luck soldiers,' the man spat the lump of tobacco on to the pavement. Then puffed on his cigar.

'Ready,' Ethan asked. I swallowed hard.

The bike shot off. Forcing us both back in our seats. The bike blasted through the streets. Swerving in and out and over the top of cars. I closed my eyes. My fingers clutched onto the side of the cart The G-force distorting my features. I screamed but nothing came out.

'Slow downnnnnnnnnnnn,' I eventually screeched.

'I cannnnnnnn'tttttttttttttttttt,' Ethan screamed louder. Just missing a truck and a bus. I shut my eyes tight and started to pray.

Without warning the bike stopped. Jerking us forward. Whiplashing us back.

'Wow, that was unbelievable,' Ethan took off his helmet.

I opened my eyes. Unsteadily climbing out of the side cart. I stared up at the impressive 19th century Dakota building. A shiver ran down his spine.

'What's wrong?' Ethan asked.

'I've been here before,' I took my helmet off. Without breaking eye contact with the architecture looming up in front of us. Flashbacks of a handsome warrior fighting with a pack of demons in the corridors of the hotel circled my mind. I somehow knew the warrior had been me. Me, in a past life. A warrior life. It was all true. Once a soul walker. Aways a soul walker.

'Ready Leo,' Ethan's words pulled me out of my trance.

'Ok…let's go and get Beth back.' I threw my helmet into the sidecar. Gripping forcefully on to the gun in my sweaty hand.

We took the front steps two at a time. Walking through a stream of men and women dressed for a black-tie affair lining up at the front doors of the hotel. Passing through the ornate wrought iron gates. Into the vast elegant foyer. In the far corner, a four-piece band played background music.

'Elevator or the stairs?' Ethan spoke over the drone of violins and half crocked partiers drinking champagne.

I tried to appear calm. It wasn't working. The machine gun shaking in my hands giving the game away. 'The elevator,' I muttered.

'You got it partner,' Ethan responded with his best cowboy impersonation. Complete with a double gun twirl.

A large group of the partiers stood waiting by the lift. Eyes glued to the lights flashing on and off above the door of the elevator. The door dinged open. The crowd pushed their way inside. Oblivious to the gun slinging soul walkers in their midst. I backed into one corner, Ethan in the other. We both stood surveying the crowd for signs of anything suspicious. The occupants called out their floor numbers to a businessman near the front. He pressed the relative buttons. No one requested the penthouse suite. I slid against the elevator wall stretching out to activate it myself. I stopped. A wiry man wearing a red and white uniform, carrying a stack of pizza boxes squeezed in just before the doors closed.

'The penthouse suite,' he grunted without saying please. He didn't look at anyone. Just staring at the floor. His back to the other occupants.

The smell of the pizza wafted around the small space. Floor by floor the elevator slowly made its way up the shaft. Ethan rolled his eyes in irritation every time the thing stopped and someone took their good old time stepping off. No one else got on. After the nineteenth floor, the elevator was empty except for me, Ethan and the pizza man. He still hadn't looked up.

'Lucky Josh ain't here,' Ethan sucked in the pizza smell. 'That guy wouldn't stand a chance.' The lift jerked to a hasty stop. The penthouse suite light flashed.

The elevator doors opened. There was an overpowering stench of demon. It was so strong even Ethan plugged his nose. I clasped the machine gun in fire-ready position.

The pizza man stepped into the stylish hallway. I followed. Scanning the surroundings. I looked out of the strange shaped window in the hallway. The view of the rest of the city stared back.

Ethan pushed a small chair in front of the elevator doors. Stopping it from moving.

'In case we need a swift exit,' he hissed.

At the far end of the hallway, the sound of rock music travelled through the set of large carved oak doors. Very heavy rock music. Very loud.

'Ready?' I whispered to my companion.

Ethan nodded, 'Yep…lock and loaded, dude…lock and loaded.'

'Yes, you better be lock and loaded boys.' The pizza man turned around to face us. A wicked grin on his inhuman face. Before me or Ethan could react, he swung one of the big doors open with his free hand. 'Honey we're home,' he yelled out. Dropping the pizza boxes onto the floor. 'The flies are in the spider web.'

Inside several demons lay on couches. Eyes glued to a big screen TV. Instantly jumping up to attention. They charged at us. Little time to react. I fired. The gun blew the first wave of creatures to smithereens. The room instantly filled with their horrible gassy stench. Ethan seemed more reserved with his ammunition. Picking the creatures off one by one.

'Die…punk…die,' he shouted over the music. Blasting one hiding behind the leather sofa.

'Ethan,' The pizza delivery demon tried snatching the gun out of my hand.

Ethan spun around. Blasting it with both barrels. The man's inner demon exploded inside of the human. Leaving the confused pizza guy standing in an empty room with the television set blaring in the background.

'Is there anyone here?' the dazed pizza man shouted out. Totally unaware of the battle taking place around him. His question met with silence. 'How did those get there?' He bent down to pick up the pizza boxes. Heading back out towards the elevator rather confused. 'What's going on?' he kept muttering to himself.

'Totally bashed them dude,' Ethan kicked a splattered demon lying lifeless on the floor.

I switched the television set off. Accidentally walking through a pile of the green sticky remains of one of the creatures. Its gunk stuck to the bottom of my shoe. Ethan reloaded his weapons.

'It's Beth's.' I bent down to pick up an item of clothing.

Suddenly from behind a curtain, a demon leapt on my back. Knocking me and my gun to the floor. We rolled about on the ground. Struggling to fight the creature off. It head butted me. Jerking my head back onto the hardwood floor. Dazed, I caught hold of its jaw. Prying it apart. 'Quick Ethan…I can't hold it any longer. Shoot it…shoot it!' The creature's teeth inches from my face.

'Hey creep.' The beast looked across at him. It didn't hear the bang as the bullet blew its head clear off its broad shoulders. Ethan blew on the barrel of the guns. 'I'll be back,' he said in his best Terminator voice.

'Thanks…again.' I wiped the horrible substance off the front of my clothes. Flicking the muck onto the floor.

The double door to the large master bedroom flew open. Zotto stood there. His left arm wrapped around Beth's throat. A long knife glistened in his other hand. A large tarantula spider crawling up the side of her head.

'Hello boys,' his manic laugh matched only by his outrageous appearance. Along with his dragon tattoo, his face was plastered with metal rings decorating his ears and nose. Behind him, a couple demons stood on the bed.

'Weapons down, boys,' Zotto jeered.

I gripped mine tighter. Several larger black spiders crawled up Beth's back. Onto her face. She stood shaking in fear. Her eyes firmly shut.

'I said put them down.' Zotto inched the blade in closer to her throat. 'It would be a shame to damage something so…so…pretty.' He licked the side of her face. She cringed.

Ethan glanced at me for direction. I threw the machine gun onto the carpeted floor. Placing my hands up in the air, Ethan did the same.

A demon scurried over. Picking them up. He rushed back towards Zotto like a chimpanzee carrying a banana. 'Be careful, don't drop…'

Bam! The gun fell to the ground. Spraying bullet into one of its demon gang members standing on the bed. His green innards splattered all over the gold and red wall paper.

'Sorry.' The demon shrugged.

Zotto gave the creature a cold stare. It turned back to me. 'I knew you would fall for it…that old tramp had more sense…but you…you are still just a rookie boy.'

I cursed myself for being so stupid. Cursed myself for falling into Zotto's trap. Endangering everyone else yet again. Jezzie was right. I was the worse soul walker there had ever been. I had broken every rule in the book of soul walking. Now I had to pay the consequences. Watching my friends lose their souls for the rest of eternity.

Two demons grabbed my arms. Positioning me by the large window. Two others tied Ethan to a chair.

'It's me you want Zotto…let them go,' I pleaded. 'Please…there are plenty of other souls out there.' I motioned towards the city.

'Forget it boy.' Zotto pushed Beth back onto the bed. The spiders scampered away in all directions. 'I'm going to enjoy this. I'm going to torture them while you watch. Then I'm going to keep you here until your human body dies….and then I'm personally going to rip you spirit from limb to limb.' His despicable laughter reverberated around the suite.

'Get me the instruments,' Zotto motioned to a stealer. It went running off into the bathroom. It returned seconds later. Carrying a small suitcase.

Zotto opened it. Pulling out the sharpest instruments he could find. He jigged around with it clasped firmly in its hand. 'I wondered if this one's eye will look good on me.' He grabbed Ethan's face. 'Oh, and they are green…my favorite colour.'

The other demons sniggered. Egging him on.

Near the hallway another demon fiddled around with an old gramophone record player. The needle danced on the plastic.

The song 'Stuck in the Middle with You,' started up. Zotto danced oddly around to the old 70's tune. Swinging the shiny instrument above his head. 'I saw this in that film. What was it called?' He left a pause. 'Oh yes…. Reservoir Demons,' he snorted.

Ethan struggled in vain to break free. Beth did the same. She watched in horror as a black tarantula crawled across the carpet towards her. Travelling slowly up her leg.

Zotto touched Ethan's face with the blade. 'Get off me freak' he spat at the demon.

'Boy…I'm going to cut both your ears off.' Zotto wiped the phlegm off its cheek. 'And then poke your eyes out.'

I searched the room. 'The hand-grenades!' I remembered the bombs in my belt. I tried to move. No good. My arms were being held by the two demons. Their main focus was on holding me still.

Suddenly the door to the room opened inwards. 'I've had enough of this. I'm going to get stuck paying for these. Punk prankster kids!' The human pizza man wandered back into the room mumbling angrily. He looked at the television set. 'Hang on…who switched that off?' He looked about. 'Ok, this is not funny…I know there is someone here.'

Everyone turned to face him. With their attention diverted, I pulled my one arm free. Punching the shortest demon in the face. I broke free completely. Smashing the other's head against the wall. Both demons fell to the carpet.

'Drop it Zotto.' I held the hand-grenade in my hands. Fingers clutching the pin.

The demon snarled. Its teeth showing. The pulse in its neck throbbed.

'Untie them…now Zotto.' I threatened to pull the pin out of the hand-grenade.

Zotto chucked the sharp instrument onto the floor. It hissed like a rattlesnake. 'Untie the scrubs,' I said calmly. His eyes burning into mine. Two demons did what they were told. Ethan picked up the weapons. Beth patted herself down. Making sure she was spider-free.

'Get the elevator Beth.'

She rushed out, Ethan and I inched backwards. Grenade and guns in hand.

'Leo…it's here,' Beth cried.

Ethan stepped inside. A rogue demon rushed out of the other bedroom. Swinging a golf club. I ducked just in time. The stick smashed into the wall. Snatching a gun off Ethan, Beth blasted the beast to kingdom come. I stepped into the elevator. Not taking my eyes off Zotto. Or the others.

'This isn't over boy,' Zotto fixed its ugly stare on me.

'We'll see.' Grinning I released the pin on the grenade. Launching it into the suite. The elevator door closed. We could feel the explosion.

'That was close,' Ethan fiddled subconsciously with his ear lobes.

The evaluator traveled the rest of the short journey down to the ground floor. We stood in silence. Holding Beth in my arms. She shook uncontrollable. Still imagining spiders crawling over her.

The lobby was still packed full of people. Dancing, Drinking. Socializing. We headed straight for the exit. Our eyes fixed firmly to the ground.

'Not so fast boy.' A large police man blocked my path.

I didn't even look up. I discharged several rounds of holy water bullets into the man's demon possessed stomach. I marched onwards. Not looking back. I knew the copper would be ok.

Once outside we rushed down the steps. Across the street to the bike.

'Beth, you get in the side car, I'll jump on the back of the bike behind the inflatable human being.' Handing her the helmet.

'Look,' Beth pointed towards the steps of the hotel. A charred face Zotto and a few of his demons emerged. A couple of them still smoldering from the explosion.

Ethan revved up the motorbike. It shot off into the night. I looked back to see an old beaten-up police car pulling up in front of the Dakota. The demons scrambled inside. Zotto jumped into the passenger's seat. His one good eye wide open. Bloodshot. 'Go…go…go,' he bellowed as loud as he could.

20

I hope I've got this right

I tucked my head into the contour of Ethan's spine. My fingertips digging painfully in his skin. The bike zoomed from side to side. In and out of the traffic. Ethan pulled it sharply to the right. Just missing a pink limousine full of girls going to a birthday party. We drove over an old rusty bridge. Back towards the Bronx. The image of Manhattan faded fast off in the distance.

'Faster…faster,' I cried. The car full of demons almost pulled up alongside. The lights on the roof flashing wildly.

One of the demons hung out of the back window. Reaching out to grab at Beth. I prepared myself to shoot. Too late. Just as I went to pull the trigger the bike hit a pothole. Nearly throwing me off the back of the machine.

'Leave it to me.' Ethan said calmly. Leaning backwards, he casually blasting it. Like he was shooting plastic ducks in the fairground. He must have been born to kill demons. The creature's gooey blood splattered over the side of the police car. Ethan blew the smoke away from the barrel of the pistol. Sliding it back into his jacket with a wry smile.

'Give me your gun,' Beth screamed at me.

'No, the kickback will knock you out of your seat,' I yelled back.

She reached across. Yanking it out of my hands. 'Kickback…watch this.' The machine gun sprayed the side of a truck passing in the other lane. 'How's that?' I nodded out of respect. Beth spun around. Kneeling on the seat. She aimed it at the approaching police car.

I reached across to try to steady her.

'Holy cow…,' Ethan spotted another police car blocking the road up ahead.

A jeep in front of the bike slammed on its brakes. Spinning out of control. It smashed head first into the central barrier. Somersaulting up in the air. Landing on its roof in front of the police car.

'Hold on,' Ethan directed the bike at the overturned vehicle.

'Noooooooo!' I screamed at the top of my voice.

Too late. Ethan used the overturned car as some kind of make-shift ramp. The bike shot up the spine of the jeep. Soaring through the air. Over the parked police car. Landing with an earsplitting bump on the tarmac. Sparks shot from the side car. Beth almost toppled out of the cart. Hanging on by her fingertips for dear life. Her feet scraping off the pavement. 'Leo…Leo…I can't hold on.'

Cautiously I scrambled into the sidecar. Seizing Beth by her wrists. Pulling her up hard until I caught hold of her belt with my right hand. With one huge tug I heaved. She tumbled head first in the side car. Her legs thrashing about like a upside down fly on a kitchen unit.

'We made it.' Ethan shouted over. Spying the church in the distance.

Beep…beep…beep…beep.

He spoke too soon. The police car skidded towards the bike for a second time. Zotto hung out of the window. A knife glistened in his hand. Ethan pulled back on the throttle. But the bike had nothing more to give.

Zotto threw the weapon. It stuck in Ethan's thigh. 'Arrrggghhhhhhhhhhh!' he yelled out. Losing control of the bike.

It wobbled back and forth before colliding into the curb. Sending us all sailing through the air. I landed with a bump on the grass, Beth luckily touched down in the sand pit. Ethan held onto the bike until the very last minute. Jumping off seconds before the motorbike crashed into the jungle gym. Bursting into flames. I stood up. My knees cut. Bruised. Battered. 'Ethan.' I hobbled towards the boy who lay slouched over the see-saw.

'You ok mate?' I gently picked up his head.

'I've felt better.' He clicked his neck back into place. 'How's Beth?'

She still laid slumped down in the sandbox. I rolled her over. Her eyes closed. Her nose bleeding.

'Beth...Beth.' I put my hand by her mouth to see if she was still breathing.

Lethargically she opened her eyes. Trying to focus on my face in front of her. 'Leo!' She grabbed around my neck. Then kissed me. I sat there stunned. I leaned in to kiss her in return.

'How romantic.' Zotto strode towards us. Clapping his grubby mitts. His face burnt. Several demons strutting by his side. 'Come on then boy,' he taunted me. 'Me and you.'

I knew I would struggle to fight him. And even if I did get the better of him, the others would probably join in. But I couldn't back down. I stood up. Took a deep breath.

'Come on then Zotto.'

'No, Leo,' Beth declared.

The doors to the church shot open. Father D paced out with enough artillery to start and finish a war. 'Get away from them or I'll blow you all back to hell, you slimy cockroaches.' He chewed on his cigar. Spat on the ground. Josh appeared on the steps along with some of the homeless souls.

The demons stood motionless. Glaring at the priest.

I helped Beth up. 'No.' I motioned to the priest. 'This is between me and him,' I said confidently. Pointing to the leader of the soul stealers.

'Just kill it!' Beth screamed.

'NO!' I walked towards Zotto. Blocking Father D from having a clean shot. The other demons took one step back. Leaving their leader to face me alone. Maybe they wouldn't be so brave with their leader out of the way.

'Big mistake, boy,' Zotto glared. 'I'm going to rip your eyeballs out. Smother them in gravy and then feed them to the dogs.'

I peeled off my jacket. Rolling up my sleeves. Why did I do this? Why didn't I let Father D blow him away?

We faced each other. Circling. Sizing each other up. Although small, Zotto was extremely agile. Fast. Bouncing around on the balls of its deformed feet. To my surprise I landed the first punch. Connecting sweetly with the side of the demon's head. Rocking it back. I stepped in. Swinging several more times. I missed with each shot.

'Pathetic,' Zotto sneered. It jumped forward. Kicking me hard in the side. Knocking the wind from my body. Zotto thumped me repeatedly. Using both hands. The half-burned dragon tattoo dancing crazily on his face. I covered up using my hands. Backing up against a wall.

The stealer swung around a lamppost. Jumping down on my back. Biting ferociously into my shoulder blade. I sank to my knees.

Some of the homeless people, who hadn't yet been through the soul stripping process, stood on the porch in shock. Beth cried. Covering her eyes.

'Get up Leo,' Josh encouraged.

'Shall I blast him?' the priest asked again.

'No.' I got to my feet. Zotto still hanging on to my back. I staggered purposely backwards. Smacking the stealer into the wall several times. The creature slid slowly down the brickwork onto the pavement.

Zotto lay dazed. I hopped on top of him. Punching him. Banging its head on the curb. Zotto slumped unconscious. I laboured to my feet. Out of breath. I headed up to the church. My entire body ached. But I felt ten feet tall.

The scream escaping from Merrill's mouth was too late for me to react. By the time I turned back, Zotto was upon me. A small compact blade in its fist.

It wasn't the pain that shocked me. It was the sight of the knife dangling from the pit of my stomach which stunned me more. I staggered back up against the wall of the church. Zotto lunged in for the kill. The gunfire propelled it backwards. The demon collapsed into the arms of two of its followers. They dragged their leader away towards the waiting car. Father D firing at will.

Beth was first to reach me. 'Are you ok…oh no, you're bleeding.'

Father D calmly strolled over. Picking up the remains of a severed stealer's arm lying on the ground by his feet. 'We won't be seeing him again.' He chucked it into a trash can.

He examined my injury. The knife still dangling from my gut. 'Close your eyes,' the priest instructed. Without another word he yanked the blade out in one movement.

My knees buckled from the pain. The colour draining from my face.

'Good soldier,' the priest whispered. Using his shirt to wipe blood off the knife.

They carried me to the steps of the church. Lowering me down on a porch swing outside the main door. I shivered. My teeth knocking together noisily, Beth watched me. Trying her best to warm me up. In the background the priest rounded the homeless spirits back up on the porch. Leading them back into the church.

Josh stood nearby. Shaking his head... 'Awesome...totally awesome.' He skipped down the steps out into the street.

'Where are you going?' Beth called after him.

He smiled. 'Hey...a boys got to eat you know...and don't worry, all the demons are dead thanks to Father Schwarzenegger over there,' he joked. Pretending to fire off a machine gun. He disappeared into a deli across the street.

I lay my head down on Beth's lap. I looked out. 'What a school trip.' I muttered, 'one to remember.'

'Yeah...a real blast,' she replied. Smoothing my forehead.

Josh reappeared several minutes later. Carrying a big brown bag full of goodies and with an extra-large candy bar sticking out of his mouth. 'Wait until you see what I've got for you.'

'Do you always think of your stomach,' Beth teased.

A dark image running near a small batch of trees caught my attention. Ignoring the sharp pain, I raised myself up onto my elbows. 'What was that?'

Beth looked about. 'What?'

My eyes searched about. Nothing else moved. I dropped back down. 'I must be seeing things,' I said.

'Just relax.' She kissed my cheek.

The Efil moved like a bolt of lightning across the grass area. Heading straight for Josh.

'Who wants a candy bar?' he called out.

'Josh!' Beth screamed. 'Behind you.'

He turned. The bags he was holding fell in slow motion to his feet. The Efil's deformed mouth opened wide. Its eyes glowing brightly. Josh disappeared in one bite.

'Noooooooooooo!' I cried. Wincing as the pain from my side shot into my brain. 'Get inside!' I screamed at Beth. 'Now!'

I started limping down the stairs. By the time I reached the middle step my head began spinning. My vision became blurred. I toppled down head first. Landing on the pavement. Facing up towards the sky. I looked at the sun. It shone so bright. Then everything went black.

'*Quick...another liter of blood,*' someone barked orders.

I lay in the dark. A beeping noise echoed around my brain.

Beep...beep...beep... The sound was steady.

'*Where's that injection?*' It was a man's voice.

Footsteps and other sounds filled the rest of my mind.

Beep...beep...beep. The darkness slowly turned into a bright light.

'*I think we are losing him,*' a voice bellowed out in panic.

Crash.

'*Nurse, will you please be careful with those instruments?*' the doctor said aggressively.

Beeeeeeeeeeeeeeeeeeeeeeeeeeeep.

The sound blended into one long noise. I tried to cover up my ears. I couldn't. I couldn't move my arms. Couldn't move anything. The bright light engulfed me. Slowly creeping up my legs. To my waist. Over my face. I tried to push it off. It forced its way in through my skin. Making my body deadly cold.

'*Hello,*' I heard myself saying.

'*Hello.*' It echoed back.

The light grew intense. Almost blinding me. My eyes shot open. I stood over a hospital bed. Nurses rushing about everywhere. The life support machine in the corner beeped continuously. The line on the display flat.

'Jezzie?' I muttered. Stepping in closer to the bed to take a peek.

What I saw made my knees buckle. I fell back. Knocking over a drip in the corner. It wasn't Jezzie lying there dying. It was me. 'On no,' I rubbed my eyes. Taking another look.

'Come on Leo, you can make it,' a nurse spoke softly above the commotion.

Another nurse walked through me. Reaching for something on the table. I looked down at my hands. They were white. I rushed over to the mirror above the small sink in the corner. My face was the same ghostly colour.

'Let's try one last time,' the doctor held some wires and paddles in his hands. The other members of the medical staff moved away.

Boosh.

The jolt of electricity caused my body on the bed to jerk violently. No good. My body fell back down limp. Lifeless.

Beeeeeeeeeeeeeeeeeeeeeeeeeeeeeeeeeeeeeep.

The beeping sound didn't waver. 'I'm dead.' Tears filled my eyes. I watched myself lying there. The doctor banged on my chest. I felt nauseas. I needed to get some air. I stuck my head out of the open window. Down in the street, I saw the hideous figures of several demons racing towards the hospital.

'Demons,' I muttered. 'They'll have a field day if they find me here.'

I glanced back at my body. Then at the open door leading out of the room. I didn't even flinch at the sight of the dark figure of the

Efil looming large in the doorway. Its features didn't alter. It just opened its mouth. Swallowing me up.

'*Efil...Efil,*' I heard the words racing around my head. My entire body spun around as if I was stuck in the centre of a hurricane. Round and round. Down and down, I travelled. Images of death and destruction appeared in the darkness as I plummeted at high speed.

I landed with a bump on something soft. Laying there on my back. Everything around me deadly quiet.

Beep...beep...beep, was the first sound I heard.

'*I think he's alive,*' off in the distance the voice of the doctor announced to the others.

I couldn't open my eyes. I just laid there in the blackness.

'*It's not over yet. We must make sure he doesn't go into another seizure,*' the doctor's voice seemed to be coming through the wall.

'*I'm alive?*' I thought. '*But how? The Efil had swallowed me up. I should be dead.*'

There was a sharp pain in my arm. '*Give him another shot.*'

'*Efil...Efil,*' I repeated the name of the creature over and over in my mind. In the darkness of my own head, I found myself in a strange looking hotel room. Like the one I had been in before. I staggered over to the window. It was dark. I couldn't see anything outside. I wrote the creature's name in the condensation on the window pane. '*What is it? What am I missing?*' I studied the word. Trying to undo the puzzle.

Beats me I thought. I turned back around. A large mirror somehow appeared behind me over the bed. I walked towards it. Staring at my face. It looked old. A lot older than my seventeen years. It was then I saw the reflection of the window in the mirror.

'LifE...lifE...' My mouth dropped open. *'I need to get back to the church.'* I concentrated hard. *'Please...please...I need to get back...back to my friends...before it's too late.'*

'His pulse is falling again,' a nurse declared.

'We've got to wake him up,' I could hear the panic in the doctor's voice.

Two large doors suddenly appeared in front of me in my head. One extremely bright. The other one very dark. Gloomy. I knew I had to choose.

'If he goes again, he's not going to make it,' the doctor's voice broke my concentration.

Make my mind up. Which one...which one. I stepped towards the bright door. Opening it up. Preparing to step inside.

'Leo...quick we have to get inside,' it was Beth. Her voice came from behind the dark door. Without a second thought, I slammed the bright door shut. Stepping in through the other one.

I felt someone slapping my face. *'Leo...Leo.'*

I opened my eyes. Beth's pretty face in front of me. 'Will you stop disappearing?'

'Sorry, but it's ok…they aren't what we think they are,' I blurted out. 'They are good. Its life spelled backwards…Efil equals life.'

She stepped away from me. Looking up at the priest.

'He's hallucinating,' Father D chipped in. 'He's lost a lot of blood.'

'No,' I struggled to my feet. 'You don't understand.' I looked around. The inside of the church was empty. All the lost spirits had gone. 'Where's Ethan?'

Beth looked across at the confessional box which stood shaking in the corner.

'NO,' I raced towards it. Trying to pull open the door. A gargoyle barked. 'Open it…open it,' I shouted at Father D.

The priest shrugged. The box stopped moving. A puff of smoke drifted out from under the door. Floating up to the ceiling.

'It's too late,' Father D put a tick against Ethan's name on the piece of paper he was holding. 'Another one's going upstairs to see the main man…I knew he was a good kid.'

He turned to Beth next. 'Come on girl.'

'No…' I shielded her from him.

'Leo…it's her turn.'

'NO!'

The priest caught my arm. Twisting it painfully behind my back. 'It's time.'

'Ok…sorry Father D…I just need to talk to her first. Five minutes…just five minutes alone…please.'

The priest rolled his eyes towards the ceiling exactly like Jezzie would have done. 'Ok…but you need to be fast, I have a mass in twenty minutes, and this place ain't going to clean itself.' He strolled away. Speaking to the gargoyle. '

We strolled back amongst the pews. I racked my brain. Wondering what I was going to do. My side hurt. I felt weak. I knew I had to fight through the pain barrier.

'I'm so scared,' Beth admitted. 'Do you think I will be going upstairs to meet the…the…the main man?'

'No…no.' She looked at me. 'Yes…no…you know what I mean.' I could hear the footsteps of the priest headed back towards us. I put both hands to my throat. Pretending I couldn't breathe.

'What's wrong Leo?'

'Air,' I copied what the thug had done to him in the church ages ago. 'I need Aiiiiirrrrrrr. I need some air.'

She opened the door. Led me outside. It was dark. The street lights lit up the pavements. Drops of rain fell on the surface of the road. A car drove past. Plowing through the puddles.

I purposely turned her around to face the church instead of the street. Way back in the shadows, the figure of the Efil appeared. It moved towards us. Its pace quickened with every stride. I placed my hands on her face to stop her from turning around.

'Are you ok now?' she asked with genuine concern.

I grinned weakly. 'I hope I've got this right,' I muttered to myself. My hands shaking. I couldn't look her in the eye.

'Got what right?' she replied innocently. The light of the neon sign flickered off her face.

'Oh nothing.' I moved my lips close to hers. She closed her eyes. Puckering her lips to meet mine. I took a deep breath. Pushing her hard in the chest. Sending her toppling backwards. Landing on her back on the grass.

'Leo…what the…' her confused words tripped from her mouth.

'I'll see you soon.' I mouthed the words.

The Efil bounded towards her. Its eyes focusing on Beth. Its fangs glistened in the darkness. Its mouth wide opened. It took only three bites to devour her. The monster licked its lips. Staring at me.

'Go…get out of here,' I threw a rock at it. The creature disappeared across the road. Into the night.

I walked into the building. Closing the doors behind me. Tears streamed down my face. I knelt by the unusual altar to pray to God that I was right.

21

can the parents of the following come with me please?

The sound of someone weeping spun around the dark abyss of my mind. I lay floating like a feather on the breeze. My heart echoed in the silence.

'*Where am I?*' I waited for an answer that never came.

A door closed. Footsteps circled around me. I strained to open my eyes. My mother's head rested on the edge of the hospital bed. Her shoulders hunched over. Shaking. My father stood looking out of the hospital window. His hands behind his back.

I reached over to touch my mother's arm. 'Hi,' my voice sounding weaker than I actually felt. 'Where am I?'

She smiled. Her eyes puffed up. Mascara running down her cheeks. 'You're in the hospital.' She hugged me tightly.

'Mam…not so hard.' I pulled back. Looking across at my dad.

I could tell he had been crying as well. 'We thought we lost you, son.' It was quite rare of him to show such emotion.

My legs ached. I felt dehydrated. I took a sip of water. Its coldness tickled the back of my throat. 'What day is it?'

My parents exchanged glances.

'Well?' I repeated the question. Pulling myself up in the bed.

'Monday,' his father replied.

I crossed my fingers. 'Monday. What Monday?' I didn't wait for a reply before asking the more important question. 'The Monday of the field trip?'

'Yes, of course...the Monday of the trip,' my mother responded slowly. Catching my father's puzzled expression.

'Yesssssssssssssssss,' I punched the air. A wide smile split my face in two.

'Leo, you've had a bad seizure, a very bad seizure.' She took the water glass from my hand. 'And you've been stabbed. But no one knows when? Or who by?'

I wasn't really listening. I looked at the clock on the wall. Quarter past eleven. 'Is that the right time?'

'Leo, don't start again,' My father hissed. I could tell he was getting annoyed. 'Of course, it's the right time.'

'It's only been about an hour.' I pulled the tube out of my arm. Swinging my legs out of bed. 'Shoes?' I bent down to look for them. Wincing in pain.

My mother tried stopping me. 'Leo, get back into bed.' her voice reaching fever pitch.

'I've got to go,' I put my socks on.

A nurse wandered in carrying a silver tray. 'Oh, Leo, you're awake.' She took hold of my arm. 'Now let's get you back into bed and I will get the doctor.'

I resisted. She was a professional and easily wrestled me back in. Hauling the sheets up over my legs. 'You don't understand.' I clutched her arm. Looking her in the eye. 'Were a group of kids brought in to emergency in the last sixty minutes?'

'What?' she enquired.

'Teenagers…their bus plunged into a lake,' I blurted out. Staring at all three of them in turn.

She shook her head from side to side. 'No teenagers. No bus. No Lake.'

'Leo, what are you talking about?' My mother started sobbing. 'Stop…please…stop.'

'It must be the drugs in his system,' the nurse added. 'he'll be ok in an hour or two.'

I persisted. 'My school friends…they're dead…no, they were dead,' I hesitated. 'It was the demons. They caused the crash. They were trying to steal their souls to get back at me. Well, me… and also for Zotto to get into Hell…but…'

'Leo…stop this nonsense your mother said,' my father raised his voice. Deflected the blame onto her.

The nurse pressed the red button near the bed several times.

'Mam…my friends,' I continued. 'It was my job to take them to the station…me and Jezzie.'

My mother's legs gave way. She sat on the edge of the bed to steady herself. 'What station? Who's Jezzie?'

'He's was my mentor. The man in the coma. But then the Efil ate him. I thought it was evil. But it was life…life.' I laughed excitedly. 'My friends are alive…alive.' I tried again to get out of bed. 'Some of them are.'

The nurse pushed me back down. Checking my pulse. She placed her hand on my forehead. Popping a thermometer in my mouth. 'Sit still.'

'What's wrong with him?' his father asked.

'Like I said probably the drugs or just shock,' the nurse replied. Checking the time on her watch. 'Sometimes it happens.'

Another nurse stuck her head around the door. 'Doris…Doris,' the nurse spun to face her. 'They need us both in ER right away. There's been a terrible accident. A bus full of teenagers crashed into a lake right outside Teatown. They are bringing them here. Pronto.' Her head disappeared from the doorway.

Everyone in the room turned slowly to look at me. I sat upright grinning back at them. 'Told you, didn't I?' I didn't wait to rub it in. I leapt from the bed. Following the nurse out of the room.

'Leo where are you going?' my father bellowed out. My parents chasing behind me.

Down in the emergency room a gang of orderlies wheeled stretchers about. Anxious parents stood dazed. Nurses rushed around frantically. A fresh-faced police officer tried hard to answer all the difficult questions from the news reporters out near the main entrance.

'Sit down in there,' a nurse instructed me to go to the packed waiting room.

I sat there still in my pyjamas. Looking across to see Mister Hubbard sitting in the corner. Shaking. Wrapped in a blanket. His face white as chalk. A large nurse and two policemen led him away to a small room.

'Leo, why don't you go back to the ward,' my mother urged. 'There's nothing you can do around here.' Her words dried up when two orderlies walked down the corridor pushing a body on a stretcher covered by a white sheet. Ethan's mother followed not far behind them. Sobbing. In a daze. Curlers in her dyed blonde hair.

'Ethan,' I muttered.

'Oh my gosh,' my mother swallowed.

I wanted to get up and hug Ethan's mother. I wanted to tell her that her son was the bravest boy I knew. And not to worry because he'd gone to heaven. But I knew it wasn't the time. She disappeared behind a door at the end of the long corridor.

Josh's parents arrived. They took up the seats next to us. No one spoke. All staring at the hands of the clock on the wall moving gradually. My knees knocked with nervous energy.

'I wish someone would tell us what's going on.' Josh's father raised his voice.

At that moment, a police officer walked in. Trying his best to fight back the tears. He called out a list of names. 'Can the parents of the following come with me please? Johnny James, Paul Cross and Sharon Bell.'

I watched the traumatized parents following the officer down the long corridor. Disappearing into the same door where Ethan's mam had already vanished earlier. My mother moved closer to me. Clenching my hand firmly. 'I love you son,' she whispered.

'Love you too, mam,' I replied. 'And you too dad.' I smiled at my old man.

Josh's mother stood up. But sank down on her knees. My mother helped her back up. 'Where's my son? Is he alive?' Josh's father asked another police man who had entered holding another piece of paper with another list of names on it.

'Can everyone else follow me please?' the man's voice sent fear into the waiting parents.

'Quick, they're ok,' I said to my mother. 'The ones left are the ones that were eaten by the Efil. The others were taken by the demons…or drowned in the crash.'

She stared at me blankly. Along with Josh's parents

'Leo,' my father muttered. 'Shut up about creatures and demons for Pete's sake.' He banged the table.

I didn't take any notice. I rushed into the recovery room behind Josh's parents. There were several beds dotted around the large room. Yvonne lay in the bed nearest the door. Her face white with shock. Her body covered in a large silver thermal blanket. She poked her hand up through the material to give me a small wave. 'Hi,' she muttered.

I waved back. I walked on. Passing Colin who lay asleep. A large lump on the side of his head.

'What happened?' Josh was sat up in his bed. Eating a cookie. 'I thought I was dead. How did I get here?'

'It was the Efil. The Efil was good after all.' I beamed at my best friend.

'What are they talking about?' Josh's mother whispered. My mother shrugged her shoulders.

'No way,' Josh sat upright. 'That big ugly thing was on our side…well I'll be damned.'

'Joshua,' his mother piped up. 'Stop swearing.'

My face turned serious. 'Have you seen Beth?' I asked quietly.

I followed Josh's eyes to a curtain at the far end of the room. I rushed over. Peeked inside. Beth lay on her side. Her hands curled up to her face. She looked right at me through sorrowful eyes. Her hair flat to her head. I sat down next to her. Holding out the palm of my hand. She pressed her hand against mine.

'I'm sorry. I didn't know what else to do,' I muttered. My cheeks growing red.

'You could have warned me,' she replied.

I leaned across. Whispering in her ear. 'You know I would never do anything to hurt you…you're my…my…' I couldn't finish off my sentence. The words sticking in my throat.

'Thanks.' She looked back through the curtain at all the crazy activities taking place in the room. 'So, I assume Jezzie is alright then?'

Her words took a while to register with me. To be honest with all the excitement I had completely forgotten about my old mentor. 'Jezzie!' I kissed her on the head and raced out of room.

'Leo, where are you going now?' my father shouted. I ignored him again. Skidding around the bend. Just missing a nurse carrying a stack of files.

'Careful boy,' she grunted.

I sprinted to the far end of the hospital. Bounding up the six flights of stairs. I threw open the door to Jezzie's room. It was empty. The bed stripped bare. I checked in the bathroom just in case. No sign of him. My entire body deflated. I moped back down the corridor. Head down. I couldn't understand it. 'Maybe it was a different kind of Efil who ate him.' Thoughts raced around my brain.

A voice rose up behind me. 'You were lucky…very, very lucky.' I spun around to find Jezzie sitting in a wheelchair, A frown on his face.

'Jezzie,' I grabbed around him. Tears streaming down my face. 'You are alive…you are.' The tramp's face was clean shaven.

His hair washed. Combed. He wore a new pair of striped pyjamas. Slippers. He looked normal.

'Get off me you idiot,' the tramp pretended to push me away. But he gripped me forcefully instead.

'Everyone that got eaten by the Efil is alive. They're all downstairs, Josh, Beth, Colin…' I sounded so excited.

A nurse rushed past carrying a bed pan. She disappeared into a room.

'That's great news, kid. What about Ethan?'

I shook my head. Jezzie tutted. He did hug me this time. 'Thanks Jezz…thanks for everything.' I began to cry again.

'You're a good kid, kid, one in a million.' He punched my leg. 'Now wheel me down to see the others. I've got something for Josh,' he announced. Pulling a Hershey bar out of his pocket.

21

'Its soul time'

'Tell him about Mister Hubbard,' Beth said. Rearranging the fresh flowers on the grave.

'Oh yeah, I almost forgot.' I looked at Ethan's headstone. 'He came back to school this week.' I stomped my feet to shake the snow off them. 'He looked terrible. Looks like he's about 85 years old. He's still wearing that old tweed jacket.'

Beth stood up. Putting the old flowers in a plastic bag. 'Do you think he can really hear us, Leo?' She looked up to the skies.

I pulled up my gloves. Tightening the scarf around my neck. 'I'm positive he can.' I placed my arm around her shoulders. 'Come on its freezing.'

We said our goodbyes. Heading off towards the cemetery gates. It had become our weekly ritual for the last nine months to come to the graveyard. To discuss life. And death. With our dead friends.

'What's that?' I saw something lurking behind the gravestones. 'It's ok…only a dog…a normal dog.' I relaxed.

'Old habits die hard,' Beth whispered. 'Anyway, what did the doctor say yesterday?'

'It was amazing,' I walked and talked. 'They did all the checks and everything looks fine…no problems. It's like I've never had a seizure in my life.'

'That's great…weird, but great.'

We headed towards the coffee shop on the opposite side of the road. Waiting at the pavement for the line of cars to pass. 'I know my parents are so excited,' I continued. 'My mam keeps telling everyone she knows about the miracle of her son. She even phoned the newspaper.'

'The miracle of Leo Young. Now that would be a good film,' Beth chuckled to herself. 'But seriously, do you miss it?'

I watched a limo with blacked out windows rolling by. 'What? Miss having fits and rolling around lifeless with everyone gawking. I don't think so.'

'You know what I mean, smart ass…the soul walking stuff?'

'I don't think about it,' I lied. I did. I thought about it all the time. It did feel strange now that it had stopped. On saying that it was something I could definitely live without.

Beth released her grip on my hand to look in a shop window. I stared at her. 'She's so pretty,' I thought. 'Perfect.' I pushed in alongside her. I suddenly jumped when something brushed against my leg. I looked down to see a dog sniffing at my ankle.

'Hey Harry. Where's your owner?' I scanned the street.

Beth bent down to play with the mutt. 'Come here boy…good dog.'

'There he is,' I saw Jezzie's backside sticking out of one of the trash bins. 'Aren't you too old for that?' I shouted across at him.

The tramp looked up. Clutching an opened bag of fries in his hand he had rescued from the bin. 'Well if it ain't my young protégé and the wonderful Beth.' He put a hand full of fries into his mouth. 'What you doing on my side of the street?' he joked. 'I didn't give you permission.'

I greeted him with a hug.

'Get off,' Jezzie pretended to pull away. 'I don't know where you've been.'

A couple walked past. An expression of disgust on their faces. Looking down their noses at the tramp. We just ignored them.

'So Jezzie, how's life at the shelter going?' I asked. Digging around in my pockets for some money.

The tramp glanced at the floor rather sheepishly. 'It's not. Well, I'm more of a street person really Leo. I was born to live underneath the stars.' He pointed to the sky. 'I love sleeping rough.'

'Oh Jezz…but the shelter had everything you needed.'

He shrugged. Feeding the dog some food from his hand. The creature's tail wagged wildly.

'It's your life,' I replied.

'Want to come for a coffee?' Beth asked. 'The old gang will be there.'

Jezzie looked at his wrist as if he was checking a timepiece. 'I would love to but I've got something important to do. Very important.' He limped away. Followed by his dog. I caught up with him. Put some money in his hand. 'You don't need to kid.' Jezzie handed it back.

'But…but.'

The old man's stare was cold. He gripped his cane. Ready to swing it 'I said you don't need to.' He walked on. 'Oh yeah,' he yelled back. 'Father D and the gargoyle send their regards…see you all soon, maybe at a soul walker's reunion party.' I could still hear him laughing to himself as him and Harry disappeared around the corner.

'Let's go and meet the others,' I said to Beth.

Josh was already at the coffee shop when we arrived. 'Hey you took your time. I'll have a semi skimmed latte,' he yelled out. 'I bought the last time.' He carried on reading a fitness magazine.

I nodded my head. I still couldn't really believe the change in my best friend since the incident on the school trip. Josh wasn't the fat kid in the class anymore. The unhealthy one at the back of the line. In fact, he had lost nearly forty pounds. Trained hard every day and had even made the school football team.

'Hey Leo, did I tell you I'm going to run the marathon,' he declared proudly.

'The New York marathon?' Beth injected.

'Are you crazy? I'm still not going anywhere near the city. No, Boston. In three months. Care to join me?'

'Nah, I don't think so.' I waited for Beth to decide what she wanted. She sat on the leather sofa. Playing with a small spider crawling across her hand.

'I didn't think you liked creepy crawlers,' Josh went to swat it off.

She protected it with her other hand. 'It's ok…after the rats and the tarantulas and the demons, little things like this don't scare me anymore.' She let the spider go safely in the corner. 'I'll have a milk shake.'

Suddenly the door shot open. Yvonne rushed in. Her body shaking. She threw her bag onto the sofa. 'I've seen him…I've seen him.'

'Who now?' Beth sighed.

'Zotto…he's over by the hardware store, carrying a ladder.' We all glanced at each other. 'It was him…definitely this time.' She stood by me. Pulling on my sleeve. 'Quick Leo…do something.'

Beth pulled up a chair for the girl. 'Yvonne, he's dead…I saw Father D blast him with both barrels.'

'Are you sure?'

'Positive.'

Josh threw the magazine onto the table. 'Yvonne, last week you thought you saw him driving a taxi. The week before he was playing for the Yankees and hit two home runs…listen Yvonne, he's dead…D…E…A…D…DEAD.'

She blew her nose in her hankie. 'Ok…Leo can I have a double espresso and a slice of carrot cake? I don't want to fall asleep tonight, just in case he does come back for me.'

I waited in line to order. It had taken time for all of us to readjust to what we had been through. Yvonne struggled more than any of us. Her nightmares followed her around everywhere.

I placed a large slice of carrot cake on the tray and moved on. 'Can I have a semi skimmed latte, double espresso, a milk shake…and …and …' I studied the menu board above the counter.

'Make your mind up boy,' the voice sounded familiar.

'Excuse me,' I looked at the young spotty kid behind the counter. 'What did you say?'

The young zit faced boy grinned at me. I dropped the tray onto the tiled floor. It clattered loudly at my feet. Some people stared.

'You didn't think you would get rid of me that easy…did you boy?' The eye patch and tattoo on the inhuman face stared back at me.

Beth rushed over. 'What's wrong Leo? You look like you've seen a ghost.'

'Excuse me,' the young kid became himself again. 'I'll get someone to clean that up for you.'

I reached over to touch the boy's face. The boy stepped back. 'Get off.'

'What's wrong Leo?' Beth asked again.

'Sorry,' I apologized. 'I need some air.' I pushed pass Beth. Staggering into the street. Ripping the scarf off my neck. I swallowed in as much air as I could.

An old woman stopped to stare. Followed by a few more people 'What's wrong with him?' I heard a man whisper.

'I think he's going to faint,' the old woman replied.

The inside of my head began to spin around. My vision blurred. I leaned against a wall to keep my balance.

KABOOM!

A loud explosion caused me to yell out. I glanced around. Everything outside the coffee shop seemed normal.

'Is he on drugs?' the old woman asked someone.

KABOOM!

I gripped the wall. Starting to inch my way to the edge of the building. Focusing my efforts to walk to the blue sign at the end of the road. My legs felt like jelly. My feet like lead. The blackness began to work its way from my legs up to my chest. I tried my best to force it back down. Keep it from climbing up until it engulfed my entire body. 'No…I'm ok now…the doctors said. They said I was ok…I'm ok.'

KABOOM!

'Incoming...incoming,' someone bellowed behind me. *'Where are our planes? Get headquarters on the radio.'*

The smell of smoke shot up my nose. I stood in a trench. My feet submerged in six inches of thick black mud.

KABOOM!

Two soldiers raced past. Carrying a boy on a stretcher. Half of the poor boy's head had been blown off. One of the soldiers slipped in the mud. Regaining his footings before walking straight through me.

'No!' Terror gripping my body. 'This can't be happening?'

Another bomb exploded nearby. Covering me in mud and small stones. I ducked down. Someone moaned quietly next to me.

'That was me on that stretcher...me... how can that be?' The spirit of a young soldier cowering in the corner of the trench. His hand outstretched.

'What?' I asked.

'That was me.' He pointed. 'On the stretcher...dead.'

'Can you see me?' I touched his shoulders.

The soldier nodded. His head twitching from the shock.

Another loud explosion filled the air with smoke. 'Where are we?' I asked. The frightened soldier wasn't much older than myself. He didn't reply.

'Where are we? Please, I need to know.' I repeated the question.

Off in the distance, a burst of gunfire rang out. Followed by cries of pain. I seized the soldier boy's face. 'Tell me.'

'France.'

'France?' Disney land France? How did I get to France?'

The soldier pulled a cigarette from his pocket. His hand shook too much to light it. I helped him with the match. The boy sucked on the rollup. Inhaling the smoke into his lungs.

I struggled to get my words out. I had seen on TV how the relationship between America and France had been strained over the years. But I didn't think it would lead to anything so drastic. 'But what's happening? Why the bombing?'

The soldier boy offered me a drag. I declined. 'It's the war,' his face slightly confused at the questions

'The war! What war?' I looked around. 'Am I dreaming? What war?'

'Um…the second world war.'

'The second world war,' I repeated the words in slow motion. I slumped back. Resting my head on a wooden beam. I couldn't take it all in. A noise above me made me look up. I saw a pair of long leather black boots. Standing on top of the trench. I slowly looked up further at the black uniform.

'Nazi,' the spirit of the soldier shouted out. Scrambling on all fours through the mud to get away.

The Nazi laughed. Another bomb sailed over our heads. I clambered to my feet. The German soldier pushed up his round helmet to reveal his face. It was Zotto grinning back at me.

'Hello boy…it's soul time!'

THE START

Many thanks to: -

Marc Phillips for the cover design (yet again)….. you are the best

To my super agent – **Derek Lynch** …. for pulling all the right strings

And to all the lost souls living and dead the world over and under

Stay free

Bunko x

Printed in Great Britain
by Amazon